Take Me Home for Christmas

Miranda Liasson ♡

MIRANDA LIASSON

Happy reading!

Published by Hawthorne House Press

Miranda Liasson, LLC

P.O. Box 13707

Fairlawn, OH 44334

www.mirandaliasson.com

Print ISBN 978-0-9986346-2-3

Ebook ISBN 978-0-9986346-0-9

Edited by Linda Ingmanson

Cover by Elizabeth Turner Stokes

Author photo @2023 by M2Photos

Published in the United States of America

 Created with Vellum

Life is hard. But everything gets better with glitter.

— GRACIE

Also By Miranda Liasson

Mirror Lake Series

Kingston Family Series

Angel Falls Series

Seashell Harbor Series

Sweetheart Series

Trigger Warning

This is a heartwarming and humorous holiday romance, and I, the author, want you to enjoy it thoroughly. The heroine works with kids who have cancer, and cancer has impacted people she loves. If you would like to know if this book contains any further elements that might be of concern to you, please check the very back of the book.

Prologue

The Christmas when I was eight, I received a magical snow globe. Within its smooth glass dome was a perfect miniature scene: a tiny Victorian house with glowing windows and a huge Christmas tree in the snow-covered front yard with lights that really lit up. A dog that looked just like our dachshund, Jack, jauntily wore a Santa hat.

But the special thing about that snow globe was that at the very center, two little girls bundled up in bright winter coats held hands, one blonde like me, the other dark haired like my twin sister, Grace.

I remember staring at it for hours, shaking it into a flurry of magical sparkles and peering in at that perfect little world that encapsulated for me all the magic of Christmas—the warmth of the glowing house, the miracle of snow, the happiness and comfort of family.

I clung hard to that magic because shortly afterward, my sister was diagnosed with leukemia, and the year that followed was a blur of doctor visits, cycles of chemo, and watching my mischievous, vivacious twin turn into a shadow of herself. All the *normal* that we knew tumbled down around us like boulders in a rockslide.

Cancer separated my childhood into a before and an after. *Before* was carefree happiness in the hugs of our mother, the winks and funny jokes told by our father, and the jostling and friendly torments from our two older brothers.

Grace got through her treatments. Later that year, on a snowy day just before Christmas, we were playing tag in the family room, scrambling around the furniture and giggling. I'd carelessly left the globe on the edge of the coffee table, blissfully unaware that it was perched on the brink of disaster. My sister had been feeling great that day, and I remember feeling so happy that she was done with her long road of chemo, that she was again my constant playmate and best friend.

It was the last time I'd felt that life was as it should be, everyone safe and tucked into place.

Right as she reached out to tag me, I twisted away, lost my balance and tumbled down, my arms splaying. The globe crashed to the floor, shattering into a million pieces as the water spilled, the magic swirling snow now just papery white flakes on the carpet.

"I did it," I immediately confessed. "I did it," I repeated, my voice a thin whisper. "I'm sorry, Mommy."

"She *didn't* do it," Gracie said, already sitting back on the couch, winded from our game. "I tagged her. *I* did it." She sounded a lot more convincing than I did. It had taken all of five seconds for her to decide on that lie, and she went with it.

My mother, hands on hips, looked the two of us over. "You girls certainly share everything, even the blame, don't you?" She sat down on the couch and pulled me next to her, wrapping her arms around both of us.

"You said no running." Grace's lower lip quivered. She was still fragile. She wasn't supposed to be roughhousing. That made me feel like I was doubly at fault.

My mother kissed my head. "I know how much you loved it, Mia. But it's just a snow globe. Just a little thing to remind us of the fun Christmas we're going to have."

Our Christmas had been more than that, really, which I didn't understand until much later. We roller-skated in the basement on new skates and on our frozen-over pond with ice skates. We made cookies and ate them with hot chocolate by the roaring fire Dad made in the fireplace. We played cards and games every night before bed. Even our big brothers seemed to pull fewer pranks than usual. Grace seemed strong and happy, and for the first time in so long, cancer had been abolished from our minds.

That was our last Christmas together as a whole and happy family.

My sister—my twin, my other half—lost her battle, and that broken globe became a reminder to me of just how fragile life is. How good fortune could turn on a dime. How happiness is a rare thing and not made to last. Somewhere along the line, I stopped expecting to find it.

Grace's illness shaped me in more ways than I could count. She was the bold one who never hesitated to speak up. I was quiet and shy, always hesitant to speak my mind.

With her death, I'd lost my lightness. And my innocent acceptance of life as a beautiful, exciting journey. Because—why her? *Why* had God taken her and not me?

I became determined to make my life count for both of us. I *would* be cheery and kind. I *would* be smart and dutiful. And I vowed to never give my mom and dad a reason to cry again.

We had to pick up the pieces after Grace left us and somehow put ourselves together again. Which we did, but ever since then, it seemed I was always looking for the part of me that she took with her.

Chapter One

Twenty years later

Mia

"Here I come, Dr. D'Angelo!" Bianca Giarelli, one of my favorite patients, sped by in her wheelchair as I stood charting at the nurses' station of the Children's Wisconsin adolescent unit, where I was a third-year pediatric resident. The chair had an IV bag attached to a pole in the back, filled with an icky green liquid and swinging slightly as she breezed by. Bianca, age sixteen, had tied red and green streamers and a string of battery-powered LED lights to her pole, completing the Christmasy effect. I waved and gave her a thumbs-up as I talked into my phone, finishing a conversation with my mom as I worked.

"So, are you all packed?" my mom asked, sounding strong and well after the ordeal she'd just been through, which made my heart swell doubly with both happiness and relief.

After what had happened with my sister so long ago, you'd

think my family would have gotten a pass on the C word. No such luck, but my mom's breast cancer was caught early. She'd gotten through surgery and six difficult cycles of chemo. But now she certainly *sounded* like herself, and this nearly made me cry with joy. The doctors were extremely hopeful that she was going to be fine. Which was still terrifying, but we were dealing. And so, so grateful.

"Getting there," I answered. It was Monday, and my four-day holiday break began after I was off the clock on Friday. "Can't wait to come home for Christmas." As my mom related what was new with my family, my eyes wandered over to my co-resident on the hematology-oncology service this month, Braxton Hughes.

Brax was actually the chief resident over the interns, the first-year residents, in our program. That meant he'd already completed his residency and had been hired on for a year where he had various duties like making the interns' schedules, arranging and helping teach their educational sessions, and keeping an eye on their professional growth and mental health.

But this week, the week before Christmas, he was pinch-hitting on the ward for a resident who had to travel overseas to see his family for the holiday. At the moment, he was standing in the middle of the hallway consulting with Joe, one of our wonderful child life specialists.

They stood against a backdrop of light strings, tinsel, and glittery paper snowflakes dangling from the acoustic ceiling tiles above their heads. Brax was tall, big-shouldered, and all lean muscle, and actually very nice to look at. I didn't realize I was staring until he glanced over at me, giving me the slightest nod, turning his dark gaze on me that always seemed to contain a twinkle of mischief—and sometimes more.

I waved and quickly looked away, trying to stop my heart from racing and the telltale flush that was already flaring its way into my cheeks. I sometimes sensed that mischief, that *heat*, was directed at me, although he'd made it clear, since breaking things off last summer, that there could only be friendship between us.

I tried not to fan myself, but the hormonal rush was, frankly, uncontrollable. But I was working on it.

As my mom discussed all the different ways she'd decorated the Christmas trees she'd talked my dad into putting up all around our house, I was distracted by what was going on in front of me on the ward. "Hey, Bianca," Brax said in a teasing voice as she rolled by. "You'd better be practicing up for ping-pong tonight." He circled his right arm around as if he were warming up his muscles for a pitch. "'Cause I'm gonna whup your butt."

"Hey, Doctor Brax," she said. "We'll see about that. *I've* been practicing too." She wound her arm around in the same way. She was weak, of course, from the chemo she'd endured, but her enthusiasm—and her sass—made up for her lack of muscle.

Brax laughed. Laughter that caused a lot of females to melt into Jell-O at his feet. Not me, of course. I was *not* a melter. But he did make my knees wobble. And a couple of other reactions that I would never admit out loud.

Bonded by the life-and-death nature of our job, Brax and I quickly fell into a friendship that was more than simply collegial, but less revealing than what we'd had before. We managed to keep the other stuff out of it. Mostly.

"So how's your guy?" my mom asked.

Brax was *not* my guy. But my mom actually thought he was. "He plays ping-pong with the teens who've been on the ward for a while." I watched Brax grab a small beanbag elf off the counter and toss it playfully at Bianca. It landed in her lap, making her chuckle. "They kind of have a pool going. They play for M&M's."

"Oh, Mia," my mom gushed. "He sounds wonderful."

A hefty dose of guilt flooded through me as I failed, as I had repeatedly through these past months, to tell my mom the truth about our breakup. Bianca cranked up her arm again and tossed the elf in Brax's direction. He made a giant show of catching it, hurtling himself in the air, making faces, and doing a football-esque victory dance when he caught it, almost running into Valerie

Beckett, our charge nurse, who'd recently celebrated her thirty-fifth year in the profession.

"Sorry, Val." Brax displayed his boyish grin, which did *not* make my heart flutter. "We were just practicing for the big competition tonight."

"In the *nurses' station*, Dr. Hughes?" Her frown wasn't really even a frown. More like a *he's-so-adorable-and-I-wish-I-were-thirty-years-younger* kind of look.

Geesh. He *was* adorable.

Brax shrugged. "To make up for it, you can join us tonight for the tournament, okay? If you're as good at ping-pong as you are at managing this ward, we should be very afraid."

Val, completely charmed, shook her head. "Mmmhmm. Maybe they should keep you residents busier if you've got time for ping-pong tournaments." But she turned away smiling.

Suddenly, the red-and-green felt blur flew through the air, directly toward me.

In a not-very-pretty but nevertheless practical move, I caught it while somehow managing to mute and not break my phone. "You suck," I said to Brax.

Bianca laughed.

Brax lifted a well-defined brow in surprise. His gaze, full of challenge, settled upon me in a way that gave me goose bumps.

To make things worse, he walked up and leaned over the counter, staring down at me with amused, warm brown eyes. "Thought you had better reflexes, Dr. D'Angelo."

"You're all bluster," I shot back. "I have great reflexes. A true teammate communicates." And then I tossed it right back. He caught it quickly and smoothly, with one show-offy hand. If only I could summon the nerve to speak with him that way—in a bold, sassy tone—about what really mattered. But Brax only allowed people in so far.

My twin, Grace, had been sassy. I, on the other hand, tended to think of smart comebacks approximately five hours after a conversation. So much for genetics.

His full mouth turned up ever so slightly. "And here I thought we had something better than words."

"And what would that be?" I couldn't wait to hear this.

"Intuition. Reflexes." He tossed the poor elf back and forth between his hands. "Being in tune with each other's moves."

Okay, it was *definitely* getting hot in here. I dropped my voice and frowned. "Are we talking about sex or ping-pong here?" Had I just said that, one finger press away from my mother actually hearing it?

I'd sworn to never bring that up again. But when did my mouth ever listen to my brain? Plus, he was being flirty. But why? We'd broken up months ago.

"Touché." He leaned on his elbows, his face so close that I could see the masculine grain of his late afternoon stubble. "I was thinking more about how we handled that case in the ER last week."

I called baloney—silently, of course. Because his eyes told me differently. They often did. But he never acted on the impulses I saw there.

And yes, we had worked together very efficiently and quickly to help a toddler with pneumonia get oxygen, antibiotics, and quick admission to the PICU, short for the Pediatric Intensive Care Unit.

"I'll be sure to communicate my plays from now on. Okay?" There was that smile again, hot lava to my insides. Oh, so painful, to be this close to him and constantly pretend we were *friends, friends, friends*. I needed a brain reset. For my own sanity.

After he'd broken things off last summer, he'd said, "I care about you so much, Mia. We'll be working together all year. I want us to be friends."

With his words, my heart cracked right in half. I should have said *Screw you, absolutely not*.

But you know what? We often happened to be on call the same nights, working closely to help very sick kids. Give us any emergency, and we were magic together. We anticipated each other's moves, had the same rhythms, even the same thoughts about what to do next.

So, I had no choice but to accept his friendship, which he offered very sincerely. That worked fine, as long as I ignored the rush of hormones that released in my body every time he walked into a room.

It had been magic in bed too. Well, in my opinion, anyway. Let's face it, if he'd felt the same, I wouldn't be searching for a fake boyfriend to bring home with me in T minus five days, now would I?

I forced myself into the here and now as Brax walked over to Bianca and handed the beanbag to her. "I've got to go but keep practicing. 'Cause Pedro and I are going to whup Mia's and your butts tonight." Pedro was another teen on the unit who happened to love ping-pong—and Brax.

"*Not*," Bianca said definitively, like the typical teenager she was, spinning her chair around and heading down the hall.

"Mia?" my mom asked.

Oh. My mom.

"Sorry," I said. She'd been relating a story about how our whole town was excited for the big annual Christmas party, where everyone got way too dressed up, ate a fancy sit-down meal, and danced to a live band—a usually fun event that happened to be hosted by my ex's parents. Except this year, it would be hosted by —bonus!—my ex and his new wife. I was definitely not going.

"I'll let you get back to work," my mom said. "Is that Braxton I hear in the background?"

"He—um—he just said he can't wait until we're on call together tonight. If it's not too busy, we're going to put together a fake Christmas tree someone donated and get the kids to make paper chains and stuff."

That part was true. But for the rest of the tales I was spinning, I was going to burn in hell.

"He sounds so...light. Fun loving. I can see why he's perfect for you."

I didn't have to tell my mom that life had sucked the *fun loving* right out of me for quite some time, starting with my longtime boyfriend breaking up with me two years ago and marrying someone else in Vegas last month.

I was okay with being single at twenty-nine, but this made my mother, who'd married my dad at twenty, worry about me constantly. Plus, the breakup with Charlie had been hard, and people in our small town, two hours from Milwaukee, asked about me a lot, which made her worry even more.

When Brax dumped me a few weeks after we'd started dating, she'd been about to start chemo, and I just couldn't tell her. And so the fantasy lived on.

I was *definitely* going to burn in hell. Since my sister had died, I'd made it my mission not to cause my parents any worry. I supposed I'd become the perfect child, determined to do everything right. They'd had enough grief in their lives. I didn't want to give them more. But inventing a boyfriend was a whopper, even for me.

"How are you feeling?" I asked. "Maybe it's too much, me coming home with someone. Maybe it's better if—" *Please,* I prayed. *Please say it's too much.*

"Sweetheart, we cannot wait to meet Brax," she quickly said. "And I'm feeling great. Ask your dad."

"Hi, honey," I heard in the distance.

"Hey, Dad." I pictured him standing there, dutifully holding an ornament box for my mom while she picked them out one by one, exclaimed over the story each one told, and hung them on our tree. I'd basically hit the parent jackpot—my dad always had my mom's back, and vice versa. Not always easy when she tended to be Mrs. Christmas.

"Tell her, Steven," my mom urged. "Tell her I'm just fine."

I heard a shuffling noise as my father took the phone. "Your mother now has a total of eight Christmas trees in our house." There was a painfully patient pause. "She's made me haul each one to its perfect place. And she's been decorating for the past two weeks." In his voice, I heard an unconscious plea for reinforcements. "I can firmly say she's back to her old self."

Stopping my mom from decorating would be like stopping the snow from coming just south of Madison, where I grew up in a quaint lakeside town dotted in the summer with crystal blue lakes, bright red geraniums, fresh June strawberries, and the squeakiest cheese curds you've ever tasted. In the winter, it was all quaint old homes and rolling snow-covered hills. And everyone trying to outdo themselves in the Christmas-decoration department.

"We can't wait to meet your young man," my dad said.

"Knowing you'll be here soon is the best medicine of all," my mom said, "so hurry home."

"'Kay. See you soon. Love you," I said as I hung up.

I took a giant breath. And rubbed my forehead. It had been so hard to support my mom this past year when I'd had so little time off, but my stories had distracted her and given her something to look forward to. Along the way, I'd invented happiness in the form of a boyfriend who was kind, funny, handsome, and treated me like a queen.

He greatly resembled Brax times ten—like, Brax if he'd never broken up with me. If he'd said he loved me instead of *Can't we please be friends?*

I marveled that, somehow, I'd managed to do what I'd never been able to do before—fool my mother. And I'd done it spectacularly. I wasn't congratulating myself for my Academy Award-winning performance or my on-the-spot creativity—every time I added onto the pile of lies, I literally broke out in a sweat.

I'd invented the perfect man. The only problem was, now I had to produce him. For *Christmas*.

I'd tried telling my parents back in November that he couldn't make it. But then my mom, her immune system already weakened, got sick with a head cold that had gone straight into her chest, requiring antibiotics and a brief hospital stay for pneumonia. She'd sounded so discouraged, so weary and tired, that I said he could make it after all.

Yes, I'd panicked. But fortunately, I now had a plan. My pal Gabe offered to play the part, which was just for a long weekend. Eventually, in a month or two, maybe, I'd tell my mom that we broke up, but it wouldn't be a big deal because by then, she would hopefully be long past this awful health scare.

So it was all going to be fine. I had it covered.

On the ward, Dr. Robin Miller, who was in her first year of practice, sat down across from me at the nurses' station. She finished a call with another doc and hung up. "Hi, Mia," she said, "how's it going?"

"You're here late." I glanced at my watch. Almost seven. I was already getting called about night shift admissions from the ER.

She sat back and rubbed her very pregnant abdomen. "Long day."

Robin was the only female physician in the prestigious BCP Group—named after the founding partners, Drs. Brunner, Curry, and Pendergast—but affectionately called by nearly everyone the Brew City Pediatrics group. Otherwise known as the most well-respected practice in town, it was the practice that ran the smoothest, stayed up to date on all the latest trends, and which invested the most time teaching the residents. It was also the group where Brax and I were both vying for the one open spot.

They were the best group with the highest standards, and I wanted that job more than anything. I loved working with people who loved their jobs, who strove for excellence, and who truly cared about making a difference for kids—everything that checked all my boxes for why I wanted to be a pediatrician in the first place.

Come July, I'd be done with residency and ready for the real world, and I couldn't wait.

She came right out and addressed what was on my mind. "I don't think we'll be making a decision about the job until after the holidays. You and Brax are both such excellent candidates." She took a sip of water from her flask. "All I can say is, enjoy third year, because that's a dream compared to private practice."

What? I, along with every other resident, was under the impression that residency might be its own form of hell, but the light on the other side was finishing and having a real job. Life balance was just a few elusive months away.

Robin must have noticed my puzzled expression. "You know how high the standards are in our practice. We all work as long as it takes for our patients. That's why we choose the hardest-working residents to join us."

I didn't want to question her too much, lest she question my dedication, even though her comment struck me as a little intense. So I settled on "Is practice what you expected?"

She hesitated. The tiniest bit. Yet that little pause took me from concerned to *really* concerned. "I'm the only woman in the practice, so I'd love more representation. Sometimes I feel that it will take bringing on another woman to bring some balance, if you know what I mean."

I was really confused, but just then, the charge nurse walked over to ask me a question about someone's medication, and Robin's pager went off, so our convo ended.

When I finished, Robin was gone, but there was Brax, giving a pep talk to Pedro, a gangly teen of fifteen, who was passing by, dragging his IV pole behind him. They talked ping-pong strategy while Brax took the pole, walking alongside him, deep in conversation.

I got up, grabbed my laptop, and headed down the hall. Brax saw me coming and glanced up. "Hey, Mia," he said in his sexy, deep voice, "hope you and Bianca have been talking, because Pedro and I have our strategy down." He fist-bumped with Pedro.

I loved being on call with him. Well, no one *loves* being on call, but the key here was *with him*. He had a way of making even the most awful nights fun.

"Bianca and I are going to win," I said with confidence. "What are we playing for this time?"

"Ice cream!" Bianca said as she passed by on her tenth lap. She smiled widely at Pedro, and he returned an equally enthusiastic smile.

Aw. Seemed like those two had a little bit of a crush going on.

"Already in the freezer," Brax said. "Waiting for me and Pedro to feast on it." He rubbed his flat stomach and licked his chops, making Bianca, Pedro, and me roll our eyes.

A visual appeared before my eyes—I'd seen that flat stomach up close. Those sculpted abs. That lovely chest. And all the rest of him. I could attest that every body part was of excellent quality. But oh, how I wish I could erase those images.

Brax's fun-loving antics with our patients had entertained my mom over the past few months and helped her—and me—through a tough time. Now, I just had to play out the charade until I could end it. My stomach gave a nervous flip, like it did when I knew I was in trouble. I reassured myself that everything was set up perfectly, if a little precariously. What could go wrong?

Chapter Two

Mia

"What do you mean you're sorry, but you can't come home with me for Christmas?" I froze in the middle of plopping scoops of snowball cookie dough on baking sheets at my friend Gabe's sparkling quartz island. It was Wednesday night, and we were in his apartment, listening to Michael Bublé belt out "Have Yourself a Merry Little Christmas." Gabe's rescue cat, Stupor Queenie (a name we'd given her after a long ICU rotation and too much wine), sat on the roof terrace of her kitty penthouse, flicking her tail and staring at us as if to say, *Your people problems are waaay too complicated.*

My other good friend Samantha Bashar, who was in specialized training at Children's to become a pediatric anesthesiologist, was uncorking a wine bottle.

I was going to need that wine, because it felt like a race car was running laps in my chest. A wave of dizziness forced me to sit down, so stunned, I forgot to set down the scoop.

"I'm so sorry," Gabe said, flicking his gaze downward in a way that I could tell he felt bad. He pried the scoop from my hand and replaced it with the glass of wine that Sam had just poured, which made me hate him a teeny bit less. "It's just...Jason's asked me to go home with him to meet his parents. That's a *huge* step." He sat down at one of his nice leather counter stools and seemed, for the first time since I'd met him, almost as bewildered as I was. "I think he's going to propose."

"Oh, Gabriel," Sam said, "that's amazing."

Tears of happiness filled my eyes despite my panicked state. Gabe and I had met the first day of pediatric residency and bonded over our mutual terror at having to care for fragile former preemies in what we residents affectionately called the Special Scare Nursery, and we'd been the best of friends ever since. He was one of those people who loved big and hard and who, because you trusted him so much, got you to overshare before you even understood you were doing it. Hence, he knew about everything—including blow-by-blow accounts of the two years of awful dates I'd endured before I'd met Brax.

"I'm really happy for you." I walked around the huge island to join Sam in giving him a giant hug. We'd all had our share of dating heartaches, and Jason, Gabe's beau of two years, was amazing. I couldn't think of anyone who deserved better.

Meanwhile, I tried to tamp down my welling desperation. I had to produce a fake boyfriend in three days. *Three.* Where on earth was I going to find one?

Gabe stopped to give Queenie, who had rubbed up against his arm, a scratch behind her regal ears. "I think this is it for me." He looked me straight in the eye, with a solemn, sure expression that I had to admit made me envious. "I think he's The One."

His happiness was obvious. And hard-earned. We'd been warriors together, on the wards and in the dating world. And he'd done it: he'd found love. Which should've given me hope that someday I might find it too. Underneath my terror and my joy, I felt a tiny twinge of sadness. "Who'll console me with ice cream and cheap but plentiful wine after I survive yet another awful date?"

"Ahem," Sam said, pointing to herself.

I turned to her and said in a wry tone, "You'd console me by taking me to a bar and finding me a one-night stand."

She lifted a perfect brow and tucked a lock of shiny black hair behind her ear past a pretty gold dangling triangle earring. I'd need to borrow those. "I can't help it if I'm a problem solver. Maybe if you'd taken my dating advice, you'd be over Brax by now."

Sam was beautiful, brainy, and sometimes brash. Adventurous and bold. Many things I wasn't. Sometimes, I thought that maybe I connected with her so much because she reminded me of Gracie. She was also one of the kindest people I knew. When she wasn't pushing me to be bolder, that is.

"I'm getting engaged," Gabe said, "not moving to Alaska."

The dizziness hit again, making the room spin. The effect of the tangled web I'd created all by myself, no doubt. Gabe coming home with me had always felt too good to be true—he knew the whole story, understood what I'd done, and hadn't judged me. He'd just settled his steady, enveloping gaze on me and said in that calm, reassuring, I-got-your-back voice, *When do we leave?*

He would've done that—been an on-the-spot boyfriend. Even though it meant pretending to change his sexual orientation to help me. I couldn't be angry with him.

Only myself. Yep, I had plenty of that pent up inside for getting myself into this stupid predicament.

"Look at it this way," Gabe said. "I don't exactly look like Brax. We wouldn't have fooled your mom."

"You're both dark haired," I said in protest. "Plus, the photos I've sent the past few months have been kind of out of focus."

"How about you ask Brax?" he suggested gently. After giving me a good eye roll, that is. "He's a logical choice. You two are close, even if you're too bullheaded to date each other again."

"Not to mention we're competing for the same job. Remember that?" Another reason to stay far away.

Gabe waved a hand in the air like the fact that we were the last two candidates left wasn't a big deal. "A job's a job, and that can be sorted out." He paused. "Did you know that the last time we went out, Brax told me that the chemistry between you two was positively animal?"

Sam covered her mouth with her hand in fake astonishment. "Shocker," she said.

I frowned. "How much did he have to drink?"

He shrugged. "Enough to tell the truth. Look, maybe it's time to sit down with him. You two have been tiptoeing around this obvious—"

I shook my head. "He made things clear." Crystal clear. He did not want to date me. Period.

"You know he's complicated," Gabe said. "Maybe he isn't sure what he wants."

I shook my head. "Last time I checked, Brax was an adult." This time around, I was going to make certain my next boyfriend was one.

"Leave her alone, Gabe," Sam said. "You know what happened with her ratty ex."

Charlie had been a straight what-you-see-is-what-you-get arrow—but when I'd left for residency, he'd fooled around on me with someone he'd met at a football party. I guess he'd finally found someone as passionate about the Packers as he was.

It hit me hard, I wasn't going to lie. Two years later, I had more perspective. My life with Charlie would have been predictable. With low-simmer arguments...and, I realized now, low-simmer passion.

And in the meantime, I'd done my best to get myself back out there.

Brax, the polar opposite of Charlie, had never put up the pretense of ever wanting to settle down, but I'd been completely swept away anyway. My brief time with him had been electric. I simply couldn't stop myself from falling hard.

"I hate men." I must've said that out loud, because Gabe came over, pried the wineglass out of my hand, and hugged me hard.

Shortly afterward, I got back to work dropping balls of dough on the cookie sheet. I couldn't resist saying, "I thought Brax spends Christmas with his sister in Philly." Brax and his sister had grown up in a rough west Philadelphia neighborhood. His ticket out had been a full scholarship to the University of Wisconsin, and he'd ended up staying on in our fine state for med school. He did his residency at the prestigious Children's Hospital of Philadelphia but returned to Wisconsin last summer to work. Jenna lived in Philly, where she was married and worked as an accountant, and Brax was very, very proud of her.

Gabe started scooping dough. "All I know is that Jenna's pregnant, and Brax is thrilled. I think he was going to make sure everything at the hospital was covered before he made a decision about going to see her." The chief residents made the schedules, which could get tricky over the holidays. We all worked extra hard so that every one of us could get either Christmas or New Year's off. It was common for the chiefs to pitch in and cover shifts to help it all work out.

I didn't know much about Jenna, but I knew she was all the family Brax had. He'd never elaborated much, but from little clues he dropped here and there, Gabe and I both figured that his upbringing hadn't been the greatest. All we knew was that he was very close to his sister.

Gabe set down his cookie scoop and grabbed my wrist. "*Ask him.*"

I rolled my eyes. "You're pushier than my Grandma D'Angelo."

Across the island, Sam nodded. "What have you got to lose?"

A lot. Also, I was making a mess of this cookie project. My balls were all different sizes and the dough was sticking to my fingers when I tried to fix them. "Hi, Brax, remember when we dated last summer?" I said in a fake-cheery voice. "Well, I kept embellishing that to my mother, and now she thinks I have a serious boyfriend coincidentally named Brax. By the way, would you like to come home with me for Christmas?" A groan escaped my throat.

"Maybe you can get to the bottom of whatever's holding him back," Sam said.

"That's the thing," I said. "Not wanting to keep seeing someone isn't a crime."

"If it makes you feel better," Sam said, "Brax doesn't do serious with anybody."

Except I'd thought we were serious. That he was maybe even The One.

Typical small-town girl goes to the big city and gets a reality shakedown.

Gabe stared at me. "I know what he says. But I also know how he looks at you when you're not looking."

I shook my head in denial. Except, to be honest, I knew exactly what Gabe was talking about. Sometimes, I'd look up to find Brax staring at me, his eyes a little heavy lidded, with fire burning in them, directed straight at me.

I might have dated my hometown honey for a lot of years, but I wasn't born yesterday.

Sam patted my shoulder. "How about we hit the town? The bars are still open."

"I'm not picking up some rando at a bar and bringing him home!" Geesh.

"Just an idea," Sam said.

"Right. A bad one!" The bottom-line truth was that Brax was a heartbreak waiting to happen (again), and I couldn't take another one. And that slow, smoldering burn that I always felt with him was just another reason not to ever bring him home—or anywhere—alone.

I must've looked completely stressed out, because Gabe said, "I have another solution. Maybe you should just come clean. To Brax, to your mom and dad. To everyone. Think of what a weight off that would be."

"Tell the truth?" Sam gave an incredulous snort. "Gabe, I bet you were one of those kids who confessed to sneaking candy in the cupboard."

Gabe shrugged. "Probably. But I didn't come out until I was seventeen. That was a whopper to hold back for all those years." He looked at me. "You don't have to carry all the burdens for your family. It's okay not to be perfect."

"I just can't," I said firmly. "My mom loves Christmas. And this year, things are so emotional." I didn't tell them, but my sister had died right after Christmas, and as you can imagine, the anniversary of her death always brought up tons of memories. But this year, with my mom's cancer...nope. I just couldn't tell my family I'd been lying for months. "I need to come up with Plan B," I said. "Fast."

Gabe embraced me from the side, rubbing my arm. I probably felt tin-man stiff. "You're really tense," he said, dropping his arm and scooping up a blob of raw dough. "That's what lying does to you," he added sagely.

Sam rolled her eyes. "I vote for the rando." Sam poured me more wine and counted on her fingers. "Exciting, adventurous, and completely out of your comfort zone. Just what you need, girlfriend."

If they hadn't been such good friends, I would've tossed some cookie dough in both their directions.

Chapter Three

Brax

Every single day as I climbed out of bed, I reminded myself to hold Mia D'Angelo at arm's length. To be friendly, yet keep her at a distance.

But every single day, I failed. Because Mia wasn't like any other resident. She wasn't like any other woman, period.

I was feeling the struggle at eight on a Thursday morning as I scrubbed my hand over my unshaven jaw and took a gulp of old, cold coffee. Mia stood in the middle of the ward conversing with one of our hematology-oncology attendings, Dr. Laura March. My good friend Gabe sat charting at a nearby computer, a refugee from the toddler ward who often snuck over here where there was less commotion.

Mia and Dr. March were at the beginning of rounds, where they would stop at each room to discuss the daily plan for each patient, basically making a square lap around the nurses' station.

I glanced up nervously, following their progress. The problem was that I knew something Mia didn't about her favorite patient. The question was, should I tell her?

Three rooms down, they'd soon stop to see an eleven-year-old named Rylee Hunter with newly diagnosed acute lymphocytic leukemia, the most common type of childhood cancer—which also happens to be one of the most curable.

Part of our jobs as physicians was to constantly walk a tightrope between caring about our patients and not getting too involved. So we could ensure our objectivity and make good decisions. Care, but not too much. Sort of what I'd forced myself to do with Mia.

Mia, for some reason, took this particular family—Rylee, with her brunette hair and big blue eyes, and her twin sister, Reagan, who had the same bright eyes but blonde hair—to heart. I worried about her because childhood cancer was a heart-wrenching roller-coaster ride—that was obvious. Yet I also knew that Mia was amazing with all the kids on the heme-onc service, big or small. She had a gift for talking with them and their families and helping care for them, medically and emotionally, that I felt was exceptional.

I wished she would see it too. That way, we wouldn't be in competition for the job I wanted more than anything. But whatever she chose to do, I knew she'd be amazing at it.

Just as I debated pulling her aside and letting her know the results I'd just gotten from the lab, Dr. Ted Brunner walked up to the nurses' station. He was the senior member of Milwaukee's best pediatric group, the "B" in BCP. "Dr. Hughes," he said in a jovial tone, "how ya doing, buddy?" He stretched out his hand for a shake. "I stopped by to say hi to Rylee's family. How's she doing medically?"

I got up and shook his hand. "She's a real trouper." She'd tolerated all the scans, X-rays, and blood tests like a champ, and they were almost at an end. "You're just in time to hear what Dr. March has to say."

"Great, great," he said. "They're such a nice family. Sorry to see them go through this."

Next to him was Robin Miller, the newest BCP associate, who also happened to be seven months pregnant.

"How are you feeling?" I asked.

"Great. Nice to see you, Brax." She looked tired, with dark circles under her eyes. I felt better when she managed a wan smile.

"Robin, how about you read through Rylee's chart and then meet me in the room?" Ted said.

"Sure thing, Dr. Brunner," Robin answered. Which I thought was a little unusual. Robin had been a resident in our program, but once you were out, you usually called your partners by their first names.

"Great," Dr. Brunner said, then turned to me. "Brax, walk with me for a sec, will you?"

When Dr. Brunner gave an order, most of us jumped. So of course I did, extra high. Hell, I would've run a few laps around the unit if that would have helped my case.

I wanted this job more than I wanted air to breathe.

It would be the culmination of a lifetime of struggle and heartache.

Dr. Atticus Pendergast, the "P" in BCP, who had been one of the founding partners sixty years ago, was the man I owed everything to. The currency he'd invested in me, despite our brief time together—how to person who strives to help others, how to not just survive but even thrive—had gotten me through a lot.

Even though he'd passed on years ago, I wanted to make him proud. Show him that despite all those years I'd spent in the foster system, all the hours of working three separate jobs and applying for every scholarship, taking every opportunity to get through college and med school—I'd finally made it, and now it was time to pay it forward.

Ted clapped me on the back and dropped his voice. "Brax, my

boy, I wanted you to know that our group is very close to making a decision about our newest partner." He beamed a big smile.

My heart began a slow, steady acceleration.

He laughed. "Don't look so serious. Of course, you and Mia are both still in the running. You know our group is all about maximum efficiency. We've got the lowest wait times for our patients, and we're the fastest at getting worried moms and dads appointments for their sick kids. That's why we take the brightest, most-talented residents who can keep up with the intense demands of a busy practice."

Dr. Brunner's gaze drifted over to Robin, who was still sitting at the computer, sipping from a water bottle. Robin had been a very high-performing resident. She was well respected and well liked. I couldn't guess what his point was.

I didn't have to wonder for long. He dropped his voice even lower. "There are certain members of our practice who feel they shouldn't have to pitch in and take call for someone just because they're of a certain gender, if you know what I mean. I'm certainly all for diversity, inclusion, and equal rights, but we're all working at maximum capacity. We want a new partner who can promise the same."

Mia and I were both efficient and hardworking, but was he actually saying something that I couldn't imagine in this day and age—that the group didn't want to hire another woman?

I swallowed my shock. Half my mentors were women whom I liked and respected. Years ago, Atticus had chosen a female physician as his first partner. And if this was about balance and humane schedules—weren't those things that were good for everyone? I got an odd, churning sensation in the pit of my stomach. One that made me wish I hadn't heard what he'd just said.

I was still figuring out how to respond when Laura and Mia walked out of the room next to Rylee's.

"Excuse me, Dr. Brunner." I suddenly knew what I had to do,

and that pushed thoughts of my would-be job right out of my brain as I took off toward them.

I mumbled something to Dr. March about needing a minute and then, before Mia could protest, grabbed her elbow and steered her a little way down the brightly lit hall. "The lab just called with Rylee's bone marrow results," I said.

Mia's breath caught. She death-gripped my arm and went pale. Her deep green eyes, the color of what I'd always imagined the hills of Ireland might be like, were filled with worry. She trained them on me, scanning my face. "It's bad news," she said.

She always seemed to read me, no matter how neutral I thought I'd trained my expression to be. "Not bad, but challenging. Not insurmountable."

"She's got cancer cells in her spinal fluid."

"Yes."

Her grip on my arm tightened, and her eyes got a little teary. I was suddenly glad I'd been the one to tell her.

"It's going to be okay," I rushed to say. Damn, why did I just say that? It was unprofessional. I didn't have a crystal ball, and cancer was scary in the best cases. She stared up at me in a way that filled me with the intense desire to do anything for her, like pull the moon out of the sky and hand it to her on a platter just to make her smile.

She called me out. "You can't know that."

"You're right, I can't." I blew out a breath. No human did. "But I do know she's getting the best care. We'll make sure of it."

She swiped at her eyes, and I could tell that she was upset. This wasn't great news, but it wasn't uncommon. Finding cancer cells in spinal fluid meant that the leukemia was present in the central nervous system. It meant more chemo, and more intrathecal chemotherapy, which was chemo injected directly into the spinal canal, but the odds were still very good that Rylee would come out okay.

"You can take a minute, and I'll cover you," I offered.

"Don't need it." She straightened up and took a deep breath.

"She's got a great shot at a cure." My words sounded weak, but I had to say something.

"I know," she said. "I also know everything this family has to go through for the next two or three years." She gave a little nod. "Thanks for telling me."

"Come find me when you're done, okay? We'll do lunch. Maybe check out that new place with the smash burgers. What do you think?" That was the thing about Mia. I'd friend-zoned her, but I kept finding excuses to spend time with her. Which was pretty messed up, but I couldn't seem to help myself.

She managed half a smile. She cared deeply about all her patients, but I couldn't help wondering what it was about this particular family that made her so emotional.

I walked back to the nurses' station. Gabe was still there working. I sat down at another computer and began to chart on my patients. After a few minutes, I turned to the sound of my name. Drake Shelton, one of the pediatric surgical residents, walked up, immediately opened a box of Christmas chocolates that was sitting out on the counter, and stuffed two into his mouth. "Have you seen Mia?" he asked in a muffled voice.

"On rounds." I gestured down the hall. He'd been coming around lately, doing what guys do when they're interested. Pretending it was a total coincidence that he just happened to be passing by the unit when he had no patients here, complimenting Mia on what she was wearing, flirting with her. I knew his game, and I didn't like it one bit.

I mean, the guy was a meathead. His muscles were the stuff of legend. He probably ingested a small cow daily to keep up all that bulk. Not to mention the Christmas cookies and homemade fudge, so plentiful at the hospital this time of year, that he was now carefully picking through as if he hadn't eaten in a year.

But the real reason I disliked him was that he had a reputation. You know the kind. Like, there weren't many female medical professionals in a three-floor radius that he hadn't tried to sleep with.

Also, did he even like kids? There was a reason children's hospitals were filled with nice people. They loved kids and somehow managed to balance the joy and heartbreak of daily life here. But Drake was impatient, short-tempered with the staff, and intolerant of spit-up, all no-nos in this world.

Whether I liked him or not didn't matter because I had no claim on Mia, which meant that I had no choice but to tolerate his presence with gritted teeth. And with my hands fisted in my pockets so that I didn't not-so-accidentally punch him.

Drake took a seat, stretching out his legs as if it were Saturday morning and not the beginning of a long and strenuous day. "I'll wait. She texted that she needed to ask me something."

Wait. She'd summoned *him*? As if that hadn't made my neck hairs stand up, Gabe looked up and went a little pale. "Can I talk to you for a sec?" He stood up and basically forced me to follow him down the hall until we halted right outside the on-call room door.

"I think you should know something," he said, concern plastered all over his face.

"What is it?" As chief, half my days began with statements like that. Which could mean anything from one of my interns having difficulties dealing with the emotions of caring for sick kids, to conflicts with other residents or staff, to the fallout from two residents hooking up. That was my job, stamping out fires. While making sure I didn't engage in any drama myself.

That was why Gabe, Mia, and I became friends. None of us were fire starters by nature, just competent, normal people who did their jobs and toed the line. Except I'd made a primary error. I broke my own rules. I'd gotten too close.

"Mia needs help." Gabe cast an anxious glance toward Drake.

"Is she in trouble?" Outwardly, at least, I practiced measured patience. From the corner of my eye, I checked for Laura and Mia. They were still in Rylee's room.

Gabe sighed. "She'll kill me if I tell you."

"Okaaay." My brain kicked into crisis mode. Debt? Eviction? A medical error? Someone giving Mia a hard time? That was doubtful, since she got along with just about everyone.

"But if I don't tell you, she might suffer even more."

My veins turned to ice. Her mom was doing great, but what if something had happened? "Just tell me already."

Gabe sighed. "She needs someone to go home with her for Christmas, no questions asked."

Irritation swelled in me, despite Gabe's good intentions. "That's why you pulled me over here? I mean, you're always matchmaking." Now Mia was back in the hall, moving on to Marc Markeson's room, a twenty-year-old with Hodgkin's lymphoma who'd had a rough night of nausea from his chemo. I figured I had about five minutes before she finished rounds and walked back to the front desk.

"This isn't matchmaking," Gabe said emphatically. "This is—"

"You know I can't." Mia and I had somehow managed friendship after what happened between us, but sometimes, things got awkward as hell. Like when she caught me staring at her. Or I'd catch her staring at me. Making me wonder if she was remembering the exact same things I was about our time together—how our chemistry had been off the charts, incredible. Too good to be true.

I'd done everything I could to stop the crazy attraction, but I might as well try to demagnetize a magnet. So maybe I couldn't help it that she made my stomach do cartwheels or made me feel like Pedro whizzing around the ward on Rollerblades, but I didn't have to act on it.

"Bottom line," Gabe explained, not letting this go, "is that she needs to show up with a boyfriend because she told her mother she had one, and I can't do it. And if you won't do it, *he* will." He nodded toward Dr. Suave, who was now flirting with one of our brand-new nurses. Ugh, no.

"She told her mother she had a boyfriend." I wasn't following.

"To help her get through her treatments, Mia sort of...embellished."

"Embellished." To handle a tough few months? Okay, understandable, I guess. Gabe somehow knew all about this.

But not me. I'd let her down, not just as a boyfriend, but also as a friend. I sucked.

Gabe was staring at Drake, who was now laughing and casually touching the nurse's shoulder.

Nice. That had taken him one minute or less. My blood began a slow simmer at the thought of Drake trying to sweet-talk Mia. Or touch her. Let alone spend an entire long weekend pretending to be her boyfriend.

Why was she even asking him?

"You *know* I can't go home with her," I said, as much for me as for Gabe. "It would be...uncomfortable."

"Maybe you'd like to talk about that sometime?" He folded his arms and cocked a brow.

I telegraphed him a look that said he was entering this discussion at his own risk.

"Okay, then, that's between you two. But while you're figuring that out, you should know that I wouldn't interfere unless I thought she really needed you."

Gabe was a fixer. He couldn't help it. He was always trying to push himself into my personal life on the pretext of "helping." He gave me a sad little shake of his head and a shoulder pat. "It's okay to let yourself feel things."

He felt *sorry* for me.

"Maybe psychiatry is your true calling?" I knew it was a bad joke, but I was on the defensive. My all-American looks fooled most people into thinking I was raised with apple pie and baseball and a fantastic family like I knew Mia had. And I did nothing to stop people from assuming that. In fact, I really didn't talk about my past at all because it would blow that squeaky-clean image to shreds, and what would be the point? "I know you think I was a jerk to her."

He'd been down this road with me before, trying to get me to talk about why I broke up with her, but I wouldn't. I *couldn't*. Talking about emotions wasn't exactly my strong suit. Or why it was so much safer for everyone to just stay friends. That way, no one got hurt.

"Do me a favor. At least talk to her," Gabe said as he left for the toddler ward. As I headed back toward the nurses' station, Mia walked out of the last room. A split second before I would've met up with her, Drake stood up and intercepted me.

"There you are," he said, his big, athletic form suddenly standing right next to her, dwarfing her more petite one. He flashed her a toothy grin, ignoring me and effectively blocking me with his body.

Every muscle in my body tensed for action. Ironically, I'd just gotten exactly what I wanted: someone helping me to keep Mia at arm's length. I wanted to push him aside and take my rightful place beside her. Yet I stood there, frozen in place, my feet glued to the floor solely by the conviction that I wasn't the one for her.

Chapter Four

Mia

When Dr. March told Rylee's mom and dad that she'd be able to go home for Christmas, they both cried with happiness. It didn't even dim their reaction when she added, "We'd like you to come back to the clinic on the twenty-sixth for the next chemo dose."

"As long as we can get her home for Christmas, it's a deal," Ryan, the twins' dad, said.

"We made you something," Reagan said to me and Dr. March as she rummaged in her pink backpack. I was thinking that whatever it was probably involved glitter, the girls' favorite among many craft supplies. That spoke to me because Gracie had loved glitter. I found myself smiling because I couldn't recall many art projects she'd failed to add it to for that extra sparkle.

"Merry Christmas," Rylee said as Reagan proudly produced a green construction-paper card for Dr. March and a red one for me.

Mine was embellished with markers, glitter, and plentiful snowflake stickers. It said, *Merry Christmas, Dr. Mia*. The snowflakes were surrounded by hearts galore.

I was thrilled. Dr. March and I oohed and aahed over the colors, squigglies, and the artistic use of glitter, half of which fell into my lap and drifted like fairy dust onto the floor. After we were done admiring our cards, I hugged both girls. "Thank you both so much. I'm going to take this home and show it to my mom."

My heart was filled with cautious hope for this family. I truly wished them all the best.

The girls' mom, Becca, pulled out her phone. "Would you each take a photo with the girls?"

"Sure. Of course." Becca took one with all of us, then one of the twins with Dr. March, and one with me. When it was my turn, I walked behind the bed and sandwiched myself between the two girls, curving my arms around their shoulders. I couldn't help noticing that Rylee was so frail and light compared to Reagan. As we held up the glittery card and posed, I said, "Everybody say 'Grinch!'" which got me a giggle.

"Okay, you two," I said, "I expect more glittery artwork from you when I see you in clinic, okay?" I pulled something out of my pocket and placed it on the bed between them.

"Glitter pens." Rylee's eyes brightened.

"Thanks, Dr. Mia," Reagan said, already reaching for them.

"Will you still be my doctor after I leave?" Rylee asked in a quiet voice.

I hesitated. A sudden sadness overcame me that I'd soon be moving on to my next rotation. "I won't be here on the ward again for a while, but I'm always somewhere around the clinic. I'll be sure to pop in and say hi."

Dr. March looked up from her laptop, where she was making notes. "Dr. Mia will definitely see you with me in heme-onc clinic on the twenty-sixth, right, Mia?"

"Oh, that's right." It would be straight back to work right after the holiday for me. "I'll see you next week."

"Thank you for all you've done for us, Dr. D'Angelo," Becca said.

"I love your girls," I said sincerely. "I'll be sure to keep in touch."

"We would all love it," Ryan said.

"Merry Christmas," I said, waving to the girls as I followed Dr. March out. "And thank you for the cute card."

Dr. March got a page and gave me a quick wave as she stopped in the hall to answer it. I was walking toward the nurses' station, dealing with the mix of emotions rolling through me—hope, happiness, fear, sadness from having to move on, guilt over my fake boyfriend problem, not to mention confusion over my career choice—had I made a mistake not going into heme-onc?—when I noticed that Drake Shelton was sitting there with his big feet up on the counter.

As soon as he spotted me, he put down his big feet, stood up, and scrambled to intercept me. I couldn't help but notice that Brax stood close by, checking his phone. He glanced up briefly as I approached, a concerned expression on his face. From Rylee's test result, or something else?

"There you are. You look ah-*maz*-ing today," Drake said as I reached the desk. "Must be that precall glow."

Brax rolled his eyes, which irritated me even though I wanted to do exactly the same thing. For one thing, I he was wrong—I wasn't on call tonight.

Also, I was anything but glowing after seeing those two little girls. Geesh. I loved my job, but sometimes I wished I could flee somewhere far, far away from reality. The same magnet that tugged me toward the Hunters, that made me understand *exactly* what they were going through, was the very same thing that made me want to escape somewhere where there wasn't any pain. I wasn't sure how to explain the terrifying push-pull that I always seemed to feel on this ward.

I turned my attention to Brax, who was now cutting into a piece of fruitcake, which I happened to know he hated. Ugh, did anyone really like it? And didn't he have patients to take care of?

He was such an enigma. He'd really wanted me to know about Rylee's labs. But now he was hovering nearby, not seeming to be doing any work. My guess was that Drake had told him he was waiting for me, and Brax was hanging around to find out what for. But if he thought he was going to eavesdrop, he was wrong. Brax didn't get to weigh in on my personal life. He'd signed off on that for good the moment he broke up with me.

I summoned my courage. I could do this. I needed help for one long weekend. Seventy-two total hours. Who knows, maybe during that time, I'd uncover a hidden sensitive side to Drake. He was a peds surgery resident, after all. That meant that he had to like little kids, right? Even though Brax believed he'd just gone into surgery because his dad was the department chief.

I'd have to lay down the rules. Be nice to my mom. Help clear the table. And absolutely no sex.

Eww. Every muscle in my body tensed. It was all I could do not to walk away from Drake, but a little voice inside me whispered one word, loud and clear: *Desperate.*

Which indeed I was.

While Gabe and Brax could possibly be taken for brothers, Drake, with his wheat-blond hair, beefy form, and rather thick neck, looked nothing like Brax. My mother, who was capable of naming the exact country from which every one of the fifty Santas in her Santas-from-around-the-world collection hailed based on the details of his outfit, would not be fooled. And while Gabe would do anything for me, including allow himself to be called Brax for a weekend, I really couldn't imagine Drake doing the same.

Maybe I should do what Gabe had suggested and just tell my parents the truth. But then I suddenly imagined my mother's face. Worried about me, as always. But mostly disappointed—so disappointed that I'd been lying for months. She'd been so excited and happy for me after all we'd been through—her cancer and these lonely years where I'd dated dud after disheartening dud.

The truth might set her back. No, she was too strong for that. But it would surely upset her.

I hadn't gotten to this point in my life because of indecision. But first things first. "Brax, don't you have something you need to do?"

He held up a plastic knife, poised to cut another piece of the awful cake. "Just getting a snack." He innocently sawed off a few chunks and placed them on a napkin.

Oh, eff it. I didn't care whether he heard or not. I took a big breath and plunged in. "Drake, I—need to ask you a favor."

"Anyone want some?" Brax held up the napkin.

I tossed him a glare. Drake reached up, took a piece, and popped it into his mouth, something that made me question my judgment even more.

"What kind of favor?" Drake asked. His gaze raked me up and down. Then he broke into a suggestive smile. "Anything for you, gorgeous."

Gag. Every feminist cell of my feminist body cringed. "Okay, it's a weird favor," I began. "It involves…"

I suddenly felt a hand at my elbow. "Hey, Drake, Mia will be right back." Brax set the entire fruitcake box in front of Drake as he whisked me off down the hall. As soon as we were out of earshot, he added under his breath, "Nothing."

"What?" I asked, balling my hands into fists.

He pushed a hand through his thick, gorgeous hair. If I did that, it would scare people. And why did I even notice that detail in the midst of being furious? "You heard me," he said in a slightly agitated voice. "It involves *nothing*." He waved his hand in front of my face, as if he were about to magically pull a bunny out of thin air. "You're not asking him anything."

"What the *hell*, Brax?" I pulled my arm back and mock dusted it off where he'd held it. As if I could dust off the attraction that flowed so strongly through me. We ended up at the end of the hall, glaring at each other, in front of a mosaic mural of children happily playing in the midst of a wild, colorful garden, one of my favorite pieces in the hospital. Did you know that children's hospitals had amazing art like, everywhere? "What did Gabe tell you?" Whatever it was, I could handle my own life. I'd been handling it for as long as I could remember, and not doing too terrible a job.

He crossed his arms. "Surely you aren't *that* desperate."

Oh, the arrogance. "I'm not asking him for a date." I didn't need to defend myself. "But even if I were, it's none of your business."

"Tell me you weren't about to ask him to go home with you."

That did it. I was going to kill Gabe. Right after I told Brax to cut the protective big-brother act. Fury coursed through me. Brax had passed on the opportunity to be a real friend. He'd rejected me romantically and then pretended every day that we'd only ever been friends. And somehow, I'd gone along with this.

"He's a tiger. A panther." He paced the stark white linoleum floor. "He's...whatever animal he is, he's on the prowl. And you know it."

I didn't understand his concern. It was pity-concern. It had to be.

"I can handle him," I whisper-shouted back. "You—you don't get to weigh in. I already have two big brothers. I don't need a third." What I really wanted to say was *Why do you even care?*

I hated him for caring. Because it made me fall for him even more. Just when I'd finally stopped asking myself what on earth had happened between us.

He snorted. "He's not going home with you."

"Excuse me?" I fisted my hands at my sides. We were all but duking it out in the hallway, a phlebotomist and a pharmacist quickly passing by and shooting us strange looks.

I tipped my head toward the nurses' station. "I've got to go, before he leaves."

Brax's gaze drilled into me. "He'll—take advantage."

I threw up my hands. "Okay, knight in shining armor, last I checked, I was an adult, capable of saying no."

"I'm thinking of your family. Your hospitality. At least take someone who cares about something other than his stomach."

"I'm a little short on those kinds of someones right now." I walked away, back to the nurses' station. Brax made me furious and something even worse at the same time—he made me hope that the reason he was so angry—dare I say *jealous*—had nothing to do with Drake and everything to do with *us*.

But that foolish hope was dashed when he said...nothing.

And I still had no one to bring home to meet my mom. My beeper was going off, I had two admissions waiting to come up from the ER, and Drake was waiting for me. Just then, Dr. March intercepted me. I was beginning to think that the universe was determined to keep Drake from coming home with me for Christmas.

"Do you have a second?" she asked.

"Of course." I took some deep breaths. Bringing my personal life to work was not working well.

"Mia, I know you're applying for the BCP job, but I wondered if you're still thinking about heme-onc?"

Oh no. We'd had this discussion last year when hematology-oncology fellowship applications were due. I knew all about the competitive program that took three extra years after residency to become trained as a specialist in childhood cancer.

"The deadline is long past," I said. Besides BCP, I had applications in with two other general practices in the greater Milwaukee area.

She smiled kindly. "I'm only mentioning it because you have such a wonderful way of dealing with our patients, and you're a great resident. And...the fellow we chose decided to join a private practice instead. We're accepting applications again—but just until we find a good match."

For a flash, I saw future-me meeting with families, getting to know kids, making the best and most cutting-edge treatment plans, all things that appealed. But then I saw Gracie's face, her young life cut short. I'd see her in every. Single. Patient. I *knew* I would, and it would slay me each and every time.

I held up my hands. "Thanks, Dr. March, but heme-onc is just not for me." I loved these kids, I loved their families, but a lifetime of reliving my own family tragedy daily through them? I didn't have the emotional stamina for that. Part of being a success was knowing your limits, right?

She searched my face. Dr. March had that gift that every good doctor should have. She listened, she saw. And she was scarily intuitive."I know you care deeply about your patients. But that's just the thing—we need doctors who care. Caring is a good thing."

No, no, it wasn't. I managed to shake my head. I loved the work when things went well. But what about the kids who couldn't be saved?

I wished I could tell her what was on my mind. But not here, not now. "I just want Rylee to get through this and lead a normal kid life."

She patted my shoulder. "We're going to do everything in our power to make that happen."

As she left, images of Rylee floated in my mind, so small and pale, lying in her bed, and her sweet sister looking lost and confused. And their parents, with desperation in their eyes. It made my fake-boyfriend problem seem trivial and foolish.

Between Rylee, Dr. March, Brax, and Drake—oh no, I'd forgotten all about him—my head was whirling.

I needed a minute. I checked my pages, making sure they weren't emergent, shoved my beeper into my pocket, and walked down the hall to the family pavilion, the place where I often snuck away for a moment of calm.

I needed a lot more than a minute, but I'd take what I could get.

I stepped onto the rooftop patio with a spectacular view of

downtown and Lake Michigan. It was cloudy with the kind of cold that slices straight through you. Of course, no one was out here but me. Even though it was morning, I could see Christmas lights in the street and on the top of the tallest hospital building, which featured a green Christmas tree with a blinking star on top.

I loved Wisconsin. The cold was harsh, but it shook me up. Made me understand what was important. Like the fact that my family was my priority. Nothing else mattered.

I closed my eyes and thought of a Christmas wish. I told God that I'd screwed up pretty badly, but I just wanted my mom to have a great Christmas. I wanted to hug her and tell her how happy I was that she was okay.

When I opened my eyes, it had begun to snow. Big, fat, sticky flakes, landing all over my hair, my face, my clothes.

I turned my face up to the sky and let them fall all over me.

It felt like a blessing. Like some kind of absolution. Or maybe it was Grace, watching over my crazy life.

"Take me," a strong, low voice behind me said.

I spun around to see Brax standing there, calmly meeting my gaze, hands in his pockets to stay warm.

All my anger vanished as fast as water down a drain. I'm not sure why. Maybe it was his expression—serious and determined. Or his eyes—he looked sorry that we'd fought.

Whatever it was, he stopped me in my tracks. Not to mention my heart, my lungs, and most of all, my brain.

I was completely off guard when he walked over, placed his hands on my shoulders, and said, "Take *me* home for Christmas."

Chapter Five

Brax

I was an idiot, and not just because I'd chosen to follow Mia outside into a snowstorm. I felt like I'd just swallowed my heart whole, where it was now lodged in my throat and obstructing my breathing. A state I almost never occupied except when I was a foot away from her.

Which was why I tried never to get close enough to smell her hair, stare at her pretty, full lips, or see all the emotions that flitted in her eyes—confusion, wariness, and maybe even a little bit of shock.

Accompanying her home was my worst nightmare. She was from, I had no doubt, Happy Family, USA, and I was the poster child of...well, I'll spare you the details, just to say I survived—I did better than survive, actually. But that didn't mean I ever talked about my past, except in therapy. Or wanted to be reminded of how I'd grown up. Or be thrown into a situation where I had to pretend I was used to affection and unconditional love, and people who always had your back.

I'd had my own back for as long as I could remember. And if I tended to keep my distance, it was because the people who were supposed to love me had kept their distance from me. It was my greatest survival skill. And Mia was threatening it.

"Come again?" she asked, her eyes blinking behind thick, dark lashes. My whole body felt funny, numb and tingly, like when your arm falls asleep. Maybe I could blame it on the blustery cold, but all sorts of weird things happened to me around her. Like muscle twitching. And sweating—I never sweated. I had the reputation of being cool under pressure, always.

"I—yeah." I swiped a hand through my hair, which I discovered was already wet from the falling snow. "You're not taking Drake."

In retrospect, I could've *possibly* phrased that just a tad differently. She crossed her arms and huffed. "And you have an opinion on this *why*?"

Just then, two of our favorite patients made their thirtieth pass of the day around the ward. This time, Pedro was pushing Bianca, which was kind of cute. They spotted us outside and put their faces up against the glass, clearly thinking that shivering out in the thick of snowmageddon was some sort of new game.

I lowered my voice. "You want *him* with your family?" Okay, that didn't come out right either. I'd made him sound sort of like the bubonic plague.

"Why wouldn't I?" She'd stabbed a pen through the complicated bun at her neck. Today she wore her glasses, which she sometimes did post-call. With the glasses on and tapping her foot, she looked like a schoolteacher. A really hot one. She crossed her arms from the cold. "He...um...he wouldn't say please and thank you." *Oh, come on, Braxton, you can do better than that.* "He wouldn't keep his big feet off the furniture." And the third reason, I kept to myself: *He'd spend the entire time trying to get you into bed.*

"Brax! Geez!" She gave me an incredulous look. My face heated. Did I actually just say that out loud?

"I appreciate the big-brother talk," Mia was saying, "but I can figure this out on my own, thanks. And you can tell that to Gabe too. " She started to walk away, to get out of the frigid cold. Good thing, because if she had any idea how *non*-big-brotherly my thoughts were, she'd be running instead.

If I were on a cardiac monitor, my pulse would be continuous bleeps. "Look, I don't know exactly what's going on, but I'm your friend. Friends help friends."

She did a one-eighty and faced me, her jaw slightly agape. I might've just shocked her for the second time in five minutes. Except I'd just managed to shock myself even worse. I was basically begging her to let me to do the thing I hated most in the world.

Her brows knit down with concern. I could see the clouds of worry in her eyes. And the doubt and mistrust. Both of which I'd caused.

But right now, I genuinely wanted to help.

She narrowed her eyes. "Why are you so eager to help me?"

I should have asked that very question before I opened my giant mouth. "Families are important." I tried to visualize what a family Christmas would entail. I'd sip a little hot chocolate, bring Mom D'Angelo something nice, hang out with everyone around the tree.

Who was I kidding? The only Christmas tree we'd ever had was the one I'd bought when Jenna was eight and I was twelve. It was right before we'd gone into foster care for the first time. I'd wanted her to remember that I loved her. That we were brother and sister, no matter if we were separated—which, it turns out, we were.

"I'm off until the twenty-sixth, just like you," I said, sounding my most convincing. "And I don't have any call until after Christmas. I promised April Green I'd cover for her if she went into labor, but she's not due until January first. So I'm free as a bird."

"I don't need your help," she said, but something in the way she said it made me wonder if she meant it.

Why was I forcing this? I'd be lying if I said I knew the answer. But damned if I was going to let that asshat go.

From behind her glasses, her astute, sharp gaze assessed me, and I quickly looked away, suddenly knowing the reason. It was right in front of me, in the form of that honest, shrewd, intelligent gaze drilling me down.

I'd failed Mia in a lot of ways, but I wouldn't now. Not when she needed me.

I saw that in her eyes. And that made it impossible for me to do anything else.

"Given our history," she said, "you would not be the best candidate."

I nodded, acknowledging she was right. I was the one who should be running away as fast as possible instead of standing here, freezing my butt off, pleading with the last person on earth I would ever want to be alone with again. Then why wasn't I?

Because Mia was a good person. A great person. And the story, while a little bit messy, sounded like something someone would do who really loved their mom. "I heard you needed a fake boyfriend."

"Yes, a fake boyfriend. I—exaggerated to get my mom through chemo. She's doing okay now, but she wants to meet him." She eyed me suspiciously. Snow had settled like a white blanket on her hair and her nose and had melted on her eyeglass lenses. She looked completely adorable.

"Well, I'm sure you'd want a really cute one." I spread my arms wide to demonstrate that I totally fit the bill. "I can definitely handle cute." Outside, I was being my usual charming self. But inside, my stomach was flipping pancakes.

"Stop trying to make light of this." She frowned and sounded irritated. Which threw me, because usually, my attempts at humor made her laugh. "This isn't a joke."

I held up my hands. Guess my charming self wasn't so charming after all. "Okay, sorry. I just want to help." That calmed me for a second. Because it was exactly true. "What's the fake boyfriend's name?"

Before my eyes, she turned as red as Rudolph's nose.

Wow, that must be a doozy of a name. "Is it Alfonso? Reginald? Obi-Wan Kenobi?"

"Brax, okay?" She threw up her hands. "His name is Brax."

What? It took my brain a second to catch up. "You named your fake boyfriend after me?" Or did she just really like my name?

She shifted her weight and looked uncomfortable. "I told my mom about you when we were dating last summer. But right when we broke up, she'd just been through surgery and was about to begin chemo. So I pretended that we didn't."

She seemed to be bracing herself for my judgment. But I got how the whole thing happened, and I wasn't about to judge. What I really got was how much she loved her mom. "Okay, so all I have to do is be myself." Despite my cut and dried logic, I got a warm feeling in my chest. Mia had told her mom about me while we were dating. What did that mean? That I'd been important enough to mention?

"You have to be yourself *times ten*." She stabbed the air with her finger. "Make that times *one hundred*. You have to be a wonderful, kind human being who is completely and totally in love with me!"

Ouch. I was going from feeling flattered to reeling from the fact that she didn't think I was that great a human when she added, "And stop looking at me like that."

"Like what?"

"Like you pity me." She turned away, fists balled.

Mia, who was an empath, a sensitive and loving soul who usually read me as accurately as a cell phone clock, couldn't have been more off course. I put a hand on her arm. "It's not pity." Even now, I could feel something between us—a pumping in my veins, a stirring in my blood, a heat all through my limbs that I could not rid myself of, no matter how hard I tried.

What was I doing?

Jumping off a bridge without a bungee cord, that was what. Still, I had to help her. It was that simple. "Look, no matter what you think, I *am* your friend." I stepped forward to show my resolve, but getting closer to her made me see the freckles she tried so hard to hide, and that made me soften even more. "And I have your back. Besides, I'm really good at Christmas carols, decorating, and eating delicious home-cooked dinners." *And shooting the bull.* Because I had no concept of what normal families did, except from the Hallmark Channel, which Gabe sometimes forced me to watch. "So...okay?"

Pedro and Bianca were now thumping on the glass. Pedro caught my eye and gave me a thumbs-up, which, fortunately, Mia didn't see.

Her jaw was so set, I could tell it was killing her to get the words out. "There are requirements," she said.

"Go ahead," I coaxed.

She counted on her fingers. "Be wonderful to my mom. No, more than wonderful. Amazing to my whole family." She poked me in the chest for emphasis. "And attentive to me. The best damn boyfriend ever. Minimal shows of PDA are expected."

I frowned. "What are you considering minimal?"

She counted on her fingers. "Sitting next to me. Smiling at me a lot. Kissing me—on the cheek." Maybe she noticed my brows shoot up because she said, "Don't worry, my parents are pretty straitlaced. They'd never put us in the same bedroom."

That was exactly what I'd wanted to hear, yet a strange disappointment spread through me. Little did she know that holding her hand and kissing her wasn't going to be the problem; keeping the PDA minimal, however, was. I managed to shake myself out of my testosterone-driven male fantasies and tried to be the man she needed me to be.

And then I felt a little nagging pull in my stomach. Brunner and his all-but promise of that BCP job. "Look, for these next few days, I think we should table any discussions about the job."

"Agree," she said cautiously. "There's nothing we can do about that now anyway."

Honestly, I didn't want to think about what Brunner had said. It was cringy; it made me uncomfortable. But would it be worth ignoring it to land the job of a lifetime? To use the leverage that came with the job to make things better? At some point, I would have to sit down with Mia and talk it all out. But for right now, she was right—tabling the discussion for the holiday seemed like the sane thing to do. "When do we leave?" I asked.

"When are you off work?" she asked.

"I have to round on Saturday." Christmas was Tuesday, and we had to be back to work the day afterward. I could survive a long weekend, right?

"Saturday afternoon it is." She looked both relieved and worried, skeptical and accepting of something over which she had very little choice. Her face was like an emotional map, with every feeling flickering across it—all of which I could read too well. I smiled encouragingly, to let her know I had this. Then I held out my hand. "Shake?"

She looked at me like I'd lost touch with reality. After all, it was a whiteout and we were shivering. She lightly tapped my hand, didn't shake it, as if that was all she could bear to do—as if the thought of taking me was so unpleasant, she could barely stand it. Then she turned to head back to the ward.

I grasped her hand before she could get away. She looked startled, like my hand was a giant alligator that had just clamped down for a tasty chomp. As for me, I was feeling a lot of things I couldn't even process. Like how in awe of her I was that she would love her family so much to do something so obviously distasteful. "Look, there's no reason for this to be awkward. We're over what was between us." Weren't we?

Then suddenly, she gripped my hand quite solidly. She looked me directly in the eye and spoke in her senior resident voice. "My only concern is my mother. Your ego is larger than I thought if you're still worried about something that happened six months ago."

Then she dropped her hand. "See you at three on Saturday."

I nodded, chastened. She hadn't been obsessing over our old relationship. This was all about her mom. "I'll pick you up," I called as she left.

I came in from the cold, stood in the hallway, and pulled out my phone. "Jenna?" I said when my sister answered.

"Braxy! Guess where I am?" She only called me that ridiculous name when she was really excited, and I could tell that she was.

"Where are you?" I rubbed my arms, hoping to get some feeling back after being outside for so long. I shook the layer of snowflakes off my now-wet hair.

"In my ob/gyn's parking lot," Jenna said. "Aiden and I just came from our ultrasound. It's a girl!"

"It's a girl," I repeated, letting the fact sink in that my baby sister was having a baby. Which I already knew, but honestly, it still hadn't really taken hold in my brain. "Jenna, I—wow. I mean, congratulations."

"Aiden just left for the office. As soon as I get back to work, I'll send you pictures. Everything's looking great and...and she's so amazing!"

I chuckled at the fact that she was obviously in total and complete love. "I'm really happy for you two." And relieved, from a doctor's point of view, that all was well.

I could hear rain pattering on her windshield. At least it wasn't blizzarding in Philly like it was in Madison. "So when are you getting here?" she asked.

I hesitated. Despite everything Jenna and I had been through, we'd never spent a holiday apart. "That's what I was calling to tell you...something came up."

"Work?" I heard the disappointment in her voice. "Please don't tell me you're taking extra call for somebody again."

"No, nothing like that." I took a breath while I figured out what to say. "I'm going to go home with a friend who needs some help."

Silence now filled the formerly chatty space. "A friend?" Jenna finally asked.

"Yes, a friend," I said carefully. That was all I was going to say. I mean, there wasn't that much more to it, was there? Okay, maybe there was. But I wasn't about to discuss it now with my baby sister.

Who turned out to be relentless. "Okay, I have one question. Is your friend a woman?"

I sighed, wondering if I could make my beeper go off so I could escape the rest of this conversation. "Yes, but it's not what you think—"

"Okay, let me get this straight," she interrupted. "You're going to help a 'friend' by going to her house for Christmas."

"Yes."

"And that's all you're telling me."

I considered that. "For now, yes."

"Well, okay, then. I'll accept that *for now*. But I'll miss you terribly."

"I'll miss you too." Could I hang up now before I confessed too much?

"But promise me something."

I rolled my eyes and braced myself for what I knew was coming. She was the younger one, but so much wiser. "You believe in yourself in so many ways, but you never give yourself a chance in relationships." Her voice cracked. "Maybe it's time for you to recognize the gem that you are."

"Hey, I'm the big brother," I said weakly. "I give the advice, right?"

"Not this time," she said firmly. "Since you're not coming to see me, I get to say what's on my mind. Promise me you'll think about what I just said."

"Okay, I promise. Now get to work so you can send me those pictures. Talk to you soon, okay?"

"Okay. I love you."

"Love you too. Tell Aiden hi." My sister had it together. I was so proud of her. I wanted to say all this, but I ended weakly, "And Jenna...thanks for understanding."

After I hung up, I stood there thinking. I'd just chosen going home with Mia for the holiday—actually *insisted* on going—over seeing my sister, my only family. But Mia was a friend in desperate need, right? It didn't have to mean anything else. I didn't want to admit that what Jenna said had struck a chord.

Chapter Six

Mia

During the two-hour drive from Milwaukee to my small hometown south of Madison, we were mostly quiet. I was enjoying the winter beauty of the forest-lined highway. Brax seemed strangely on edge—too quiet for him—but that wasn't my concern. My goal was simply to survive the next three days and pray they passed as quickly as possible.

He'd insisted on driving, showing up at my apartment with an eight-year-old Honda CR-V that he'd bought from a senior who'd rarely driven it and that he took impeccable care of. It struck me as a practical choice for someone who needed a reliable car and who was also trying to save money. Which was fine with me—practical was my family's middle name.

He helped me load my suitcase, cookies I'd made, presents, boots, and snow gear without complaint. When I got in, I patted the seat beside me. "My grandma has seat liners just like this," I said with an evil smile.

"I want to get full resale value, okay?" he said half joking, half defensively as he pulled away from the curb.

"I think they're cute," I said to let him know I wasn't poking too much fun. "In a retro kind of way." But I felt that I'd hit a nerve. I wanted so badly to know more about his childhood, what drove him to such practicality—but I knew he'd have to offer that up in his own time. So I kept the conversation light.

"So, what do I need to know?" he asked out of the blue.

"Beth's my mom. Steven's my dad," I recited cheerfully, "and you've heard me mention my brothers Liam and Caleb. You already know that Caleb's an orthopedic resident at UW. Liam's married to Dina, and their little girl is Emma. And our dachshund is Cooper —he's the real boss of the family.We've always been a doxie family."

"Doxie?" I appreciated from the side how his nose crinkled up the slightest bit in confusion.

"That's short for dachshund. I was working in a realty office the summer of my sophomore year of college, when my parents got Cooper from a rescue organization, and we bonded for life." I looked over and smiled. "He really counts as my favorite sibling."

Brax laughed. "What about grandparents, aunts, uncles, cousins?"

"Yes, yes, yes, and yes." Judging by his expression, I thought maybe it was good that over the next few days, Brax wouldn't be overwhelmed by my whole family at once; he'd just experience a few wild ones at a time.

"A few days after Christmas, all four of my grandparents are flying in from Florida, and everyone's getting together at my aunt's in Green Bay. We usually have everyone at our house, but this year, no one wanted my mom to have to host. I'm sad to miss everyone." I shrugged. "But I'm lucky to have Christmas off, so I'm not complaining." We both knew how tight the call schedule was around the holidays, how everyone sacrificed for their few days off.

Brax seemed to take all that in, repeating everyone's name like the good student he was. "Got it," he said. "Anything else I should be prepared for?"

"No, not really." So maybe I accidentally-on-purpose left out a few things. I wasn't talking about how my parents enjoyed piling on food and love to nearly anyone who walked through their door. Or how my mom loved Christmas more than Frosty on steroids.

What I left out was the big Christmas bash Charlie's family threw every year, that he and his new bride were hosting this year. After all, I wasn't going, so that wasn't really an omission, right?

I also didn't mention how my very tall and burly brothers were *extremely* protective of me, especially after what had happened with Charlie. I focused on imagining the expression on Brax's face when we pulled up the driveway, and there my brothers would be, big arms crossed, waiting for us. No matter what happened over the next few days, it would be worth it for that one moment of seeing Brax's face as they checked him over.

"Whoa," Brax exclaimed. "Why are you smiling like that?"

I didn't mention it was caused by the fact that my family had my back, no matter what. I might have been unlucky in love, but I'd hit the family jackpot in spades. "Just that you're soon about to be hugged by a woman who is known to put a Christmas bow on anything that can't move fast enough to avoid one. Just a warning."

The corner of his mouth lifted up. "Good thing I was on the track team."

"Stop," I said jokingly. "I didn't know that."

"Sprinter. College scholarship."

"Cool." That made me sad. We were "friends," yet I knew so little about him. Against my will, the image of a sweaty, shirtless, and very buff Brax jogging along our country roads flashed into my mind. *Whew, that car heater must really be cranking out the heat!*

"There you go again, still smiling." He tossed me a quick glance from the driver's seat. "Hope you're not plotting my demise and planning to leave my body in a snow-covered pasture."

"Only if you're mean to my mom or do anything out of line."

"Anything?" He raised a brow and sent me a look that sent another ball of heat barreling through me, clear down to my toes.

I wasn't going to react to double entendres that might or might not be purposeful.

I wasn't going to fall for him again, especially after trying so hard to un-fall.

I *was* going to be a freaking wall of self-discipline. I knew I could do it—after all, I'd had the cojones to survive four years of med school and a hair short of three more of residency. I would not let a man of all things get under my skin. No sirree.

I tried to focus on my excitement at going home and finally, finally seeing my family instead of my rogue feelings for Brax. Or the fact that I'd spent the past two hours trying to stop my heart from racing every time he smiled or said—well, anything, even something simple like "great coffee" in that low, deep voice of his. As a result, I felt a little shaky. My throat was dry and my nerves were jumping. Maybe it was from the giant coffee I'd consumed on the drive.

Or worry. Because once a person sees you with your family, it changes things. Makes them understand things. Makes them get to know you in the truest sense. I wasn't sure if I'd be able to keep hiding the intimate details of my past from him.

Not that I had secrets, but honestly, Brax had broken up with me. You don't confess your deepest wounds, your deepest feelings, to someone who's rejected you.

What was I worried about? He couldn't stay charming and affable forever. This weekend, I would see his true colors. And his imperfections. Like maybe he had stinky feet. Or didn't floss regularly. Or picked his nose.

"So, is Oak Bluff a small town?" he asked as he surveyed the view out the window, miles of farms and rolling countryside. As he drove, I took the opportunity to scrutinize his profile—strong—a nice forehead, a defined nose, a good chin, and a square, stubborn jaw. He sat straight but didn't tend to hold tension in his neck or shoulders like I did. The thick layers of his dark hair curled a little over his coat collar, his open coat revealing a gray crewneck that matched well with his faded jeans.

I could've chosen worse.

My heart sank. Because I realized that I *had* seen him when he wasn't charming and affable—I'd often seen him when he was exhausted and yet focused beyond belief trying to save a child from dying. And you know what? That Brax was pretty amazing too.

But who knew? Even the most affable, laid-back person could go bonkers when trapped with someone else's family for a long weekend.

"Yes, a very small town," I said. I felt that same little kick of excitement in my stomach whenever I thought about home. This was a region of water and forests, of sleepy little lake towns with Victorian summer getaways from a century ago, of forests and cherry trees and big blue skies. I almost said something like *You'll have to come back in the springtime when everything's in bloom. We can go out on the lake. We can hike and bike and pick cherries at the cherry farms. Visit the farmers' market and buy fresh veggies and bouquets of flowers bursting with rainbows of color.*

I stopped myself from getting caught up in my own fantasy. The part where I found someone to love, who loved me back. That someone, I reminded myself sternly, wasn't Brax.

Maybe he was the one who'd broken it off, and that had stung, but honestly, I didn't want someone who'd straight-out told me he didn't do serious. So there.

"Your family's got a little farm?" he asked. If it were anyone but Brax, I'd say I detected a little waver in his voice, a bit of nerves.

"Okay, so it's actually a big farm," I began.

"Like, with crops and stuff?"

"Yes, Brooklyn boy, a real farm. Five hundred acres," I said proudly. I counted on my fingers. "Corn, soybeans, wheat. And we have cherry trees."

"Cool." He seemed to be mulling that over.

"You've been to a farm before, right?" I didn't think I was prodding too much by asking.

"Does a petting zoo count?" he shot back a slow, charming grin. "And of course I pass a lot of farmland when I drive from Philly to Milwaukee."

I saw what I was dealing with. But I tried to be nice. "Okay, that counts—a little. But seeing our farm is going to knock your socks off. It's...beautiful. All rolling hills and fresh air and..." How could I describe what a great place it was to grow up? "You're going to love it."

"All right, then, farm girl," he said, still grinning as he turned to me. "I'll take your word for it."

From the passenger's seat, I could feel the familiar heat spread low in my abdomen, straight through my body, and flare out as a burn in my cheeks.

I hated that heat. It reminded me of our third date, when we'd brought pizza back to my apartment, sat on my couch, and turned on the Packers. When our hands grazed, he took my hand and held it. My breath caught, and suddenly the game commentary might as well have been in another language, punctuated by whistles and cheers in the background.

It all faded into nothingness as our lips met.

The way we came together wasn't tame, and it wasn't slow, but rather wild from the beginning, our mouths greedy, our tongues tangling. We clutched at each other until we ended up horizontal on my couch, his mouth devouring me, me sinking my fingers into the wavy thickness of his hair and pulling him over me.

He smelled like shaving cream and simple bar soap, his bristle pleasantly rough on my cheek, his hands sure as he wrapped his arms around me.

And then his phone went off. It was one of the residents with a question about transferring a patient.

The call didn't last too long, and I was about to suggest we take this to my bedroom when he sat down—now on the opposite side of my couch—and nervously tapped his fingertips together.

"What is it?" I asked. "Is someone really sick?"

When he looked up, I saw the heat that had so recently flamed in his eyes was replaced by conflict—maybe even misery. A premonition of cold dread shot straight through my overheated body.

"What is it?" I asked. "What's wrong?" Clearly something was.

He stood up abruptly. "Mia, I like and respect you so much. So damn much. But I have to tell you now that I never do serious."

I really liked where that was going until the last sentence.

"Do I—look like I just do serious?" The answer to that must have been yes. Six years with Charlie. Then two years of dating regrets. And now...him. And tragically, I was half in love already, after just three dates.

"I don't want anyone to get hurt."

Oh, that was the worst line. The line of rejection. I didn't want to believe it. I wanted him so badly, more than I'd ever wanted anyone. Maybe my loneliness had made me desperate, but I could feel the pull between us as deeply as you feel the deep, booming bass on someone's cranked-up car stereo at a red light. It felt different from anything I'd ever experienced with Charlie.

I wanted to joke, but I was nervous. I'd had a big breakup. I didn't want to get hurt again. Was he just not into me? But he looked so pained. I could see it in the fine lines above his eyes. His mouth was pressed shut, his lips a straight line. He shook his head. "I'm sorry," he whispered.

He got up to leave, but before I could think about what I was doing, I grabbed his hand and tugged on it. "Wait," I said. He turned slowly around. "Don't go."

I held my breath. His gaze was conflicted, burning, agonized. Before I could let out that single breath, he stepped forward, swept me into his arms, and kissed me hard.

And he didn't go. He stayed.

In the car, I shuddered from a sudden chill. I realized that Brax was calling my name.

"Where'd you go?" He touched my arm, which unfortunately started that tingling sensation again.

"You okay?" he asked.

"Yeah. I'm just—" I took a deep breath and tried to remember what we'd been talking about. Oh yes, the farm. My family. "I'm so grateful my mom's doing well. And my dad—he's been there every step of the way. I'm anxious to see for myself that they're back to their old selves." I was so full of emotion, I had to pause. "I have a great family."

"Wow," Brax said.

"What is it?"

He gave a slight shrug. "Most people have issues with their parents, you know? Or they don't get along with their siblings. You know, typical family stuff."

I understood what he was saying, but I think that Gracie's death had made us all appreciate each other a little bit more than typical kids appreciate their parents. Oh, we still had our teenage issues, but somehow, Gracie had made us older and wiser. Her death made us understand how lucky we were to have each other.

Speaking of Grace, I thought about mentioning her, but I just couldn't. Her memory was so personal to me. Maybe I should have, but I just...didn't.

I pretty much forgot everything I was worrying about as we finally turned into the long gravel drive. My family's vintage Queen Anne house was nestled in soft, snowy hills, and came complete with turrets and Christmas lights and garlands with red bows and an electric candle lit in every single window. Clearly, cancer had not beaten the desire to decorate out of my mom, thank goodness. And I still just couldn't stop grinning.

Home at last.

Chapter Seven

Mia

As soon as we pulled up to the house, the front door opened, and my family came flooding out. First Caleb and Liam. Then my Dad and Liam's wife, Dina, who was holding my little niece, Emma. They stood there and waved excitedly as we approached.

"It's like the fricking Waltons." Brax definitely sounded a little panicked.

I lifted a brow. "Like the old TV show?"

"Yeah, you know. They were a family with like, six kids from Depression-era Virginia who all, like, loved each other." He shook his head incredulously.

"Seven kids," I corrected. Before I could tease him that I knew all about the show my mom had watched as a child, much less grew up watching nearly every episode myself, he said, "But they sure didn't have brothers who looked like *that*."

I bit down on my lower lip to not laugh and then patted him on the shoulder in sympathy. "You should be more scared of my mom. She's a real hugger. My dad's a bit calmer, but if you start him talking about fishing, you're going to be hanging with him for quite a while."

My attempt at humor didn't work. "So, who are the linebackers?" he asked as he stopped the car at the top of the driveway.

"Caleb's the taller one, and Liam's the one with the big beard." I stuck my arm out the window and waved back.

"I should've brought my shoulder pads." A shadow of worry clouded his face. Unflappable Brax suddenly looked very...flappable. And I was loving every minute.

"Don't worry," I said, opening my door. "They'll only tackle you if you fumble." And then I got out.

My brothers whooped. Our little dachshund Cooper bolted straight down the porch stairs and ran all the way across the driveway to greet me.

"Cooper!" I bent down, my arms open wide.

Beside me, Brax emitted a low whistle. I think I understood why. Our house was picture-postcard perfect, complete with pine boughs draped around a picket fence that surrounded the large yard, and around that, fields, stretching for acres in three directions. The backyard, with its red barn, faced a little lake and some woods. And the front was...well, magical. With the snow and the lights, it took *my* breath away too.

I received an amazing welcome from the dog. What did it matter if all men sucked? Cooper was literally licking my face all over with doggie kisses, almost as thrilled to see me as I was him. I couldn't stop laughing. "Cooper! Coopy baby! I missed you so much. Yes, I did."

After a minute of intense mutual affection, I dusted myself off and stood up.

"I never heard you do that before." Brax gave me an amazed look.

"Do what?" I asked. "Baby talk to my dog?"

"Giggle."

I rolled my eyes, but to be honest, his comment startled me.

Did I giggle at work? Or anywhere? I hadn't exactly been feeling carefree these past few months.

I kept riling up the dog, and he was jumping, sniffing, and running in circles around me. As I lovingly bent to ruffle the fur on his neck, I said, "Cooper, meet Brax."

His big brown doggie eyes were full of love for me. *Me, me, me.* Not Brax, to whom he gave the complete cold shoulder.

I'm not going to lie. It felt great to be somebody's favorite, loved unconditionally. I wondered if Brax knew what that was like? I mean, not just from a dog. From people.

"Hey, buddy," Brax said, bending low and extending his hand a little. Copper barely sniffed it, returning to lick my face instead.

I have to say, Brax looked a bit put off. How many people didn't like Brax? He was one of those charismatic people who never lacked for the right words, and when he smiled—oh, Lordy, when he smiled, half the female population of Milwaukee swooned. I bit back a laugh as I straightened up. "Don't take it personally," I said. "He just misses me."

I felt Brax's hand on my shoulder. "If your dog's this excited, I can't wait to see how the rest of your family acts."

"Ha." I looked up and grinned. "Just you wait."

Just then, the front door opened again. My mom ran out, wearing a blue checked flannel shirt and a Christmas apron that said *We Whisk You a Merry Christmas.* Her hair was very short, cut in a pixie, and it was gray and curly—I was used to it being dark brown, straight, and layered. The last time I'd been home, in early fall, it had barely started growing back. I shouldn't have been shocked because we talked on FaceTime a lot but seeing her in person made tears sting behind my eyes. I ran to meet her, and before I knew it, I was wrapped in her familiar, vanilla-scented embrace as the rest of my family gathered around.

She kissed me and drew back to look at me, smiling widely, just as always. "Sweetheart," she said, and that one word, coupled with her beaming love, made me grateful beyond words to be standing here, in this snowy gravel driveway, surrounded by everyone I loved.

There is nothing in the whole world like an embrace from your mother. And mine had just made it through hell and back. She was thin and a little pale, but she was here, and as full of life as ever.

She soon moved on to Brax. "Braxton," she said, looking him over at arm's length and then clasping both his hands in hers "We are so thrilled to finally meet you. Mia's told us so much about you."

A pang of guilt needled me in the gut. To Brax's credit, he didn't so much as steal a questioning glance in my direction. Or blink at the sound of his name on my mom's lips. While he got caught up in a giant hug, my mom said something low to him that I couldn't quite hear. I could only see his cheeks color, and he nodded and smiled.

That was interesting. What did she tell him?

"Call me Beth," she said warmly. Then to me she whispered, "I like him." Threading her arm through mine, she added, "He's so handsome."

"Yes, he is." I smiled at him in a way that said, *And he knows it too.*

He must've heard, because he looked pleased, grinning so that one of his dimples showed.

Yes, he had dimples. The man had zero unattractive features, okay?

Brax smiled at me and gave an easy, nonchalant shrug that seemed to say, *Can I help that I'm so hot?*

Before I could parry him, my brothers bear-hugged me, and then my dad gathered me in. I squeezed him hard, wordlessly acknowledging all he'd gone through with my mom.

"I'm so happy to see you!" Dina said. She wore a beige cowl-neck sweater—cashmere—and black leggings, looking as put-together as always. Dina was in fashion merchandising, and her sense of color and style extended to, well...just about everything.

Emma, in her arms, had her light brown hair was in pigtails with one red and one green scrunchie. She wore a bright pink sweater, Barbie leggings, a pink tutu, and red and green fuzzy socks. And lest I forget, a little pink rhinestone crown hanging at a lopsided tilt on her head.

"Auntie Me-Me," my very bright and intelligent and beautiful niece said, "are you going to color with me?"

That was our special activity that we always did together even though she was more creative than I was with crayons. "As soon as possible, my precious. I can't wait." I hugged Dina, then kissed Emma on the cheek and gave her foot a little shake. "Nice socks."

"Great to see you, sis." Liam smiled and gave me another giant hug, then gave his daughter's right pigtail a playful tug. When he was single, he wore brown cords and sneakers every day, an ode to his job, as Mr. Smarty Pants was a brainiac software engineer for Epic in Madison. But thanks to Dina, he wore a smart-looking sweater and tapered tan pants, looking shockingly stylish.

Liam was four years older than I was, and he'd dated Dina in high school, so I'd known her for a long time. She'd always been like an older sister to me and was a born nurturer. If it hadn't been for her, I'm not sure how I would have made it through the Charlie-and-Erin thing.

My dad, less exuberant than my mom and clearly the calming influence in our family, shook Brax's hand solidly. Caleb, who was two years younger than Liam and two years older than me, clapped Brax sturdily on the back. "So, Brax, my man, what are your intentions?" Great. He'd wasted zero time putting Brax on the spot. "Toward our baby sister, that is." His gaze drifted over to me.

Like a true baby sister, I punched him in the arm. He had so much muscle, he didn't even flinch, just grinned and made a face like *Did a fly just land on me? I thought I felt something.*

It was jerky of Caleb to try to make Brax flinch. But that was how Caleb showed love. He was as protective and brash as Liam was quiet and thoughtful. Brothers. I loved both of them to death.

There was a sudden hush as everyone seemed to hold their breath for Brax's answer. Even the dog stopped barking.

Brax stood his ground. As the two men stood toe to toe, they seemed to be sizing each other up. Then Brax smiled at me and looked me straight in the eye. "I love Mia," he said smoothly, with feeling. "I'll do anything to make her happy."

My poor, lonely heart quivered. Like a droopy flower hungry for water, I soaked all that sap right up. For just a few seconds, I felt those words. Felt what it must be like to have someone really, truly love you. *Someday*, I promised myself. Someday, I wanted to hear them for real.

Then the guilt set in. I was lying to my family. I'd never done that before, and it didn't feel great.

It got even worse. "That's the most precious thing I've ever heard!" My mom clapped her hands in glee. "Steven, isn't that the best?"

My dad gave a slight nod to be polite, but I knew he was reserving judgment for when he really got to know Brax.

Oh, except he wouldn't really get to know him, would he? I'd just caught myself getting swept up in my own fantasy.

"Well, all righty, then," Liam said. "Welcome to Casa D'Angelo."

Just then, Dina met my gaze. She smiled and gave me just a flicker of a look that I took to mean *We need to talk later*.

Emma held out her arms to me, so I took her from Dina. She slid off her crown and put it on my head. I twirled her around until we were both dizzy. Then she took my cheeks in her little chubby hands. "Is that your boyfriend?" she asked—loudly, I might add.

"This is Brax," I said, replacing her crown. "Brax, meet my super-smart, super-kind, super-pretty niece, Emma."

"I'm this many fingers," she said, suddenly ducking her head shyly into my shoulder.

"Wait a minute," I said, realizing she was holding up five

fingers. "You're *this* many fingers." I held up four. Apparently, she thought that was the funniest joke ever.

Brax bent his head to say hi. "Nice to meet you. I'm Brax."

"Mia's my favorite aunt," Emma said, unducking her head. "You could be my favorite uncle. *May*be."

Thank you, girlfriend.

"I sure hope so," Brax said, his gaze sliding over to mine, his full lips tilted up into the slightest smile. Like we shared a secret. Like he was up to the challenge of being her favorite uncle. Or was he just hamming it up in front of my family? I was completely caught off guard. How would I ever know which of his reactions were real and which were fake?

I told you, he could captivate 'em. He was a natural-born charmer. Which made me shake my head and force myself back to reality. "Hey, can someone help us unload the car?" I called out. "I've got cookies."

I busied myself with the task, reminding myself that falling under Brax's spell could only bring disaster.

Chapter Eight

Brax

Mia opened the trunk and started to hand over cookies, presents, and other Christmas stuff to the males of her family. I stopped her at her suitcase and my duffel and took over. She looked a little startled, like she didn't expect me to do that. I didn't know what that said about the ex Gabe had briefly mentioned—Chuckie, Chad, Charlie, whatever his name was.

Judging by the way she interacted with her two very tall, very built brothers, both of whom were eyeing me like I was something that the dog had dragged in, I could see how she was, in a lot of ways, one of the guys. Which was one thing I really liked about her —she had zero sense of entitlement.

For some strange reason, that made me want to do even more for her. Besides, that's what a good boyfriend did, right? I wouldn't really know since I never let my relationships last long enough to find out.

The D'Angelo house looked like it had jumped right off the Hallmark channel, only to land in a rolling landscape dotted by pine trees. Mom D'Angelo hugged me like I was one of her own. The first thing she said—whispered, actually, was "Thank you for making my daughter so happy."

For someone who'd been through hell and back, I marveled that she was completely keyed in to her daughter's well-being. She instantly made me feel like she was the kind of mom who would be just fine with her clan putting their feet up on cushy ottomans in a big, beamed family room with a crackling fire, or helping themselves to food in the fridge or falling asleep on the couches after an amazing dinner.

The bros had taken our travel bags as soon as I'd set them on the ground, so I tried to take some of the packages brimming over from Mia's arms. Apparently, she'd brought presents for everyone, something else that amazed me. I was starting to think that she loved Christmas as much as her mom.

"I'm not helpless—hey!"

That was from me subtly tickling her side and then snatching the pile of gifts. "Hope you brought one for the dog." I couldn't resist poking fun.

"I would never forget Cooper," she said adamantly.

I laughed and shook my head. "Of course you wouldn't."

Mia's mom stood near the front steps as we piled into the house. Despite all her friendliness, she also looked at me with shrewdness—a carefully assessing gaze. I sensed that she'd seen our interaction and was sizing me up, seeing if I was good enough for her daughter.

Of course, I, Brax, was not. But Brax, Boyfriend for Hire, would have to be. And so I shifted the packages and placed a hand gently on Mia's back like maybe a good boyfriend would as she headed up the front stairs to the wide front porch and tried not to notice her great ass. She instantly stiffened under my touch. Yeah. Awkward. But hey, I would play my part to the max, because a promise is a promise.

Thank goodness her parents were absolutely not going to

tolerate any hanky-panky in their home. Sharing a room would be really uncomfortable, considering we'd actually *done* said hanky-panky.

Speaking of that, it was the really, really awesome kind. Like, the kind that comes around only in your wildest dreams. Where you're so in sync, you start to think that this person really understands you. *Gets* you in ways no one had before.

Good thing I'd decided long ago that getting serious wasn't for me.

As I walked up the steps and passed over the threshold, the dog rushed to squeeze through the doorway with us, and I was so busy avoiding stepping on him that I immediately clunked my head on a giant ball of mistletoe.

Mia, who was next to me, righted the swinging ball. "Are you okay?" she asked with concern. She was close, right next to me. We both became aware of the mistletoe, the logjam of family, and Cooper barking excitedly, not to mention each other. And we both sort of froze.

Kiss or not?

I cleared my throat.

"Don't you two even know what to do with the mistletoe?" Caleb said, shaking his head. He'd been sizing me up ever since I'd stepped out of the car. I didn't think I'd met him before, but I knew *of* him—being an orthopedic resident from UW, he'd definitely rotated through Children's as part of his program. He had the reputation of being levelheaded and friendly, although I'd never guess that from the evil eye he was giving me.

"Shut up, Cay," Mia fired back. She grabbed the packages from my arms and handed them over to Caleb. Who promptly shot me a dirty look.

I wasn't one to avoid a challenge. Before I could think, I closed the gap between us, bent my head, and kissed her. Mistletoe was mistletoe, right?

Her lips were tense with surprise, but then suddenly yielding, soft and warm. She tasted like coffee and cinnamon and cool December air. I tried to keep the kisses short and brief, but she pushed closer to me, closing the gap between us. She kissed me deeper, moving her lips against mine, wrapping her arms under my jacket, around my waist. I felt their heat and the soft brush of her hands through my shirt.

We just fit together, our bodies, our lips, our hands. For the sake of decency, I finally pulled back, sucking in a breath of air to try and calm my pounding pulse, disguising my shock at the intensity of those few PG-rated kisses. (At least I hoped we'd kept them PG.)

Mia looked dazed, her eyes soft and unfocused. She managed a quick smile, then backed up before following Beth into the foyer. Caleb mumbled something and walked ahead of me.

I was grateful to direct my mind to the house and trail behind Caleb to recover my senses. Its Victorian character was evident from lots of woodwork in the foyer and a large staircase with a shiny lacquered banister strung with lighted garlands. The banister was the kind that made me imagine kids sliding down it, screaming with glee. I tried not to let my pediatrician brain interfere by imagining ER visits for sprained ankles and fractured wrists.

A small peek into the family room gave me a glimpse of the largest Christmas tree I'd ever seen, glowing with multicolored lights. And a big fireplace just like I'd imagined, complete with a roaring fire. It was like another universe for someone like me. Sure, the foster families I'd stayed with had their trees and their traditions, but they were always someone else's. As a teen, I'd grown to hate traditions, resentful for never having had any of my own.

I rubbed my forehead, certain that I'd fallen down Alice's rabbit hole into this close-knit family. As with a few of the foster homes I'd had so much hope for, I had to be careful not to like this home, this family too much.

"This way, come on." Beth led us up, up, a grand staircase and into a hallway with high ceilings framed by carefully crafted moldings. The house had lots of quirky nooks and crannies, mostly filled with Christmas decorations like Santas, floral arrangements with pine and berries, and little lit-up ceramic trees, and it felt cozy and lived in.

We stopped in front of a tall wooden door that must have weighed a hundred pounds off its hinges.

"You and Brax can share your room," Beth said. With a flourish, she opened the door to a room done up in red-and-white bed linens, complete with a small Christmas tree glowing with red and pink lights. A giant window offered a panoramic view of the backyard, complete with the hugest hill I'd ever seen, covered with a blanket of snow so pure white, my eyes hurt.

Wait...did she say *share*? The room was more amazing than a hotel. And the big poufy bed made me think of all the things we *weren't* going to do here.

I could not share this room with Mia. Period. I didn't have the self-control to keep my hands off her. I knew this to be a fact.

"Wait," Mia said, looking a little alarmed. "Where's my bed?"

There was a bed in the middle of the room. One with a nice white wooden headboard. The dog immediately made a leap for the cushy pillows and settled right in. I didn't see the problem.

Mrs. D shrugged. "We decided it was time to upgrade to a queen. It's hard to fit two people into a double bed."

"It looks really nice, Mom," Mia said. "But, um—I thought we'd put Brax on the pullout in the library." I lifted a brow, surprised at her slight stammer. Apparently, someone else was nervous about the sleeping arrangements too.

"A couch would be more than fine," I chimed in a little too eagerly. I had to get myself out of this room somehow.

"That's where Emma's sleeping." Beth put her hands on Mia's shoulders. "Listen, we're so thrilled to have you two. We just want you to be able to come home and relax and...and we know what it's like to be in love." She winked at me. "We're not that old."

Mia's cheeks turned the same exact red as the bed linens. We were hosed. So at the very least, I had to antagonize her a little more. After all, I was here to do a job, and dammit, I was going to be the greatest Boyfriend for Hire *ever*.

I walked up behind her, wrapped my arms around her, and tucked my chin over her shoulder, unable to ignore that she smelled sweet, fresh, and clean, and...addictive. After nuzzling her neck longer than I should have, I looked up at her mom. "It's a great room. Thank you." Then I pointed straight ahead to the poster taped to the closet door. "Hey, Nick Jonas. Cool." Apparently, tearing him down had not been part of the reno project.

"He is cool," Mia said while poking me in the stomach. Which made me hide my *oomph* with a laugh.

"I figured I'd let you decide what to do with him." Her mom smiled and, with a twinkle in her eye, said, "You two are the cutest."

I could tell Mia really wanted to flee from my arms screaming, but she relaxed back against me, and when she did, her hair brushed my cheek. Again, I had the sensation of her somehow fitting perfectly against me. She was warm and soft and...

Oh no. My body was showing the evidence of being very close to her and touching her, and how did *that* happen so quickly?

I pulled away, but not without some side effects from the closeness. Like a weird tingling in my hands from where I'd held her. And a slight pounding in my chest that I quickly rubbed away. My senses being filled with that soft, powdery scent made me imagine all kinds of things I had no business imagining.

I stepped back just as her mom said, "I'll leave you two a few minutes to settle in. Then come down and have dinner, okay?"

The dog jumped down from the bed and trailed Beth out. And then suddenly, Mia and I were alone.

"Look, don't worry. We'll be fine," she rushed to say, staring nervously at the bed. "I'll sneak out once everyone's asleep and crash on the family room couch."

Her forehead creased in worry, and I had the impulse to reach over and smooth it out. Maybe take her back into my arms and kiss that worry away. Because those kisses under the mistletoe had lit me on fire. But no, that would be the worst thing. What was I thinking? Just being in this room was making my hormones go wild.

"You're not sleeping on a couch for three nights," I said. "I can sleep anywhere." I absently examined some photographs on her bookshelf. In the center, there was one of two little girls with birthday hats that said "5" on them, sitting in front of two pieces of chocolate birthday cake. One of them had curly blonde hair like Mia, but I didn't recognize the other one. A best friend or a cousin, maybe? The dark-haired little girl had cake all over her mouth and chin—like, she'd probably dipped her entire lower face into the cake to take a bite. Mia's cake, on the other hand, was missing a tiny bite, and her mouth was free of crumbs, but she was smiling just as widely.

So much of Mia was a story I didn't know. Puzzle pieces that I had no clue how they all fit together. Worried I was staring at the photo too long, I turned around. "Your family's nice."

"I *know*."

I heard a *pfffft* sound and turned around in time to see Mia sinking down onto the quilt, her eyes filled with tears.

Usually, in the hospital, she performed with toughness and the strength of steel. Granted, she had a few tears when I'd told her Rylee's test result, but now she was full-blown crying.

I sat next to her. "If it helps, I get what you're doing." While I didn't fully understand it, I knew that Mia loved her mother. A lot.

"I'm glad *you* do, because I'm really not sure how it all came down to this." She swiped at her eyes. "I've dragged you into this mess, *and* I'm an awful daughter. I should have just told my mom the truth. I should have told all of them the truth."

"Actually, I think you're an amazing daughter." I nudged her elbow in a playful way. That made her smile. A little.

If she were anybody else, I would've put my arm around her. But that would have been like lighting a match to a fuse. If only I could stop thinking about touching her. Instead, I gave her another paltry nudge.

She looked up, and I realized that tough, strong, impervious Dr. D'Angelo looked uncertain. And very much like she could use someone on her side.

I shrugged, disguising my almost desperate need to make her feel better. "You kept up your mom's spirits at a really hard time."

She made a dubious sound. "Thanks for seeing some good in this."

Trust me, I saw more than that. Her soft, full lips, those big, full-of-feeling eyes, and the glow of the Christmas tree lights on her hair were making me forget why I'd ever let her go.

"Brax, what did my mom say to you before we came in?"

"Say to me?" I asked, stalling. I knew exactly what she'd said, but repeat it? No, thanks.

"I know it was something. She whispered in your ear, and then you turned sort of red."

"She thanked me for making you so happy," I finally said, figuring I shouldn't lie. I instantly regretted it. Why, oh why, didn't I lie? Because that started Mia crying all over again. In a panic, I ran to the bathroom to grab a box of tissues. "Hey, it's all right," I said. "Better wipe those tears, or she's going to accuse me of making you really, really unhappy."

She didn't even crack a smile, instead pulled out a couple of tissues and blew her nose sort of loudly. "She thinks I look happy. All a ruse."

I sat down and put my arm around her, squeezing my eyes shut and trying to pretend she was Jenna. It didn't work. "It's not a ruse." I opened my eyes and forced myself to be the friend she needed. "Look, you have a great reason to be happy. Your mom is doing great. Your family is here together. And when the time is right, you'll be strong enough to tell her the truth. If I know your mom, she'll understand."

"I'm not strong enough to do it now. I'd ruin everyone's holiday."

"All right, then," I said, giving her the most platonic squeeze I could muster. Believe me, it took everything I had to pull that off. "For the next few days, I'm going to be the best fake boyfriend you've ever had."

That finally got me a tiny crack of a smile. And even that made me ridiculously relieved.

I was grateful for a rap on the door.

"Yo, Braxton," one of the brothers called out before I could even open it. Hopefully the nice one.

I swung the door open to reveal Liam, all six feet five of him, grinning and quietly rolling up the sleeves of a red flannel shirt. With his beard, he looked like a burly lumberjack ready to chop something—hopefully not me, figuratively or not.

"Hey, Brax," he said, giving me the once-over. "Mia, we're borrowing him right after dinner tonight, okay? We'll have him back by midnight."

Borrowing? Was that code for taking me out to the barn, getting me drunk, and making certain I was worthy of their little sister?

Mia walked up behind me, her hand resting lightly on my upper arm, where it felt like a firebrand. "You're not taking him out to the barn and getting him drunk."

Great. I was right.

Mia's mom came by. "Nobody's taking anybody anywhere until the dishes are done." She tapped Liam on the shoulder. "And by the way, I could use a few hands to help set the table."

"We'll be right down, Mom," Mia said. Closing the door, she leaned against it and heaved a sigh.

I rubbed my neck. "The barn, huh?"

"Listen," she said in a coach's voice as she paced in front of the bed. "My brothers are going to interrogate you. We have to get our stories straight, or they'll see right through everything."

I leveled my gaze on her. How hard could this be? I knew her. I mean, maybe I didn't know the details of her past, but I knew who Mia was on the inside as surely as I knew, well, myself. So, piece of cake, right?

Worry creased her face. "There are critical things you don't know about me. Things my brothers will bring up."

I counted on my fingers. "Jail time, previous marriages, grinding your teeth when you sleep?"

"Ew, gross," she said, her nose crinkling up adorably. But she still looked seriously concerned. Why? Could she possibly have even more secrets than the whole fake-boyfriend thing? Could she be a pathological secret keeper?

And I thought *I* was tight-lipped.

"Okay," I said, the problem solver in me wanting to fix whatever was wrong. "Tell me what foods you hate. Besides peanut butter."

She jerked her head up. "How do you know I don't like peanut butter?"

"Because you don't ever eat Valerie's famous chocolate-peanut butter-oatmeal cookies."

"I always take one," she said defensively. "Because she insists."

"And then you toss it."

"*No one* sees me do that," she said. "I'm very discreet."

I lifted a brow. "What else should I know?"

"I always win the sledding competition."

"Sledding competition?" This was getting more and more terrifying.

"You'll see."

Right. "If I were you," I said, "I'd be more worried for me. I mean, you've got oak trees for brothers. What are they, like six-five and two-fifty?" That was the trouble with being a doc. Your main weapon was your brain a lot more than your brawn. Not that I didn't work out, but I had more of a runner's build than a body-builder's. And these guys...well, they were big and beefy and as full of muscle as WWE fighters.

She smiled. "They really were linemen in college."

Of course they were. "Exactly what are they going to do to me in that barn?"

It was her turn to count on her fingers. "Brand cattle. Pick up the tractor and see how far you can move it. Make newbies shovel horse poop." My eyes must have gone wide, even as I was glad she was back in fighting form. "Don't worry, city boy," she said with mischief in her eyes. "They're usually mellower after they've eaten, so you're safe. Probably."

I couldn't take that sitting down, so I grabbed her in a fire-fighter hold and tossed her over my shoulder.

She let out a squeal, pounding me on the back and demanding to be put down.

So then I tossed her onto the bed.

Unfortunately, a side effect was that I landed with her, right on that bed, our bodies tangled up together, so close I could see the vibrant spring green of her eyes. They were the kind of green you see in May when it's eighty degrees and the sun is streaming brightly through the leaves, and they were wide and round with surprise.

And then things got quiet.

A shock ran through my body. An awareness. A slow, steady quickening of my pulse.

I sat up quickly, struggling to pretend I hadn't just experienced an inner earthquake.

I couldn't shake the memory of her in my arms, laughing and out of breath.

"You need to laugh more," I said. My voice came out low and gravelly.

In that one moment, the world seemed to stop. And I saw her. What I mean is, I saw the raw, honest feeling in her eyes. The attraction I'd tried so hard to hold at bay zapped between us like a hot wire.

I tore my gaze away and forced myself to get off the bed. I busied myself opening my duffel bag, trying to find a nice sweater to wear to dinner. Which made no sense since I already had on my nicest sweater, but I had to focus on something, anything else.

"By the way, they make you do that with one hand," she said, a mischievous grin spreading over her face.

I frowned. Mia was lying on her side, propped up on an elbow. She mimed bench-pressing a heavy object—the tractor, I presumed. Then she laughed again, sending all the tension inside me breaking like a dam.

Something inside me loosened. Go ahead, brawny D'Angelo brothers, tear me apart. Hearing her laugh—twice—had been worth it.

Chapter Nine

Mia

While Brax went downstairs, I pulled myself together. Yes, I was upset about the lying. But something else was bothering me. I'd made light of my brothers whisking Brax away to the barn, but the truth was, I had to stop them at any cost.

Oh, I didn't mind if they gave Brax a little bit of a hard time—they were just doing what brothers do, protecting their younger sister. But I needed to tell them that the subject of Charlie was off-limits. It would surely come up because my entire family was going to that Christmas party.

But I was not. And I did not want to discuss the details with Brax. At all.

Unfortunately, I couldn't commandeer either of my brothers because the kitchen was bustling as I walked down the stairs to find everyone busily helping to prepare for dinner. Caleb was setting the table. Liam and Dina were filling the water glasses while letting Emma help drop the ice cubes in with tongs. The fire was blazing brightly in the little brick fireplace. A smallish tree decorated with antique cookie cutters my mom had collected over the years glowed softly in the corner. Mom had woven pine boughs through the arms of the chandelier and lit candles all down the table. It smelled like a pine forest and a delicious beef dinner, all at the same time.

Watching the pre-dinner bustle gave me time to ponder the other problem I was having, which was that I couldn't help liking the handsome, fun, annoying man I'd brought home to my family. I thought I'd managed to put my attraction to Brax in its place. But being near him, bantering, watching him interact with everyone, was starting all my rogue feelings up all over again, and what was I supposed to do about that?

Not to mention those kisses that felt anything but fake.

I'd been so worried about my mom, wanting to do anything not to disappoint her, but what if I was the casualty here? It had taken my poor heart months to get over Brax, to accept that we were just friends. What if this weekend did me in for good?

Speaking of Brax, he was standing at the island chopping pecans. I had to smile because he wore the same intense look of concentration as when he was studying a chart, examining a patient, or playing Wordle on his phone. Next to him, my dad was adding cranberries, cubes of orange squash, and feta cheese to a bowl full of greens.

"My favorite salad," I said to my dad.

I walked over to the sink and poured a glass of water. My dad had gone to the fridge, where he rummaged for dressing ingredients. "You are quite the chopper," I said to Brax as I walked over to him.

He shrugged and gave a half-curved-up smile. "Don't underestimate these good looks," he said in a voice meant only for me. "I'm multitalented in other areas besides medicine."

I rolled my eyes to disguise the fact that I was already imagining *what* areas. "Humble too."

"You bet." With his knife, he raked the pecans down the

cutting board and into a bowl. "Your dad and I had a heart-to-heart."

"Already?" The thirty seconds of relative peace I experienced devolved into another adrenaline spike. "What about?" I took a sip of water to calm myself.

"Oh, the usual. Business. Sports teams. When we're setting the date."

I choked on the water.

"Just teasing." He tossed me a smile filled with mischief that made me love-hate him. Love because his smile was, well, nothing short of dazzling. And hate because it reminded me that he was not averse to giving as good as he got. He'd be just fine with my brothers.

I helped Caleb finish setting the table, and we all sat down. My mom brought a giant pot of boeuf bourguignon from the stove and set it next to the loaf of crusty, warm bread my dad had baked himself earlier today.

Liam was helping Dina get Emma settled, and my mom and dad were preparing the food. Caleb was staring at Brax. Like, really staring at him. Before I could figure out why, my dad raised his hands, a signal for all of us to join ours together.

Oh no. I knew what was coming. I didn't mind grace. But I could exactly predict what my dad was about to say.

"Let's all bow our heads," he said, giving a definitive nod.

My dad was about to do what he always did every time all of us were home. Say grace, yes. But a very personal, very extemporaneous version that I really didn't want Brax to hear. I didn't think my dad would go there with a guest present at the table.

"Dad, I—maybe we shouldn't—" My brothers looked up, looking at me like, *What's the big deal?* Liam shifted in his chair. Caleb tossed me a sad little smile, as if he, too, wished Dad would keep it simple.

My dad was about to get super personal. I suddenly didn't want Brax to learn of the tragedy that had split our family, that had taken my sister away, that had frozen her in time so that she was eternally nine years old.

It was too intimate. It was as if, by knowing about Grace, he would know other things about me that I tried very carefully to hide.

"How about a generic version, just for tonight?" I asked. More like pleaded.

"It's okay, honey," Dad said, smiling a kind smile. "I'm sure Brax won't mind what we usually say."

"All good," Brax said, scanning my face carefully. Panicked, I looked away.

"I just wanted to keep it light, you know?" I said weakly. Because Dad's prayer was always a tearjerker. I supposed I'd have to get used to spending this entire weekend in tears.

"Dear Lord," my dad said, ignoring me and plunging in as everyone folded their hands. "We thank you for the blessing of this food. For the blessing of family." He glanced at each person around the table, and then rested his gaze on my mom. "For the blessing of good health. For the blessing of love." Then he looked at me and Brax. "We thank you for bringing us new people to love." Lifting his gaze upward, he said, "We know that our Gracie is looking down at us from your loving arms and is with us in spirit as we celebrate. Amen."

"Amen," everyone echoed.

"To Gracie," Caleb said, holding up his wineglass. For being as tough on the outside as Caleb was, he couldn't hide his mushy heart.

"To Gracie," Liam seconded.

My mom lifted her glass and nodded, her lips pressed together. I could only nod as well and lift my glass. Brax lifted his glass and simultaneously took my hand, leaving me to swipe at my eyes with the other one. And then do you know what he did? He squeezed it. Just like that. No questions. Just a tiny little *I got you* squeeze.

My mom dabbed at her eyes with her napkin. "She's always in our thoughts," she explained. "We like to say her name."

Leave it to my mom to tell it like it was. As a family, we acknowledged out loud the one who wasn't with us.

"That's amazing," Brax said. And he sounded sincere.

I glanced over, and there he was, giving me the softest smile. And that made me feel...like he got it. Without even knowing who Gracie was, he sensed something personal, private, and sad, and he acknowledged it. He acknowledged *her*.

Then suddenly, Liam was digging in. He passed Brax the peas, who took some for himself and then handed the bowl to me. "Peas?" he asked.

Studying me closely, Caleb said, "Dude, she, like, hates peas."

Brax froze with the peas in midair. I could practically feel him wondering what to do next. On the outside, Brax was calm, but a telltale flush was creeping up his neck. He hated screwing up: I knew this well from work. I took the bowl from his hands and said the most difficult words I'd ever had to utter. "Peas have antioxidants and..." And what? "and I, um...I love them now." I scooped out a generous serving on my plate as I smiled, I'm sure quite maniacally, as my entire family stared.

Why didn't I tell him earlier I hated peas? And even worse— what else didn't I tell him that mattered? *A lot*, it turned out.

"You love peas now?" my mother asked in an incredulous tone. "That's...amazing."

I shrugged, dying on the inside, knowing that I would now unfortunately have to put my money where my mouth was. I levered a dreaded green spoonful up to my mouth. "Yep. Love 'em," I said, then forced myself to take a bite, smiling while the sickening pasty vegetable filled my taste buds with its mushy *blech* flavor.

Then I did the only thing that would make this bearable. Washed it down with my wine. Lots of it.

And then almost my entire glass of water. Trying to do that

subtly, while your brothers are watching you openmouthed in disbelief, is not an easy feat. Especially Caleb, who was piercing me with that astute, sharp gaze of his.

I drank more wine to help me get over the trauma. But even then, the aftertaste...ugh. Good thing I didn't bring home fake boyfriends often, because that had been *really* painful.

The worst thing was, how many peas could I hide in my beef stew or under the mound of mashed potatoes? Because I still had a giant heap left on my plate. And unless my family wanted to witness someone throwing up all over the pretty Christmas table, I was in big trouble. I had reached my limit.

"What's your family like, Braxton?" my dad asked. "Mia tells us you're very close to your sister."

"I am. She lives in Philly with her husband, and she's expecting her first child," he said. I could hear the pride in his voice. "Both our parents have passed."

Not for the first time, I wondered why he wasn't with his sister. Why had he agreed to bail me out in the middle of Snowville, Wisconsin, instead?

"Oh, honey," my mom said. "I'm so sorry."

"No, it's okay." Then he looked my way and smiled a wonderfully smitten boyfriend smile that was so good, it sent goose bumps up and down my arms. Or maybe that was just a reaction from the dreadful peas. "That's why I was so excited to come home with Mia. It's been a long time since I've had a family Christmas."

What kind of Christmases did he have? How had his parents passed? He was like the blank pages of a book I wanted desperately to fill in.

This was such a dangerous game we were playing. One that made me greedily want to know more, more, more. The truth and the lies all blended together so that I was losing track of which was which. I felt like I was on the edge of a precipice, ready to fall into the trap of crossing the line between real and pretend. And it was only dinnertime.

Guilt and confusion flooded me. But that awful pea aftertaste kept me grounded in strict reality.

"You've come to the right place," Caleb said, shaking his head as he cut a bite of the beef that was so tender that it literally fell apart on his fork. "Mom loves Christmas more than Mrs. Claus."

"What I love is having you all here," my mom said with a crack in her voice.

My heart swelled with happiness and gratitude that my mom was on the road back to health. And that I was with the people I loved most in the world.

"Santa's coming," Emma said, her tiny voice almost a whisper. "In this many days." She held up three fingers.

"What did you ask Santa for?" Brax asked with the practiced nonchalance of someone who talks with kids all day long.

"Mommy and me took my old books to the kids at the hospital," she said. "So I got to ask Santa for more."

"That's really kind of you, Emma," Brax said. "Having fun books to read is really important for kids."

Emma beamed. Yet another woman succumbing to his spell, no doubt.

"She loves books," Dina explained.

As I glanced down at my plate, I noticed my peas had vanished. Just like that. As Brax was dazzling me with his smile, he must've scooped them right up.

I felt—well, a little dizzy, to be honest. I wasn't used to somebody having my back. I was used to having my own back, which was working out just fine, thank you. But still, what he'd done floored me. And also made me relieved, because I knew that I was one pea away from a giant hurl.

I shifted my gaze to Brax, but he was laughing at something my mother said.

As dinner wore on, I braced myself for embarrassing anecdotes from my brothers, like the time I'd tossed a half-peeled potato at Liam and given him a black eye, or how I'd been able to outrun both of them for most of my teen years, until they turned into bricks of solid muscle, or a more touching one about the time I'd gotten into med school and both of them spontaneously showed up at my college dorm with champagne. All classic family lore, which got told in one form or another during that dinner.

"Tell everyone that funny story about how you two met," Mom said, setting down her fork, propping her elbows, and tenting her fingers, all ears.

Brax seemed to be all ears too.

Panic closed my throat as I considered what to say. We'd actually met twice. The first time was at a bar. We'd each gone with friends, and our respective teams had gone head-to-head in a trivia game.

He'd told me that night that he'd just moved from Philadelphia, where he'd done his residency at CHOP, to take a position in the clinic at Children's Wisconsin because he loved to teach. And because of his mentor, Dr. Atticus Pendergast, whom he'd met while he was an undergrad at UW. Dr. Pendergast was a legend, a beloved pediatrician who was still revered in town. I loved that Brax had been lucky enough to know and be inspired by him. Brax hoped—like many of us residents who were planning to stay in Milwaukee—to land a prime spot in the impressive practice that he created.

Our connection was instant, raw, and electric. That night was followed by two glorious weeks where I was certain I'd found my soul mate.

I decided to stick with the G-rated version. I racked my brain to remember precisely what I'd told my mom, what exactly that version was.

Our next "meeting" had been at the hospital, at the welcome-new-residents meeting in July where Brax introduced himself as the chief resident in charge of interns.

Yeah, not a meet cute. Because as I sat there, it dawned on me that he was the guy I thought I was in love with, the guy who hadn't called me in the week since our last date, who hadn't been answering my texts. Then Sam, who was seated next to me, whispered, "I'd like to have a private morning report with him." She chuckled. "At his place."

I sat there frozen, my heart practically fibrillating in my chest. Because I had *been* at his place. As recently as last weekend, eating Chinese and having hot, wild sex in his bed...and other places.

I smacked my head. Suddenly, I got it. Why he hadn't called me.

Could it be he'd discovered that he was my colleague? He'd been going to teach in the clinic, but now for some reason, he ended up as a chief resident in my program. But even with the job switch, he had no authority or power over me. He wasn't my boss —he was in charge of the brand-new residents, the interns, the ones fresh out of med school. Not. Me.

Was he merely ghosting me in the cruelest way possible, one that would mean we'd see each other every single day despite having broken up?

I felt like a fool.

And I was angry. Why hadn't he told me? Been an adult about it?

Brax seemed completely unperturbed, not acknowledging me in any way other than as a present and accounted-for resident. A warm body to take call and keep the wards orbiting in their usual state of contained chaos.

This was not a meet cute. It was a fricking nightmare.

After the meeting, everyone scurried away to do their twelve-plus hours of work. I told Sam I needed to stay and discuss some business.

How could Brax blindside me like this? Also, how on earth were we supposed to work together after all this?

Brax and I walked down to a tiny used-to-be medical supply closet, which was now his office. He unlocked the door and gestured for me to go inside.

It was a tiny space with a bare desk, white walls, and glaring fluorescent lighting that whitewashed everything. A blank slate, waiting for the next person to move in. As soon as the door clicked behind him, he let out a huge sigh and said, "Mia, I'm sorry."

To his credit, not the worst way to begin. But still. "For what? Dating me, having sex with me, or ghosting me without a word?" Fists balled, I braced for his answer.

"I could never be sorry for dating you." He met my gaze. "I just can't keep doing it."

I swept my arm around the antiseptic-smelling closet-office. "Is this why you ghosted me? Why didn't you tell me?"

To his credit, he looked pained. But I had no sympathy. I was being dumped—again. I'd fallen head over heels, but he clearly wasn't feeling the wonderfulness, the euphoria, the magic. *Ouch.*

"The person they chose to be chief left suddenly for family reasons, so they offered me the job. I took it because it was academic, and I'd get an opportunity to interact with the residents. Now that I'm the chief," he said, "dating would be awkward."

"You're not *my* chief." I knew what he was doing. Using this as an excuse to get out of...us. "If you weren't feeling it, you should have told me. Before now." I shook my head. I wanted to kill someone— specifically him. But I was a professional, and suddenly, we were in a professional relationship—one where we would not only be seeing each other every single day, but also working closely together, taking call, working to save lives.

The enormity of that revelation nearly brought me to my knees. The entirety of a year. Every. Single. Day.

I'd felt things with him—things I hadn't felt during my million years with Charlie. I'd been completely, unabashedly myself. I was totally blindsided, and that hurt like hell.

I turned to leave.

He called my name. Put a hand on my arm so I would turn around. And I did. I looked into his eyes. I saw conflict. Remorse. Probably from the regret of starting things up in the first place.

Stupid, stupid me.

He spoke calmly and softly. But that didn't stop me from being furious. "I want you to know you're really special," he said. "But doing a relationship under these circumstances won't work for me. I can't show partiality to you. I can't let my emotions impact decisions." He paused a long time as we stood there, staring at each other. "I hope we can still be friends."

It was the typical blow-off line. I hadn't been the recipient of that because of dating Charlie for forever, but all my friends had. Now it was my turn to experience this special form of humiliation.

Bitterly, I realized that Brax had warned me. He'd straight-out told me from the get-go that he wasn't the type to settle down, but I'd fallen for him anyway.

He looked miserable, and I was glad. I straightened my spine and pulled out my courage. "I won't say a word to anyone, and I'll treat this like a working relationship." And then I left.

He called my name. Tears were already leaking from my eyes, but there was no way I was going to let him see them.

Back at the table in my parents' house, I was a mess of emotions, all because of the most simple, straightforward question. I hadn't wanted to remember that day. It seemed incredible that we'd somehow become friends after that—but we worked so well as a team, and we often found ourselves on call together, bound by the adrenaline rush of life and death. I was trying to figure out how I got from there to here, with Brax at my home, sitting around the table with my family, when he touched my arm, bringing me back to reality.

"I'll tell the story," Brax said, completely unruffled by my spacing out. "It was after midnight one night last July, our first night on call together, and we were getting hit with admissions left and right. The cafeteria had closed, I'd missed dinner, and I was starving. I walked up to the toddler ward to maybe steal some graham crackers and apple juice to tide me over until morning. It was dim and quiet, and there was Mia, sitting on the floor in her scrubs, reading a book to a kid and unwrapping a sandwich."

My heart began a slow but loud thump-thump-thump that surely everyone at the table could hear.

I remembered that night. We'd gotten killed with relentless admissions, one after another, until around 2:00 a.m., when the constant panicked rush of stamping out fires finally slowed. Brax wasn't the only one who'd missed dinner. I'd had to break out my emergency food supply. And as for the little kid...he couldn't sleep in a strange, unfamiliar place with the wheezing and a fever and a snotty nose, and the book was the only thing that had stopped him crying.

As Brax continued, I hung on every word. "I walked over, and as she kept reading out loud, she reached into the baggie, pulled out a half of her sandwich, and handed it to me."

"What kind of sandwich was it?" my dad asked, laughing. Because he already knew the answer.

I shrugged. "Almond butter and strawberry jam."

My dad flashed a knowing smile—because how many of those had he made for me in my lifetime? "That's my girl," he said with a wink.

I thought I was the captive audience, but when I looked at my family, they were all totally swept up in the story.

"I guess I made a face," Brax said, "because I'd never had almond butter before. But that night, it tasted like prime rib." As my family laughed, his gaze strayed to mine and held. "That's how I knew Mia was not just a competent resident. She'd shown me that all night. But now I saw she was also kind."

Our gazes locked. How did he do it? His sappy story had held my entire family spellbound and made my limbs suddenly turn to warm molasses, all the silverware clinking and laughter and murmuring fading around me as I felt that same relentless connection surge between us.

Such a simple story. But he told it in such a way that he had me believing that it was fricking love at first sight.

Geesh.

Of course, he'd left out a few details. Like how at first, he refused, but I could tell how starving he was, and so I pushed the sandwich at him as I continued reading about the little green room and the cow jumping over the moon. He took a bite and then made a terrible face that told me he literally had never tasted almond butter before, which prompted me to say, "Beggars can't be choosers."

"Yeah. You're right," he said, chasing it with a little container of apple juice. "Actually, it's not bad. In fact, it tastes as good as a loaded pizza right now because I'm famished. Thank you."

"I have to finish the story," I told my family. To Brax, I said, "You felt bad that you ate half my sandwich. So a few hours later, you showed up with a warm sausage and egg sandwich and coffee."

He shrugged.

"You two are the cutest," Dina said.

Brax was quite the storyteller. But as I returned to my mercifully pea-less plate, I sternly reminded myself that it was just a story. A simple act of taking care of each other between people who were in a kind of war zone together.

And a nice thing to tell people when the truth was way too painful.

It didn't mean anything more.

But part of me couldn't help wishing that it did.

Chapter Ten

Mia

As dinner ended, I shook the stardust from my feet and got back to reality because I had an important fire to put out. I cornered Liam in the kitchen while he was loading his plate into the dishwasher and pulled him over to the little nook near the back door. "Maybe you two shouldn't take Brax..."

He gave me a sweet, older brother smile. "Don't worry, we'll go easy on him, sis." He chuckled at my concern. "We just want to get to know him better." He extended his arms and cracked his knuckles ominously just to torment me.

"Okay, but—" I opened my mouth to say—no, to beg—*Please don't tell him about Charlie*. But then I stopped myself. What kind of girlfriend wouldn't tell her serious boyfriend about the Charlies in her life?

I mean, I would have if we'd had more than a handful of dates. After that, I purposely kept the personal info to a minimum. With all the trauma of getting him here, I'd avoided giving him the course on Mia 101. How were my brothers not going to see straight through this sham?

"What's going on?" Caleb asked from the top of the stairs. "What's the huddle for? Is Mom okay?"

"Mia's worried about us roughing up Brax tonight." Liam's mouth turned up in a smile. "I told her we'd be nice—for the most part."

"I just—I just don't want you guys to get into the past." I tried not to plead, but I could hear it in my voice.

"The past?" Caleb looked puzzled. "As in Charlie?"

"Yes, numbnut," Liam answered. To me, he asked, "What'd you decide to do about the party? That's got to feel awkward."

"No, it's not," I said firmly. "Because I'm not going. I wish Charlie well, but I don't need to show up to do it."

"That's okay," Liam said. "Do what you want."

"You don't have to show up," Caleb said. "But *should* you?"

I rolled my eyes. This was why I loved Liam and hated Caleb. Caleb always poked the bear.

"Back off, Cay," Liam said, giving me that concerned older brother look that almost made me spill everything. If I confessed it all now, maybe they'd understand. But they'd never be able to keep it from our mom. "You found someone better. Screw Charlie, right?"

With a sinking feeling, I realized that I would have to tell Brax about Charlie, fast. "Don't discuss Charlie, okay?" I asked. "It's—over and done with. I just don't want—"

Liam gave me a giant side hug. "Hey, we won't embarrass you. Brax seems like a nice guy." He flashed a handsome grin. "And if he's not, we'll find that out in the barn. Then we'll take care of him." He laughed just as Brax sauntered over. "You ready?" Liam asked. "You can help us with the firepit."

"Okay," Brax said. He'd gotten his jacket and was wearing a multicolored knit ski cap with earflaps and a giant pom-pom. He saw me staring at it. "What?" he said, giving it a tug. "Caleb let me borrow it."

I caught Caleb's eye just as he turned to leave. He was biting the insides of his cheeks to keep from laughing. Because Caleb had given him, of all the hats, my mom's. But I didn't dare tell Brax. Besides, I was too busy trying not to laugh myself to be able to talk.

He looked dopey and silly and somehow very earnest, and for a second, I just wanted to run into his arms and kiss him. For being a good sport. For being willing to subject himself to the whims of my brothers. For sneak eating my peas and making up a sappy story at the table.

But then I thought of all the secrets my brothers would spill.

I grabbed his down-padded arm. "We've got to talk," I whispered. Panic made me a little dizzy, and I clutched the back of a chair to steady myself. Why did I hate discussing my screwups so much? I'd been like this as long as I could remember.

"Okay," he said with the smile of a guy who was going to go out and have a few brewskies with the guys.

"All set?" Caleb called from the door.

"Be right there," Brax said, oblivious to my pain. "Is this about any other foods you might hate that I don't know about?"

I shook my head. How to tell him about the biggest mistake of my life in ten seconds or less? "If they mention a party this weekend, I'm not going, okay?"

Brax stared at me, probably wondering why my voice sounded an octave higher than usual, or why I was making a big deal, as if I were a slighted teenager who didn't get an invite.

So I did the worst thing, kept on trying to explain. "Some people we know got married in Vegas, and they're having a big get-together."

"That sounds fun." I could see him processing. "'Some people'?"

"Old friends." That was certainly not a lie. "But I'm not going. It...wouldn't be fun for me."

"Okay." Not only were my parents lifelong friends with Charlie's, but also, my brothers had gone all through school and played sports with his brothers. That was the thing about small towns—everyone knew everyone, and relationships were as entwined and twisted as orchid roots in a pot.

That was what I used to love the most. That people knew and cared for other people. But now—well, it was the worst thing. The very worst. To see all my old friends and be pitied or felt sorry for, to congratulate Charlie and his new wife and smile and pretend nothing awful had happened—no. I just couldn't do it.

Brax was looking at me funny. Like, I wasn't exactly giving him a lot to go on. And what about Gracie? I hadn't told him anything about her either. "I have to tell you more. I—" My heart sank. How did I describe the essence of the person I held close in my heart, who I carried everywhere with me, in ten seconds? It was impossible.

"Hey, we're sweating in these jackets." Liam walked past and playfully tugged an earflap of Brax's hat. "Let's go, bro."

He tipped his head to one side and assessed me carefully. "Everything okay?"

I dropped my voice. My brothers were standing near the door, Liam's hand on the knob, and I could tell Brax was eager to follow. "My ex is having a party, and I'm not going. *That's* what you need to know."

"Okay." He shrugged. "All good." He reached out and squeezed my arm. "Talk later, 'kay?"

He smiled and gave me a peck right on the lips. It was quick and decisive, just like him. Maybe he did it to distract me. Or because my brothers were watching. Or maybe he just didn't see any of this as a big deal. His kiss sent sparks spreading all through me like a warm blanket, wiping my mind as blank as Emma's throwback Etch-a-Sketch toy.

Charlie who?

A moment later, when I recovered, I knew I'd made a huge

mistake, throwing Brax into the throes of my family without an instruction manual.

"They won't rough him up too badly." My mom had somehow snuck up directly behind me.

Liam laughed. "Not *too* badly," he said, patting Brax on the back on their way out the door.

I forced myself to smile back. For the first time, I realized that this game I was playing wasn't a game at all.

I'd avoided sharing my vulnerable spots, avoided telling Brax about my past. So now he was going to hear all about it from my brothers instead of me.

In our house, everyone traditionally pitched in with the dishes. Tonight, the guys had cleared and loaded, so I started in on the washing. My mom had insisted on helping until my dad intervened and made her go put her feet up in the family room in front of the big tree. I took a second in the now-empty kitchen to try to stop freaking out. All I knew was Gabe had better return from his holiday engaged and ecstatically happy. I was a private person, especially as far as Brax was concerned. This weekend was costing me a lot more than I wanted to give.

"Hey," Dina said, returning from giving Emma a bath, startling me just as I finished. She was wearing Liam's faded red UW hoodie, which practically came down to her knees.

"Go Badgers," I said back, giving the rah-rah sign with my fist in response to the giant Bucky Badger mascot on the sweatshirt. "Mom and I were going to sit down in front of the fire. Join us?"

"Your mom just ran upstairs to read Emma a story. I just have to tuck her in, and then I'd love to catch up." She looked at me— really looked, for the first time since I got home. "You okay?"

She'd always had this way of seeing through BS, starting from the time I'd broken up at age fifteen with Harry Styles, my first boyfriend. Okay, his name was really Evan Thomas, but his hair looked just like Harry's. Anyway, Dina knew me far too well not to sense when something was up.

Instead of words, a tear came out. *Drat.*

She ran over to me. "Honey, what's wrong? Is it Brax? We think he's so nice, but if he's causing any trouble—"

"It's not Brax," I said, swiping at my eyes and letting her guide me to a chair at the table. The first thing she did was grab the wine bottle from dinner from the counter and pour some into the only clean cup left in the cupboard—ironically, a sparkly Disney princess cup of Emma's. As I knit my hands together, I realized I was shaking. It felt good to sit down. It felt even better to have a friend to talk to.

Dina patted my hand and waited in her patient way. She'd always been there to give boy advice and makeup and fashion recs. She was the one who made sure I didn't overload my freshman schedule in college with courses so I could have some fun too. Basically, she was the older sister I'd never had.

I swallowed. "You can't say anything," I managed.

"You know I won't." I did know this. When she caught me buying beer with a fake ID as a teenager, she drove me back to the convenience store to return it but didn't tell my parents. And she covered for me once when I'd stayed out too late with Charlie, telling my parents that I'd been with her. I wasn't exactly a kid who pushed boundaries, but those times she'd saved my butt without hesitation had meant a lot.

How could I even begin to explain this giant mess I'd created? Ironically, the mess seemed to be more about me than my mom. How had that happened? Maybe Dina wouldn't be sympathetic. After all, I'd lied and then brought the lie home in person. Not exactly adult behavior.

"Brax is amazing," she said. "The way he looks at you." She fanned herself and mouthed a silent *whew*. "And he's so personable and nice. And Emma adores him. She's a very good judge of character. He's a keeper." She paused. "Right?"

"He's not a keeper," I whispered. I cleared my throat and forced out the words. "Because he's not my boyfriend."

First, she looked perplexed. Then her mouth dropped open. To her credit, she quickly closed it. When Emma and her other future children were teenagers, she'd be a great mom, slow to judge. "What?"

"We did date for a few weeks last summer—long enough for me to really like him." *Maybe even fall in love with him*, a little voice inside me whispered, but I pushed it aside.

"Wait, you—"

"I'd been telling Mom all about him—I mean, after the thing with Charlie, I guess I thought I'd never feel that way." If I was going to spill the tea, I'd better spill hard. "I fell for him. But then we discovered we were going to be working together, and he told me he thought we'd be better as friends." I took a big breath. "He dumped me."

Her expression changed from confused to *You did go to med school, didn't you?* "And you brought him here anyway?"

Right? What was I thinking? "I was desperate. But I'm okay. To be fair, he'd warned me from the start that he doesn't do serious. But I thought—" I sighed. "I thought he might be *it*."

She sat down next to me and held my hand.

"Right around the same time, we found out about Mom's cancer and..." Underneath her frown, I could practically see her pulling the whole terrible story together. "I couldn't bear to tell her the truth. I did the exact opposite—lied my head off until I ran into a big problem."

Her eyes got wide. "What big problem?"

"Christmas." I buried my head in my hands.

Stupid, stupid Christmas.

She lowered her voice. "Did you sleep with him?"

I didn't deny it. My this-is-a-complete-debacle look must've tipped her off. "Oh, honey."

"The cancer was such a shock. I couldn't think of any way to make it better."

"Wait a minute." She crossed her arms. "If he blew you off and broke your heart, why are you still friends?"

"At work, getting along is sort of a necessity."

"Now I want to kill him."

"I can handle Brax," I said hurriedly. I really wasn't sure of that, but I had to sound grown-up here. "My friend Gabe was supposed to come, but he was about to get engaged, and Brax ended up helping me out. But right now, Liam and Caleb are telling him everything about me."

She frowned. "What can they possibly tell him that matters?"

"I never told Brax about Charlie. I'm not going to the party, so I didn't think it was necessary to explain."

She got up and shut the door between the mudroom and the kitchen. "You brought your fake boyfriend home, and he doesn't know your ex-fiancé just got married?"

I crossed my arms. "After Brax friend zoned me, I didn't want to discuss personal things. But now he's going to find out anyway. I feel like a coward."

She was pacing the kitchen floor in front of me, tapping her upper lip in thought. "You should go," she said. "To Charlie's party. Everyone goes. You shouldn't let Charlie stop you from seeing people."

"What? No. Not going." Charlie and Erin had written me a note with the invitation, asking me to come. I'd burned it in the flame of my White Barn Tranquility candle. "I'm over what happened," I said. "I wish them a happy life, but I'm not doing it in person."

What I did feel bad about was that ever since the breakup, I'd been avoiding my old friends, avoiding going places where I might run into them. It was like I wore a cloak of shame, which made no sense.

Dina took a sip of wine and kept pacing. "Well then, there's only one thing to do."

I looked up at her, not expecting a solution, but suddenly hoping she had one. "What's that?"

"We get to Brax first." She placed her hands on the table and leaned in. "*You* should be the one to tell him, not Liam or Caleb."

I checked my watch. My brothers were probably cozied up by the fire, plying Brax with liquor as we spoke. "I lost my chance to do that."

She shook her head. "Not if we show up with sleds."

The sleds. Of course. The perfect diversion. I stood up and hugged her. "You're a genius."

"If I was a genius, I'd tell you how to fix this mess. But we can start with something simple, right?"

As Dina ran off to tend to Emma, I felt a huge relief. Like I wasn't alone. And that somehow, I might be able to navigate through all this chaos I'd created.

Plus, it was a fantastic night for sledding down our giant hill and then flying clear through the pasture, like I'd done as a kid a million moonlit nights before. When you were sailing through the icy cold air on a sled, you didn't think about anything. You just closed your eyes, hung on for dear life, and enjoyed every wild, fleeting, free moment. And prayed that you survived the ride.

While I was waiting for Dina, I found my mom in the family room, sitting back in the recliner she'd sequestered from my dad, her feet propped up near the blazing fire.

I handed her one of two mugs of tea I'd brought in from the kitchen, tossed my grandma's colorful crocheted afghan over her legs, and took a seat on the couch. Cooper hopped up and snuggled in right beside me. Within seconds, he went belly-up, begging to be rubbed, his favorite thing in the world. Of course, I complied.

"You did too much." I waved my hands around the room. "Making everything look so Christmasy, making all our favorites for dinner." I made a note to cook dinner tomorrow, regardless of how awful the consequences were. She flashed me a smile that I read as *You silly girl, don't you get it?* I've always been able to read my mom, probably because we are alike in many ways. We're attuned to others' feelings and emotions, we're do-gooders when we can be, and we tended to wear our hearts on our sleeves. Except she can't—or won't—fake what she's feeling.

Well, with that last one, she was far braver than me.

"Okay, okay," I said.

"Don't treat me like I'm too weak to do what I want," she said in a firm tone. "You know I love this more than anything—having you kids home, watching you finally find happiness."

Guilt hit me again, oozing its way around my stomach like thick green slime. I knew how badly she wanted my happiness. She'd mentioned it frequently in our conversations, often before her own health.

That said more about my mother than anything else. She was selfless. More concerned about others than herself.

"It's wonderful to be home." And to have her with us, God willing, for many more Christmases to come.

My mom looked at me, her eyes a little watery, her expression earnest. "Mia, I think Brax is wonderful. Every time he looks at you, your whole face lights up."

I felt my cheeks blaze, the curse of the pale complected. Sadly, I knew she was right. When I caught Brax glancing my way, it was like lighting a match. Heat skyrocketed uncontrollably through me, head to toes. But it was just the same unholy attraction I'd gotten used to fighting from the start.

I wished everyone would stop telling me how in love I looked when I was doing everything possible to protect my heart. Next time our eyes met, I swore I would frown deeply, even scowl. I'd glower and toss daggers at him with my eyes. Then we'd see if anything could break through that force field.

My mom blew on her tea, cradling it in her hands. "I've always said that there's not much to a relationship without chemistry." She tapped her teacup thoughtfully. "Anyone can see that you two have it in spades. You seem well matched."

Well matched. Chemistry in spades. Creepily, I pondered again how easily my mother had bought my lies. Clearly, I'd added a darker bent to my personality since that time when I was ten and couldn't sleep until I'd confessed to being the one who'd pillaged every last crispy chocolate egg from my siblings' Easter baskets.

She took a sip of tea. "Are you and Brax going to Charlie and Erin's party?"

The question was as loaded as our twelve-foot Christmas tree, every possible branch and bough weighted with some storied ornament from our pasts, yet the expression on my mom's face was as placid as if she'd just inquired about the weather.

"No, Mother." I hadn't used that tone—or called her *Mother* —since I was eighteen and she made me return the dress I'd bought for prom because she said it looked less substantial than a '40's pinup girl's bathing suit.

She laughed. "You haven't gotten irritated with me since I got sick. It feels sort of good."

I frowned instead of laughed. "I'll send a card."

"Charlie worries a lot about how you feel," she said carefully, like she was tiptoeing around this awful topic. "His mom tells me he's waiting for your blessing."

Clearly, Charlie hadn't waited for anything. "To absolve him of guilt?" I snorted.

She gave me a stern look. "Now that you found someone who's right, maybe you can find room in your heart to forgive."

I set down my mug, no longer wanting any tea. "I forgive him because I've moved on. But as far as showing up there...maybe you could do that, but not me."

I'll bet you're thinking that I seemed like a nice person, concerned with helping others—my patients, my family. My friends would likely say the same. I didn't cut people off, or alienate them, or hold grudges. But I couldn't simply pretend with Charlie that nothing had happened, as my mom actually seemed to be suggesting.

My mom would always think of him as that cute, little, chubby-cheeked, curly-haired toddler. Even now, she talked as if what he did—what *they* did, Charlie and Erin—had been something easy-peasy to get over and move on from.

She shook her head adamantly, as if I wasn't understanding. "I'm not saying what he did was right. I'm saying that you can't avoid all your friends, everyone—even Charlie—forever. Why let him dictate what you do? But that's for you to decide."

So my mom had called me out—and unfortunately, the sinking sensation in my stomach told me she was right, as she usually was. The whole situation was so awkward. If I went to the party, I'd feel like I was under a microscope, with everyone watching for my reaction. But how long was I going to hide for? And didn't that give Charlie power, if what he did kept me from my old friends and neighbors?

Just as I was about to get up, my mom threw off the afghan, got up, and came to sit beside me. She slid her hand in mine. I initially frowned, but she made me sit there like that until I calmed down. Which of course I eventually did. Because I understood that having my mom by my side, holding my hand, was a precious something that I could have lost. And that thought made all my worries seem much more insignificant. "I'll think about it," I finally said.

"Good," she said, squeezing my hand. We sat for a few minutes, enjoying the fire and the tree. Before long, my mom's sheer force of stubborn will made me forget that stupid party and just enjoy the moment. Cooper opened one eye and shut it again, wanting nothing more than for me to continue the nonstop belly rubs I was still providing. Oh, to be a dog.

My mom patted my knee. "One day, no one will care what happened, and none of this will even be important to you anymore."

My head knew this. It knew that *this* was what was important —being here with my mom, my family. That one day Charlie would be a dim line from my past. I just wasn't completely there yet.

Thankfully, just then, Dina walked down the stairs and into the room wearing a hot-pink cap with silvery threads shimmering through it, looking more like a kid herself than the mom of a toddler. "Ready to sled?" She turned on the monitor on the end table. "Emma went out hard. Thanks for listening out for her while we're gone, Beth. We won't be too long."

My mom laughed. "I'm perfectly happy sitting here with my tea and my book." She picked up a hardcover with a glossy library cover from the end table next to her. "Have fun sledding."

Dina gave me a nod. *Let's do this.*

Time to rescue Brax from interrogation by my brothers. So that I would get to tell him all my secrets instead.

Chapter Eleven

Brax

I was actually excited about going to the barn with the big boys because I was interested in learning more about Mia—things she didn't tell me herself and that I couldn't glean from Gabe's hesitant confessions. I got it—why would she trust me with the important little details of her life after what I'd done to her?

Like who, exactly, was Grace? "*Our Gracie*," the D'Angelos had called her. They'd toasted to her. She certainly wasn't a pet. And maybe some people called their grandmas by their first names, instead of MeeMaw or Nana or Grams, but this family didn't strike me as having a grandma named Gracie. Which made me wonder the worst. But if they'd lost a sister/child, wouldn't Mia have mentioned *that*?

I knew that any info I would glean would come with a price. I had a feeling they'd be testing me, especially the suspicious one, Caleb.

The barn was clean and warm and smelled like hay and, well, animals. I passed a few cows that were chomping on straw and a horse that whinnied. I'm not sure I'd ever been so close to actual animals. As a kid, I'd never even gone to a county fair.

Liam found me staring at a giant black horse who snorted and stuck his snout threateningly over his stall. He rubbed the horse's head and ears, and in response, the horse whinnied and stomped in his enclosure. "Hey, Diablo," he said. "How you doing?"

Diablo? As if the horse wanted to prove it was worthy of its namesake, he snorted and bent down to...either nuzzle me or take a bite out of me, I'm not sure which. I hedged my bets by ducking and trying not to look startled.

Liam laughed. "You haven't been around horses?"

I shook my head. Not many of those near our apartment in Philly.

"I'm just messing with you. His name is Fred." He ran his hand along the animal's back and fluttered its mane. "Hey, Freddie boy, you wouldn't hurt a flea, would you?" Fred responded with some kind of noise that seemed collegial, as well as nudging his snout into the palm of Liam's hand.

Looked like I was going to need my secret weapon—a bottle of Crown Royal I'd tucked into my duffel bag for emergencies precisely like this. I'd placed it on the top of a low barrel, and Caleb was now pouring a round of shots. A large electric heater and a battery-powered lantern sat nearby, casting a warm yellow light. They'd opted not to light the firepit because it felt like was below buckass zero out, but it wasn't half bad in here, once it warmed up a little and once you got used to the potent scent of hay and horses.

As we took our seats on hay bales, Caleb started right in. "Mia's worried about that party tomorrow night."

"Party?" As soon as the word flew out of my mouth, Caleb glanced up at me and frowned. "I mean, yeah, the party," I said, trying to correct course. Given by her ex? I wished she'd given me a little more to go on here.

"It's not our place to tell Mia what to do," Liam said, tossing down his shot.

Not even five minutes in, and I was already lost. And here I'd thought I'd just have to hold my liquor to earn their trust.

Caleb turned to me. His posture, his expression—everything read as a challenge. He smelled a rat, and he wasn't going to stop until he ferreted me out. "What do you think, Braxton?"

Come clean or play along? "I, um—Mia's very strong-willed. I think she's going to do what she wants." All very true.

"See, here's the thing," Liam said. "I have to agree with you, Brax, that going to the party is a show of strength. She's been avoiding people."

Caleb tossed back a shot. "Charlie's the one who should be seeking her forgiveness after what he did. She has nothing to be ashamed of."

"Charlie sucks," I said, because it seemed like the right thing to say. This was like putting together the pieces of a puzzle...blind.

Caleb poured me another shot. "I never liked Charlie anyway. Never could hold his liquor."

I downed the shot, just to show them I wasn't Charlie.

Gabe had never mentioned what had happened with her ex, but I was getting the vibe that it wasn't good.

Caleb filled our glasses and pointed at his brother. "It's hard on Mia because we all hung out together. Aaron was Liam's best friend all through school." Caleb turned to me. "That's Charlie's brother."

Liam shook his head. "I should've known better than to let that effer date my sister."

"Don't beat yourself up," Caleb said with a dismissive gesture. "She's over him. But if she went, everyone would stop talking about it—about her, you know?"

"We'd all be there to support her," Liam said.

I lifted my glass. "I will be too."

Caleb frowned. "Yeah, but what about...what about Erin?"

Erin? I'd better stop with the shots, or I wouldn't be able to untangle any of this.

Liam poured me another shot and jostled me in the ribs with his elbow. "Keep up, Braxton." Liam shook his head. "He met her one weekend when he was visiting Mia right after she'd moved to Milwaukee. Then Erin moved out here and went after Charlie."

"Hey, don't blame it all on her," Caleb said. "It was him too."

My heart skipped a beat. Charlie had cheated on Mia while she was in the middle of her internship? That sucked.

"Why didn't Charlie move to be with Mia?" I asked. Because... why would you want to be apart from someone you loved?

Liam gave a little shrug. "Farmers don't leave their land."

Charlie stayed; Mia left. And then Charlie got busy with someone else. Got it.

Caleb set down his shot glass with enough force to make the wood plank over the barrel vibrate. "We'll help her through this."

I nodded. We clinked shot glasses and downed more whiskey, which sank down as a warm fireball in my belly. Silence descended. Liam and Caleb moved on to talk about old friends home for the holidays whom they hoped to catch in town. As I sat there next to the heater, I listened with one ear, my mind wandering to a night around six months ago.

From the first time we met I'd somehow sensed that Mia was vulnerable, even though she was as pro as I was about hiding her past. But it was that sense of vulnerability that made me warn her about me as we sat on her couch during our third date watching a movie.

Well, we were doing more kissing than watching, and I knew where things were heading. I couldn't get it out of my head that everything about her signaled that she was looking for connection and relationship, not a quick fling. Don't get me wrong; I wanted her badly. But I wanted more not to hurt her. And if she stuck with me, that was bound to happen. So I sat back and told her I wasn't the guy she was looking for. I firmly repeated my usual mantra that I didn't do long-term anything.

I scrambled up from the couch, took a big breath, and grabbed my keys, pressing them hard into the palm of my hand so the pain would somehow stop me thinking about how turned on I was. Slow my motor down. Give me some sense.

As I walked over to grab my jacket from the back of a chair, she touched my arm. Tugged on it until I turned around, coat in hand.

Just put your arm in the sleeve and button up, my inner voice said. *Do it now.*

But then I made the mistake of looking into her eyes. Those big, green, mesmerizing eyes that I just fell into. I fell into the honesty, the feeling, the pure transparency that made me understand one thing alone—that she wanted me just as much as I wanted her.

But I saw something else—that she'd been hurt. I sensed it and saw it, and I still didn't leave.

Mia was a time bomb—my personal time bomb. She made me feel too much, and if I continued, I knew this would lead to disaster. I was *certain* of it. And yet I remained there frozen, unable to move, unable to look away.

"Don't go," she said. Those two short words were all I needed to step forward and erase the distance between us, take her into my arms, and press my body and my lips to hers. She was soft, and she smelled fresh, like lavender, and tasted wonderful, and I couldn't let go, couldn't stop. I was addicted to every single thing about her, every enthusiastic caress, every deep but quiet sigh. We kissed, kiss after endless kiss, until all my good intentions dropped from me along with my coat and my keys, and I was lost.

For the next two weeks, we had a great time together, and not just in bed. She was intelligent and funny, and we shared the same views about a lot of things. We never ran out of topics to talk about. And the sex...well, that was over the top. I found myself riding on a high that I'd never felt with anyone before.

When I reported for duty two weeks later, the head of the Peds department handed me a list of all the residents in the program. As I perused it, my blood turned to ice. One name stood out as if it were set in flashing lights. *Dr. Mia D'Angelo, third year*, right smack in the middle of the page. Please, God, I prayed. Let there be two Mia D'Angelos who were pediatric doctors in the city. Not the green-eyed, curly-haired beauty I couldn't get out of my head.

I knew in my heart there wasn't. And I also knew I had to cut things off immediately.

I didn't want to watch our relationship fade away and dissolve in the middle of our workplace, in front of all our colleagues. How would I keep the residents' respect if I was involved with her, even if I wasn't directly in charge of her? I didn't want angry emotions and hurt feelings when we had to perform jobs that needed us unquestionably to be at one hundred percent.

The truth was, I wasn't being honorable. I was running away, as I'd always done, from every relationship I'd ever had. Things were getting to be too much—too intimate. Too...everything.

So I deserved not knowing about the important events and people in Mia's life.

Bitterly, I realized that good ol' Charlie and I had something in common. We'd both been assholes to Mia.

～

Mia

Dina and I burst into the barn, sleds trailing behind us. The three guys were sitting around a barrel-and-bale setup, and they'd done some serious damage to a bottle of Crown Royal.

Whoa. My brothers were beer people, so where did that come from? I couldn't say, but from the chilled-out smiles on their faces, it appeared that Brax had passed the initiation phase.

I bit my lower lip and raised a silent prayer that they'd spent the time discussing books, good booze, fly fishing, politics, or literally anything else besides me.

Dina handed Liam a toboggan rope. "Come on, you guys. The snow is perfect."

The three men looked at each other. "I'm in," Caleb said without hesitation, standing right up.

"Ready?" I asked Brax, giving a nod toward the sturdy red toboggan I'd left near the door. I knew he'd grown up in the city, but even city kids went sledding, right? But I was coming to sense there were a lot of normal kid things he never got to do. "You've been, right?"

One corner of his mouth tugged up enough that I could glimpse his dimple. Drat, those dimples. Every time they appeared, they made me a total goner. "Does sneaking trays out of the cafeteria at college and using them to hurl ourselves down a hill behind the dorms count?"

I grinned. "Counts. Want to give it a try?"

"Yes?"

"Yes, with a question mark?"

"Well, I usually never drink and sled."

"I got you." I grabbed his arm and led him out of the barn. As soon as we were out of earshot of the others, I asked, "Did my brothers behave?" What I really meant was *What did they say about me?*

"The convo went down as smoothly as the Crown Royal."

Nothing like confidence, I guess. "So, did they spill any secrets?"

The snow crunched below our feet as we headed out. "If they did, I won't remember them in the morning."

I couldn't help laughing. They'd probably just been discussing guy stuff anyway, and Dina and I had likely gotten here before the conversation turned serious. We trudged the short distance to the hill, our breath making puffs of white in the moonlit night. Everyone was laughing and talking, making me miss all the times we came out on nights exactly like this.

The stars above were like Christmas lights in the sky, lit just for us. And our house glowed in the quiet darkness with colored lights that outlined the rooflines and dotted the pines in the yard. Brax's sudden *"Holy shit"* made me smile.

"It's a fricking mountain," he said under his breath. Below our feet, the hill sloped down, down, down to a long, flat pasture.

"It's perfect," I said. I chuckled at his obvious discomfort as I pulled the sled to the brim and scuttled onto it, digging my boots into the snow, breaking into the crunchy top layer that I knew would be perfect for speed.

Caleb, always the daredevil, took a running head start and belly flopped onto his sled. With a large whoop, he slid easily down the slope and then coasted far out into the open field. A smooth, graceful run.

"Survival rate one hundred percent," I noted. Brax looked hesitant, his lips drawn into a thin line as he rummaged in his coat pockets for his gloves.

I scooched to the front of our sled. "Come on." I patted the back with my mitten. "Unless you're chicken."

"Not chicken," he mumbled as he dropped into place behind me.

Of all the emergencies we'd handled, all the sleepless nights that were so busy we'd barely had time to pee, I'd never seen him apprehensive of anything, except maybe of the bad fried food in the cafeteria at midnight.

And then suddenly, it hit me—we were sitting together. More than that—he was essentially wrapped around me, his long legs stretched out alongside mine.

Despite the fact that he wore old, faded jeans and I wore insulated snow pants, I swore I could feel his body heat searing through the layers.

Forget him. I was the one who needed reassurance.

It brought me straight back to last summer. His familiar nearness. His big, solid arms grazing my arms. His body encompassing mine.

I thought I'd banished those memories, but they came slamming back with a vengeance. Not unlike the chicken pox virus, which lives on in your nerves long after you're through being sick, only to create havoc years later.

He was too stiff and silent. Steeling himself, I thought. "Are you by any chance...afraid of heights?"

"Of course not," he said, sounding offended. He scooched up farther behind me, resting his hands at my sides. This put his chest inches from my back. He seemed to be taking great pains not to allow any part of his body to touch me. Like that was going to help my nerves. Underneath my jacket, I was in a full-body sweat.

I looked back. His face was so close that I could see the late-day stubble on his cheeks. He was so handsome. A wave of longing passed through me so intense, I sucked in a breath.

Liam pushed Dina off, the toboggan scraping over the clean snowpack. Calm, practical, wise Dina screamed the whole way down.

"Holy shit," Brax said again.

"You might be too inebriated," I said.

"I'm not inebriated enough," he corrected.

"After this, you're going to wish you were." I was thinking of another comeback when Liam pushed us off.

"Okay, kids, see you at the bottom!" I had just enough time to gather the rope and what I could of my senses as the sled suddenly plummeted down the giant hill.

Brax let out a curse as he grabbed my waist, more from survival instinct than anything else. I leaned against him because, well, I had to, didn't I? It was either that or risk being tossed off into the cold unknown, also known as a giant hilly meadow that was known for its rainbow bursts of wildflowers in the spring, but was now a sleek, silver-coated racetrack with multiple dips.

I couldn't think. But I could feel his lean torso against my back, solid and comforting, his arms now encased tightly around me. I leaned back even more to brace myself as we flew down,

down the hill, the snow flying up in our faces, the cold air nipping at our cheeks and making tears stream from our eyes as we barreled down.

Then, as we careened and dipped along the curves and flew down the incline, Brax laughed.

Not a tentative, nervous laugh, but a full, real one. Carefree and fun.

I'd been down this hill dozens—if not hundreds—of times, and I always felt the rush of absolute freedom, the fresh sting of the winter air, and the intense, quiet beauty of a moonlit hillside in the dead of winter.

But this time, I experienced it with fresh eyes. And ears, as we both yelled and screamed as we navigated the roller coaster of dips, the snow spraying up onto our faces.

The terror turned quickly to relief as we glided smoothly into the pasture, the wild ride coming to a much calmer end. "That was amazing," he said, untangling his legs and lifting himself up. Holding out a hand for me, he grinned. "Let's do it again."

So we did. Again, and then again. In fact, we outlasted the others, who brushed off their backsides a final time and went inside to get warm.

"One more time," he said. He looked boyish. Sweetly excited. And purely happy in a way I'd never seen him before.

I shook my head, smiling. My butt was wet, and I was a little freezing, but I loved seeing how much fun he was having, like a little kid sledding for the first time.

Then it suddenly occurred to me—maybe it was. The first time, I mean.

The very last trip down, we nearly wiped out at the bottom of the hill. When we'd almost slid to a stop, he purposely tumbled over to one side, taking me with him.

"You're a terrible driver," he teased, looking down at me. Our legs were tangled together, both of us sunken into the snow, where

I could feel the shock as an icy chunk hit my bare back and sank under the waistband of my pants.

"You're a bad passenger," I shot right back. The moon was full, lighting up the hill and making the snow sparkle in spectacular shades of blue and gray. It was breathtaking, but not as breathtaking as Brax's face above me, full of mischief and teasing.

"I shouldn't have let you steer," I complained weakly.

"You're right," he admitted. One second, we were laughing and joking. But then something happened. Maybe it was staring into his eyes for too long, watching them turn darker, more somber, and very focused—on me. The only sound was my quick intake of air as we both got caught up in a moment where everything stood still. The earth became totally silent, the moon softly shining down on the snow, the lights from the house at the top of the hill glowing warmly.

"You're a sledding virgin, aren't you?" I was trying to be funny, but somehow, the mood had shifted. The intense look in his eyes told me so.

"Yes," he admitted. "That was amazing. Thank you."

For a moment, we stared at each other. His face was so perfect, so masculine, his eyes unreadable as they searched mine. His breath released in a puff of white. Before I could stop myself, I brushed his snowy hair back with one wet mitten.

His gaze dropped to my lips.

I sucked in a breath. My body froze in place. My heart was pounding so loudly in my chest that I was certain he could hear it.

"Mia," he whispered, full of longing. I tilted my face upward in response. Snow had crept between my boot and my sock and the icy wetness was sinking in, but I forgot all about it as a slow, building heat pumped through me and Brax lowered his head to mine.

At first, he kissed me tentatively, his lips softly brushing mine. But I sought his mouth, unable to disguise how badly I wanted this, how badly I wanted him. The next time, our lips met in a clash of need, our lips parting, our tongues meeting. He gave a little groan as he kissed me deeply and tenderly, making me dizzy and hot.

I got lost in his taste, the feel of his mouth, in the solid, encompassing way he held me. I felt like the focus of his every thought, his every feeling, his every need. And I savored every precious moment of it.

I don't know how long we lay there, but finally he lifted himself up, his full lips drawing up into a little smile, and rolled to his side. I missed his warmth immediately. For a moment, we lay there together in the snow-covered field. The world was hushed, the moonlight casting a silver-blue light as it slanted across the snow.

He reached across and grasped my hand. There were so many stars shining, they looked like tiny Christmas lights, twinkling from far away. "Mia," he said softly, turning his head toward me. "When were you going to tell me about Charlie?"

Chapter Twelve

Mia

I stood up abruptly, despite all the layers restraining me, and adjusted my hat. Snow fell off me in chunks. Some of it ran down my back. "I—because it's not important." I sounded ridiculous to my own ears. It *was* important. Things needed to be said—lots of things. And I had to muster the courage to say them.

Brax shook off the snow from his jeans. "Okay, well, were you planning on talking about it ever? Or were you just going to let me hear it from your family?"

I glared at him. His hat fell off, and he bent to retrieve it. He looked as discombobulated as I felt.

I'd given up trying to read his body language long ago. But I was tired of the mixed signals. And I needed answers too.

How did we get from kissing on a starry, snow-covered night to icy-cold reality? I did the only thing possible—began trekking up the hill. "Come with me," I called back over my shoulder.

He jogged and caught up with me, dragging the toboggan behind him.

Both of us were silent, either because our digits were about to freeze off or because we knew we were about to have it out.

Once again, I'd gotten flummoxed by his kisses. Consumed by them. The man definitely knew how to kiss.

The first time we were together, it had been all about connection and passion and the magic of feeling that someone really got you. For me, anyway.

But that was finished. So why had I let this happen now? Who had kissed whom first? I knew the answer. *He* had. And I hadn't even hesitated, getting swept right along with it.

I walked up the concrete steps to the stone patio, unzipped my coat, and tossed it onto the ground.

"What are you doing?" He sounded more incredulous than angry. His dark brows were knit down, his arms crossed, tall and stark as a winter warrior in a fantasy novel. But this time I wasn't going to let him distract me from the truth.

"Take off your clothes," I said. "Your *outer* clothes," I amended as I tossed a boot to the ground, then shed a sock. When I was down to my thermal shirt and pants, I hopped quickly over to my parents' hot tub and lifted the lid.

Wonderful, balmy, chlorine-scented steam cut the icy air with smoky tendrils. I took one glance back and then hopped in. He was right behind me as I sank into the hot water, feeling the burn, grateful for the insta-thaw.

I looked up at him, hesitating on the brink.

He wanted answers, but so did I. "Why did you kiss me?"

Brax

I faced Mia. Tendrils of steam rose up between us into the frigid night. Moments ago, we'd been horizontal and lip-locked. Those kisses were among the best I'd ever gotten...and the worst. I'd managed to stuff all my feelings in a box for the past six months, and the lid had just been blown right off. By me. I'd done it. I'd gotten swept up, unable to stay away—again.

Despite everything, I wanted to take her back in my arms and tell her I'd meant every kiss. I wanted to give her a thousand more. I had the sinking sense that everything I was feeling wasn't just attraction but something far more complicated, a journey I had no map for.

This was why I never should have come. I had no control when it came to her.

I had to say something, so I steeled myself. "We were close, we were touching. And I've had a couple of shots. It was an honest mistake." Lies. I was as sober as Job. I'd known what I was doing, and I'd done it anyway. I'd wanted her too badly to stop myself. I tried to shove all the emotion back inside as I forced myself to look in her eyes. "Rest assured, it won't happen again."

She crossed her arms over her chest. Good thing, because through her gray thermal underwear, I could see the soft outline of her breasts. I wrenched my gaze back up to her face. "So you're telling me that was all an accident," she said. "Nothing more to it."

"Correct."

She blew out a big breath. "Now that we're being honest, I wasn't going to tell you about Charlie, ever."

All the cool I'd been trying to command dissolved. "You weren't going to tell me anything about a guy you dated for, what...six years?" I didn't have a right to be angry, but I found that I was.

She stabbed the air. "You're acting like we *tell* each other things."

"I thought we were friends." I sat on an underwater ledge and folded my own arms. "Friends tell each other important things."

She snorted. "Don't look like that."

"Like what?"

"Like you're hurt that I don't tell you big things about my life. We started out being friends. And being *more* than friends, remember that? When you broke things off, you lost the privilege of hearing my stuff." Her gaze blazed with defiance.

I blinked, chastened and surprised.

"Stop messing with my emotions."

If only I could tell her that I'd kept her at arm's length for her own good. Somehow, I had to find the strength to stay away, but how? "I deserve everything you're saying. But now I'm asking as your friend. Someone who cares about you a lot." I felt desperate, needing her to know that I meant every word. "Please tell me."

We sat there, glaring at each other. Above our heads, snow began to fall, thick, giant flakes hurling silently down and melting once they crashed into the hot water. It felt like we were in a giant snow globe, duking it out.

"Fine." She sighed. "Charlie and I dated for six years. When I left for residency, the distance wore us down. I was working all the time and on call, and it was difficult to see each other, but I always thought we'd get through it. At our engagement party, he took me aside and told me there was someone else." She shrugged and met my gaze. "That's it. That's the story.

She ran a hand lightly over the effervescent water and focused her gaze on it, not me, as she continued, "Anyway, I'm here for my mom, not for Charlie. People can talk all they want. And I don't need to give him my blessing in person. Why should I? *He* cheated on *me*. I hope he has a good life. Isn't that enough?"

"I'm sorry." I felt helpless. I didn't know what else to say or do. My desire to do anything to comfort her battled with my need to hold my distance, and I was a mess.

She stiffened, clearly not needing my paltry words of comfort. "It's not your problem, so no reason to be."

"Mia." My voice cracked when I said her name. I had to say something, anything, to let her know that I cared, even if I couldn't be more than a friend to her. "You deserve to have fire and passion and...and everything. Every last piece of someone's heart and soul."

Her mouth dropped open. She stared at me, thrown and speechless.

"He doesn't deserve you," I continued, my voice cracking with emotion. "I'm glad you didn't end up with him."

Up at the house, the back door opened. "Hey, you two," Liam called. "We're heading to bed. I wanted to make sure Dad didn't lock you out."

"Be right there," Mia called. "Hey, could you grab us a couple of towels?"

"Sure thing," Liam called.

She moved to get out, but I stopped her with my words. "Before you leave, please tell me who Gracie was."

She sank back down. Blew out a sigh. "Gracie was my twin sister. She died when we were nine. Of leukemia."

My head reeled. Died? Of cancer? My mind went instantly to the trials I survived with my sister, how we might've been separated, but our bond was never broken. What would it have been like to lose her permanently? I couldn't imagine the tragedy that this family had suffered, that Mia had suffered.

I remembered the birthday cake photo, the two little girls side by side. The little brown-haired girl full of mischief. Her *twin*. Of course!

And of course, Mia had become a doctor—a pediatrician. I thought of her attachment to Rylee and her sister. And about how wonderful she was with the kids on the heme-onc unit, yet how difficult every single day on that ward must be for her.

Click click click. The pieces of the puzzle that was Mia snapped into place.

The back door opened. "Towels are right here," Liam called.

Mia called out a thanks. "It's all right," she said softly to me. "Now you know. So I've been honest with you, but I still feel that I don't know anything about you. That's your choice. But Brax, I don't want what happened to happen again—those kisses." She waved her hand in the air. "Whatever that was."

"It won't."

She got out of the tub, wrapped herself in a towel, and walked into the house.

I stood in the hot tub watching Mia leave, thinking about how I'd just messed everything up. *Again.*

My hands were clammy, my throat was dry, and I felt like a complete a-hole. She was right. I hadn't opened up at all.

I'd panicked, just as I had last summer.

It wasn't because I had nothing to say.

Mia was different. She'd always been different. If I'd been honest, I would've told her that I thought about her constantly. That no one I'd ever met could compare to her in kindness, brains, or beauty. But something inside me told me loud and clear that I couldn't deliver what she deserved to have.

She deserved everything. A guy who'd had a normal upbringing and knew how to be part of a family. How to be a good husband and father.

I didn't have a clue how to live like normal people. *Love* like normal people.

In my misery, I heard something above the hot tub motor and the bubbling of the swirling water. It was my sister's voice, telling me that I'd had the confidence to push myself to be successful in so many ways, to never give up, but that confidence didn't seem to extend to my relationships. I'd always believed that my upbringing had been too chaotic for me to take the chance. But what if I somehow found the strength to fight my past?

Mia deserved so much better than Charlie. I never would've done what he did to her.

Yet she hadn't even felt comfortable telling me about asshat Charlie. She hadn't trusted me enough to. And that was the worst thing of all.

Chapter Thirteen

Mia

I went up to my room and took a shower. At one point, I heard Brax rummaging around in his duffel. When I reentered the bedroom, he was gone. And so was the down comforter from my bed. I was relieved to have my room all to myself. *Good*, I thought. *Be like that*. It wasn't any kind of friendship if only one person revealed difficult things. Or feelings. Or...anything.

I climbed into bed, snuggling in between fresh sheets and a blanket that smelled of fabric softener, but I couldn't rest, and it wasn't because Brax had taken off with my warmest blanket. Christmas peace evaded me. Things weren't right, and I couldn't even pretend that they were.

I threw back the covers, grabbed my plaid flannel robe, and opened the door to the hall.

The house was as silent as falling snow. A slight chill hit me, always the case in winter in the old house, so I ran back into my room and shoved my feet into my plaid fleece-lined slippers.

Brax was nowhere. Not on the family room couch, not in the

kitchen. I pulled back the drapes on the front window and was relieved to find his car still sitting in the driveway, covered with a thin coating of new snow. So he had to be somewhere. The grandfather clock struck one.

I'd walked through the kitchen and halfway down the basement stairs—would he really resort to heading down there?—when I stopped myself. What was I doing? How many books had I read where looking for someone in the basement was a very, very bad idea?

As I ran back up the stairs into the kitchen, I rationalized that I was looking for him because I was worried about him. Trapped in a house full of D'Angelos with nowhere to go.

All right, all right, the truth was, I was thinking about those kisses. They were…amazing. Wonderful. Full of hope and promise. They'd been the real thing, I felt *sure* of it.

The thing was, when you work so closely with someone and lives are on the line, you get to read the other person—their moves. Their thoughts. You anticipate their actions. Some part of you senses what is real and what isn't.

So here was the real reason I went looking for him: no matter what Brax said, his lips said something different. His words to me were full of passion and longing. And I needed to know why.

I walked over to the antique hutch in the kitchen where my mom displayed my grandmother's dishes and some photos and searched for one in particular. There sat my sister and I, side by side at the pond, both of us grinning wildly. Two cute twins with identical grins. Gracie had just caught a fish and was holding it up, close to our faces. She'd been so proud of catching that ginormous fish herself.

I'd begged my dad to throw it back in the lake. He'd gently told me that it was big enough to keep, that we didn't have to toss it back in. Gracie begged to be able to take it home for dinner.

I'd worried endlessly about killing the fish. I asked about its family. I even imagined its mother looking for it. Needless to say, I didn't eat any fish that night.

My sister had been so bold and unafraid. She'd known what she wanted and she went for it. Whereas I was the overthinker, the overplanner, the one more governed by fear.

I closed my eyes and conjured Grace as I thought she might look today. A little like me, of course, only more stylish, more artsy, more boho, like the free spirit she was.

"I get what you'd want for me," I said to the photo. To be courageous. To not back down, which I'd gotten really good at, especially after being hurt by Charlie. To realize my power. To make things happen in my life.

Brax's actions didn't match his words. Why?

Using my phone light, I sat down on the top step leading down to the basement, a little freaked out that I'd actually started to check it out. And I was talking to photographs. But that was better than lying in my bed crying, right?

My phone went off, and I jumped.

Want to talk? the text said.

I was instantly filled with the most intense relief I'd ever felt. Accompanied by something far more dangerous—the thrill that Brax wanted to talk too. That he thought we had unfinished business too. That being on the same wavelength might not be a fantasy after all.

Worst of all, I was buoyed by the wildest hope—that we weren't done.

Where are you? I texted back.

Where are you? He countered.

The basement stairs.

That's creepy.

Followed by: *So you're walking around the house in the dark looking for me.*

I didn't answer that.

I'm on the third floor, he texted. *Please come up.*

The third floor? How had he even found the third floor?

I bolted first up the main staircase and then a more narrow one to a room under the dormers, my mom's sewing room. It had a peaked roofline and a killer view of the surrounding hills out a big palladium window. It was also completely freezing because the furnace just didn't do a great job pumping heat all the way up here.

From the landing, I could see a lump on the couch, huddled in my down comforter. Aha! As I shone the light, the lump moved, and hands lifted to shield a face.

"Brax?" I was halfway too full of hope. The kind you feel when things aren't right with someone you really care about, and you'd do anything to fix them. "What are you doing up here?"

He popped his head up. "I figured going back to your room would be a bad idea, and I wasn't sure where else to go." He looked —well, "adorably rumpled" was the descriptor that popped into my head. No. I wasn't going to think he was adorably *anything* until I got some answers.

"Can we talk?" he asked, sitting up.

Oh, how my heart jumped at that. "Are you actually going to say something this time?"

"I promise." He lifted the comforter, beckoning me to come sit next to him.

He didn't have to ask me twice.

I clicked off my phone light and sat down. The comforter was warm from his body heat. Our shoulders and legs grazed lightly as he pulled it back down over us. And he smelled nice. Well, okay, he smelled a little like chlorine, but it wasn't unpleasant.

My heart was softening. Make that melting. I'd tried so hard to prevent that, but it was just like left-out butter. *Inevitable.*

"I have something to say," he began.

"Okay," I said cautiously. I wanted him to share his heart with me. Tell me what he was thinking, like during the hundreds of conversations we had at work, when we had downtime, and when we weren't pretending to be dating. Except even with all that talking, he'd rarely mentioned his past.

He rubbed his neck, taking a long time to choose his words.

"You had a long relationship with that guy," he said.

"Charlie," I confirmed. "Yes."

He cleared his throat. "My longest relationship lasted eight weeks." I could feel his eyes on me more than I could actually see them in the dark. But I could sense that he was struggling, and I could hear the emotion in his voice.

I knew all about his lack of steady dating, how popular he was with all women everywhere. But I wanted to know who the real Brax was.

He grabbed my hand. A pleasant shock that I didn't see coming in the pitch blackness. His long fingers closed around mine, warm and secure. Like someone I could count on. Yet everything he was saying was the opposite. "I want to explain," he said. "I understand why you don't trust me. I just want you to know that I always thought you were different from anybody else I'd ever met. But I felt it was a mistake for us to keep going."

"Because of the working-together thing?" I asked.

"That was an excuse."

Aha! I knew it. "An excuse for what?"

He gripped my hand more tightly. "I was protecting you. From me."

I grabbed a pillow from the couch and swatted him with it. He protected himself with his arms before he grabbed it from me and tossed it aside. "Hey! Why'd you do that?"

"Because that's the most arrogant thing I've ever heard." I realized I was sort of shouting, so I dropped my voice. But not my indignation. "What are you, from the '60s? I don't need protection."

"Trust me, you don't know my upbringing. Listen to me," he said in a whisper-yell. The moon must have peeked out from behind a cloud, suddenly throwing silvery light everywhere, illuminating the couch, the sewing machine, and the man in front of me.

He got up and paced in front of the old couch, raking a hand through his hair. "I should have stopped this before we slept together."

"So why didn't you?"

He'd stopped pacing in front of the window. From the moonlight flooding the room, I could see his eyes spark. "You blew me away. You were the whole package—smart and fun and kind and pretty. I couldn't stop."

"I *chose* to sleep with you," I said. "I knew what I was doing." That sounded mature, but it was only half-true. I really had no idea what I was doing with Brax. I was crazy about him. And did he say that he thought I was kind? Yet I tilted up my chin to brace for a blow that I felt sure was coming.

"Mia, you need to hear what I'm saying."

"I'm listening." My stomach was flipping. We might finally be getting somewhere—or he was going to tell me something terrible. I couldn't tell what was coming.

"My mom was addicted to meth, and my sister and I were put into foster care. I was twelve; she was eight. She got adopted. I didn't."

"Oh, Brax." That horror seeped into my bones and made my heart ache. My impulse was to hold him, to hug him, to try to take away the unfathomable hurt. But I wasn't sure he would want that.

He was standing in front of me, still spotlighted in moonlight, speaking so emphatically, it was breaking my heart. "This isn't something I talk about—to anyone. But I need you to know that I'm not a good bet for a boyfriend. For your own good. I'm not the kind of guy anyone takes home for Christmas."

I shook my head, seeing this in an entirely different way. "You *are* that guy because you're here now. You came when no one else would." Well, except for Drake, but he didn't count.

That was when I swatted him again with another pillow to knock some sense into him. And for some comic relief, because, man, we could've surely used some.

"Would you stop with the pillows already?" He sounded a little irritated as he sat down and grabbed me by the arms, causing the upcoming pillow to hit the floor with a *pffft*.

His hands were warm, his grip firm. And his gaze was drilling into mine in a way that raised goose bumps on my arms.

"You know what I hate the most?" Even as I spoke, I was getting lost in his eyes. He was so intense, so conflicted, so loveable. The opposite of what he thought he was. I didn't see a person unworthy of love. I saw someone full of it. "You didn't give me a chance to decide about us," I said. "You decided for me."

"It was an easy decision," he said stubbornly. "I don't know how to...how to do this."

"How to have sex?" I feigned a puzzled look, desperate to make him laugh. "I thought you were pretty good at that, actually."

He didn't laugh at my terrible joke. "How to be with somebody. As in—really be with someone. I spent too many years only being able to trust myself. No one else was reliable enough."

My heart was thrumming, thrilling, threatening to beat right out of my chest. I tried to comprehend. He'd stayed away because...he felt like he didn't have the skills? He was dead serious.

What had he endured that he would say such a thing? I pictured a lonely, sad, very handsome boy, left entirely on his own. If that were the case, then look how he'd thrived. I was awestruck at his strength, his fortitude, his endurance.

Also, I was aware the universe had somehow given us this strange, miraculous do-over. A Christmas miracle of sorts. This time, I wasn't going to accept what he said without a fight.

This time, I didn't hold back. Without thinking, I wrapped my arms around his lean waist and laid my head on his chest. The soft, warm cotton of his gray T-shirt grazed my cheek. His heart thumped, strong and regular in his chest.

Such a nice chest. So wonderful to be here next to him. And for the first time, I felt that he was happy to be next to me too.

Except he was stiff. When I looked up, he looked wary. But also like he wanted me too. "You came home with me because you knew how important to me this was. You sacrificed your time with your sister for me. What you did means a lot to me. And I don't...I don't need anything else." I paused. "Except...except if you might want to try again, I'd be willing. I mean, I could work with you, you know?" I smiled. "I heard you're a quick study."

Then I reached up and kissed him. Brief, quick, but *wham*.

Wow, he had great lips. Soft and full and really, really nice.

I rarely did anything without thinking. That made me chuckle a little.

"What? What is it?" he asked.

I shook my head. "I've never kissed someone who'd dumped me and was maybe trying to do it again." But he'd looked so forlorn. More than that. He looked—well, miserable. Like he really believed what he'd said about being a liability. And that made me hurt for him. And created a million questions I desperately wanted the answer to.

But right now, I did what my heart was compelling me to do.

And that was cover his lips with mine.

To show him that maybe we hadn't been a mistake.

He didn't fight it. He kissed me back tenderly, slowly, seeming to savor every second, moving his mouth over mine, drawing me into his arms.

I backed up far enough to say, "We could take it one kiss at a time, you know?"

When he stopped my chatter by kissing me some more, I felt only absolute relief. Now we were getting somewhere.

He smoothed my damp hair away from my face. "You're so beautiful," he said. I could see in the watery light from the window that his eyes were full of warmth, his touch light. And then he held me. "I don't want to dump you. I just want to *deserve* you."

I went boneless. Tears welled in my eyes. What he'd just said—was it real? Was any of this real?

Then he kissed me hard, and thoughts ceased. He felt so good, his mouth so clever, his hands wrapping around me, stroking my back, our bodies pressing together as we desperately sought each other in the darkness.

It was pure magic, the kisses, the connection, knowing that I was wanted back. I'd never experienced anything like this during all those years with Charlie. I wanted to take all of Brax's pain away. I wanted to show him that love was something freely given, not given to someone because they are worthy.

Brax drew me down to the couch. Or maybe I pulled him down. I wasn't really conscious of space or time. I lay back and tugged him over me, and there he was, his weight over me, his warm, strong body on mine, his kisses ardent and all-encompassing. I ran my hand along his shoulders, his back, feeling the strong planes of muscle, thinking how long I'd yearned to do this, to touch him, to learn all his angles and lines. I kissed him hard and drew him to me when I suddenly heard a soft whimper.

I froze. "That wasn't you, was it?" I whispered into his neck.

A low, soft woof was the answer, as Cooper, sniffing and chuffing, poked his cold, wet nose between us.

Cooper, who'd somehow jumped between us just at the right time. Or rather, the exact wrong time.

Who knew my old dog would become my chaperone?

I made a strangled sound, halfway between a laugh and a groan.

"Hey, Coop." Brax gave me a shrug and welcomed the dog, petting him the way guys do, a kind of roughhousing rubdown that the dog adored so much, he immediately rolled over on his back between us and begged for more.

And with that, Cooper was won over.

I couldn't be too upset when watching Brax love my dog was

so much fun. I loved how he took the interruption in stride, without a trace of irritation.

And then the stairwell light flicked on.

"Cooper?" My dad's voice. Then, my dad himself, in a flannel robe and wool-lined slippers.

He took a look at us, and oh lordie, what must he have seen? Us, tangled in the blanket, the dog between us, our disheveled appearance. *Disaster.*

His brow lifted. He let out a surprised "Oh." Followed by a pause that spoke volumes. "Hello." He looked from me to Brax to Cooper, his face politely blank. "I was looking for the dog. He needs to go out one more time. Trouble is, I thought I heard a coyote out there."

Brax immediately flipped back the comforter and stood. "I'll take him, sir."

I'll take him, sir? I wanted to slide back under the comforter. Brax might as well have said, *We were about to get naked in Mom's sewing room, sir.*

But in typical chill-dad form, my dear dad didn't say a thing. He just smiled and turned toward the stairs.

"Good night, kids," he called over his shoulder.

"Now what?" I asked as Brax put on his shoes.

He grinned. "They didn't have coyotes in Philly. At least that I know of. If I happen to run into one, I'm screwed."

Someone cleared their throat. I turned to find Caleb standing at the bottom of the stairwell. Cooper tore down the stairs to greet him. "Hey, Brax," Caleb called up as he petted the dog, "I'll join you, if that's okay. We can take a little walk—together."

"Be right there," Brax called, tying his other shoe. He smiled at me. "Coyotes, big brothers...all good." Then he kissed me on the lips and left.

Chapter Fourteen

Brax

I woke on the couch just as a thin line of reddish-orange light from the rising sun appeared in the frosted-over window. I was freezing, and something hard was stabbing me in the back. I reached a hand back into the crook of the couch and felt something thick and scratchy...aha. Dog chew. Thank you, Cooper.

Cooper had been my roommate, not Mia. Caleb had been extra chatty in that interrogating way of his, and I still had the feeling that he was vetting me, trying to find the cracks in my armor. By the time we got back from walking the dog, it was way past midnight, and Mia had been curled up in bed, fast asleep. So I crashed in the sewing room.

And maybe I also took advantage of the time to think.

I felt a warm, dead weight on my feet—like, my actual feet, nothing in between. "What the—" I sat up and tossed off the comforter. The dog looked up from the well between my feet, where his snout had been happily resting on my ankle. Without a tinge of embarrassment, he wagged his tail and climbed right up, hovering over my face, licking me—basically letting me know that he needed to relieve himself again and that I was now the selected friend lucky enough to go with him. At least Caleb wouldn't be joining me, which he was way too enthusiastic about last night. I took a peek at my weather app. Twenty degrees. This time, I was adding more layers before I ventured out into the frostscape.

I tiptoed into Mia's room, as stealthy as the Grinch stealing Christmas, and managed to find a thermal undershirt, a flannel shirt, and some pants. And then I caught my breath.

In the dusky gray of the early morning, she was snuggled in the bed, the red plaid flannel sheets tucked under her chin, her hair splayed out on the pillow.

I stopped dead in my tracks. She was asleep, peaceful, her expression serene. Her beauty floored me. I mean, it always did, but even more seeing her like this, unguarded.

Then I had the weirdest out-of-body experience. It was as if it were any early morning, as if I'd just gotten up for a prework jog, and I got stopped in my tracks by the fact that there was someone beautiful in my bed—no, more than that—*special*—and I could swoop down and kiss her and be with her because...because she was mine.

What would that be like, I wondered, to know that you had someone to wake up to every morning? Whom you could tell your secrets to, who would understand you, who might even love you back if you were willing to take the chance?

I would never take a miracle like that for granted.

But then, miracles didn't happen to damaged people like me.

Except—maybe one already had. One that I'd nearly let slip out of my hands.

I stared at her for so long, I forgot what time it was or what I was doing. Until her lashes fluttered, and she stirred. My heart pounding, I froze until her breathing returned to the deep, slow rhythms of sleep, gathered my stuff, and hightailed it out of there, careful not to make a sound. All that was loud was the sound in my ears of my pounding heart and a deep, visceral yearning I couldn't quite snuff out.

The scent of cinnamon and warm dough hit me as I descended the back stairway into the kitchen. As I turned the corner at the bottom, I saw the warm reddish-golden blaze of a fire in the brick fireplace. Mrs. D was sitting at the table with a mug of coffee, flipping through a book. The Christmas tree with cookie cutter ornaments and red ribbons in the corner was already lit up.

She looked up and smiled, then patted the seat next to her. "Brax, come sit. Unless you're on your way out?"

"Just going out with Cooper here so he doesn't get eaten by a coyote."

She rolled her eyes and chuckled. Then she got up. "You just sit down. Coopy, come here." The dog followed her obediently to the door. As soon as she opened it, he bolted out. "Thank you for being willing to freeze your backside for our dog, and don't tell Steven, but it's way too cold for coyotes. Now, how do you take your coffee?"

I smiled, grateful for her laid-backness. "Black is fine, but cream is nicer if you've got some."

She grabbed a Santa mug, filled it up, grabbed a carton of creamer out of the fridge, and took her seat next to me.

She pushed a spiral book between us. A photo album. "I love remembering our early Christmases. Maybe you'd like to look at the photos with me?" She looked up, her bright blue eyes searing through me, as if she could read all my secrets.

"Sure." I sensed that she really wanted to share these photos, whatever they were. And I felt honored to be invited. What better way to understand Mia better?

Beth heaved a sigh. "Sometimes I feel that my kids would rather pretend nothing tragic happened to us. But I find I need to remember the love—it helps me to dwell on that and not the pain. I *sort of* succeed at it." She eyed me carefully. "Otherwise, our Grace is forgotten, and I can't have that."

Our Grace. I couldn't imagine the loss. Instantly, I thought of Mia with Rylee and Reagan. How she always made sure to bring Reagan into her interactions with Rylee. Always chatting with her, asking about her, including her. She was so great with those little girls. Now, I was beginning to understand that it just might be a mission.

Beth tapped on a photo. There were her kids—all four of them —cross-legged under a brightly lit Christmas tree, all wearing red Santa hats and their Christmas morning pj's. "I asked them to pose with their favorite gift."

There was Liam wearing Harry Potter glasses, not unlike the pair he wore now, clutching a book. Caleb held a lightsaber somewhat threateningly over his brother's head. Guess nothing much changed. Grace clutched a doll. Mia—who was all of eight or nine, I guessed—had glasses and a halo of blonde hair curling everywhere. Notably, she had bunny slippers on. She had one arm wrapped around Grace, and she was smiling at the doll in Grace's arms. There was a round, glass object in her free hand, but it was obscured by the folds of her robe. "What's that Mia's holding?" I squinted hard to see.

Beth leaned over. She smelled like cinnamon, and it made me wonder, is this what mothers smell like? She rested a hand lightly on my arm and pointed with the other. How could she be so welcoming to a stranger? I'd known lots of foster parents. Some were really nice, others more aloof. All I knew was that it was easy to feel the warmth and affection Beth seemed to so readily hand out to everyone. Having it directed at me felt strange, but I admit, I absorbed it as hungrily as sunshine on the beach.

"Mia did love that snow globe." She peered carefully at the photo that she must have looked at a million times. "I think we bought it at the Kris Kringle market."

Before I could ask her what that was, she told me. "That's a market they have in the Main Street shops each year. All the artists make special wares for the holidays, and they serve hot chocolate and warm gingerbread and, of course, warm cheese curds."

I'd never heard of cheese curds before coming to Wisconsin. Unbelievably, I'd never tasted them. As an undergrad, I was always pinching pennies. And as a med student...well, I just wasn't very food-adventurous. But a lot of people said they were the state's best-kept secret.

"Anyway," Beth continued, "the globe was very Christmasy, swirling with snowflakes. In the center was a house with Christmas lights and a couple of little kids holding hands that Mia always thought of as her and Grace, and there was a little dachshund in it that did really look like our little doxie at the time, Jack. The globe broke a year later, when the kids were chasing each other around the family room. Mia cried and cried. Shortly after, Grace got sick again and..." Her voice got very soft and choked up. "And we lost her."

Instinctively, I put my arm around her. To my surprise, she let out a sob and hugged me tight. At a loss, I stayed stock-still, uncertain of what to do, but sensing that she somehow needed me to stay right where I was.

I thought of little-girl Mia, so in love with the lovely fantasy inside that globe. One that was shattered right along with her family as she knew it.

Suddenly, it dawned on me—Mia's mom had just explained to me who Mia was. And I saw the evidence of it in that photo.

She was the little girl wanting to do anything to protect her sister, wanting the cancer to go away. Trying to help but feeling helpless.

Was that why she'd gone into pediatrics? So she could obtain the tools to help? It made sense why she was so taken with Rylee and Reagan. Maybe she was seeing another pair of twins so similar to herself and Grace and wanting desperately to change their fates.

Maybe that was also why she was so determined *not* to do heme-onc, despite having such a passion for helping those kids. In some way, each family's circumstance would be a version of her own personal nightmare—trying to save kids as she'd wanted to save her own sister—and couldn't.

After a moment, Beth drew back. "Oh, goodness. I'm sorry," she said, sitting up a little straighter and wiping her eyes. "No, I'm not," she said resolutely. "I needed someone to listen to me tell that story. I needed you to understand how close Mia was to her sister, how a twin bond is so very, very close, and when it's broken, it feels like a piece of you is missing. And maybe it always will."

I nodded because I got it, what it was like to feel that hole. I totally did.

My mother was an addict who couldn't hold down a job, couldn't provide for us. Despite all that, I knew that in her way, she'd loved us, even as she'd continued to hurt us. I'd long since forgiven her, but the sense of *what if* would always haunt me. What if she'd stayed clean, what if her last stint in rehab had worked, what if we could've had the chance to be a normal family? I would never stop wondering.

"Tell me about your family, Brax," Beth said.

Oh boy. If she was expecting the discussion to switch to something more lighthearted, I was in trouble. Unless I did what I usually did. "There's just me and my younger sister," I said.

Stop there, I warned myself. *Like you always do.*

Beth was looking at me kindly. Like she somehow intuited that there might be more. "I told you my secrets," she said. "Now it's okay if you tell me yours." She paused. "I don't mean to joke. Just that you seem like you might be a person who's been on his own for a long time."

That took me aback. I must have given her a puzzled look.

"Mia's told me as much, but I also see the signs." She closed the photo album and sighed. "My dad died when I was eighteen, and my mom sort of fell apart. That left me in charge of my three siblings. I felt responsible, like I had the world on my shoulders, but I was determined to help them to turn out right. I was tough on them. But I'm proud to say they all turned out to be great human beings. And as for me...sometimes, I longed for someone to turn to myself. But I learned to be strong on my own. Maybe sometimes too independent." She looked at me long and hard. "Forgive me if I'm being pushy, but I sense that same trait in you. Not that I know you that well, but you seem to minimize the hardship you must have gone through."

Yeah. This woman saw straight through me. Just like her daughter.

"My mom—had problems," I found myself saying for the second time ever. "I was placed in foster care from twelve on."

She set down her mug and made a soft exclamation. "You stayed with your sister, then?"

I shook my head. "No." Was I really going to spill it all? "A nice family adopted her. I made sure we always stayed in touch."

She shook her head sadly. "And what happened to you?"

"I aged out of the system, but I made it to college. School saved me, really." My smarts had given me a new life.

"You need more than intelligence to thrive the way you did."

I shrugged, embarrassed. It was hard to take the compliment. She didn't see the scars. "I had a sports scholarship, and then academic ones. That's how I made it to UW. And I worked a lot of part-time jobs."

"Like I said, more than smarts. Strength of character." She smiled. "Will you see your sister over your break?"

"Not enough time off, but I plan to go see her as soon as I can."

"You came here with Mia instead of seeing your sister."

I nodded. Mia needed me. That was a no-brainer.

Beth gave me a side hug. A good one, full of warmth and unspoken solidarity. That's what got me. That she sensed what I needed even more than I did. To be listened to. To acknowledge that I'd survived despite all I'd been through. No one had ever said that to me before.

"I see much more than your survivorship. I see your kind heart," she said softly. "Just like I see the way you look at my daughter." She squeezed harder. "From all that Mia's told me, you treat her like the jewel she is. I've never seen her so happy. For a while, I suspected that maybe she was embellishing to keep my spirits up. But now I see for myself that it's all true."

I waited for a wave of guilt to cut through me. But it never came.

I just felt...grateful. To be here. With Mia. With this amazing family. With this kind woman who was so willing to take me into her home and give her friendship. I shouldn't have been surprised, because Mia was the exact same way.

I cleared my throat. "Well, you have a very special daughter, Mrs. D." I found myself wanting to say so much more. Even ask her if she thought it was possible for someone like me—

"Call me Beth. And yes. Yes, I do." She gave me that deep look again. "And she's found someone who brings out the best in her. As I think she does for you. That's really what love is all about, isn't it? It repairs old wounds. It makes us our best selves. And it helps us to move on from the past and create a brand-new future where anything is possible."

I desperately wanted to believe that. I looked down to find my hands fisted, tense. I'd hung on her every word.

Beth released my arm and stood up. "Well, here I am blathering on. I love chatting with you, but now we have something very important to do."

That distracted me from my thoughts, but also put me on edge. "What's that?"

A sparkle appeared in her eyes that made me feel like I was about to be asked to do something waaay out of my comfort zone. "We're going to make cutout cookies."

We? "Right now?" flew out of my mouth. It was—well, it was the butt crack of dawn was what it was.

"Yes," she said cheerily, walking across the kitchen and pulling ingredients out of the cupboards. "We'll get most of them done before everyone wakes up. Are you up for it?"

"I've never baked a cookie in my life." Confession seemed to be my word of the day. But I wanted to make sure she knew exactly what she was getting herself into.

She winked and scurried to pull the cinnamon rolls out of the oven. "Well, you're a smart one, and I'm sure you'll catch on fast." She gave a giant grin. "And you're gonna love it." On the way to the oven, she opened a drawer and tossed me something red-and-white striped. "Put that on."

It landed in a heap on the table. As I untangled it, I saw that it was an apron. It said in big green letters across the front, *Let's Get Elfed Up.*

I raised a brow. "It was from a gift exchange," she said. "It'll do just fine, right?"

"Sure. Of course." Right. As I placed it over my neck and tied it behind my back, I heard footsteps on the wooden stairs.

Mia stepped into the room wearing her glasses, an oversized sweatshirt, flannel pants, and fuzzy socks, her hair wildly doing what curly hair does. Seeing her made me fumble tying my apron. How could she be, hands down, the sexiest woman I'd ever seen, even rolling straight out of bed? Even if her sweatshirt said Packers, and I was all about the Eagles.

I read her look as wary. A combo of *Where did you go last night/can I trust you/why are you baking with my mom?*

Wanting to reassure her without words, I poured her a coffee and brought it to her.

"Good morning," I said, handing her the steaming cup. Beth had managed to vanish at just the right time, a move I felt certain was strategic.

"Hi," Mia said, eyeing the coffee. "You're up early."

"Your little dog apparently has an equally tiny bladder."

That made her laugh. "Please don't blame Cooper for you not showing up," she said.

I held up my hands. "Caleb wanted to talk. And when I checked on you, you were fast asleep." I paused. "Maybe even snoring."

Her brows lifted. "I do not snore."

"Okay, maybe not. But I...I just—" I thought about what I really wanted, which was her. I'd spent a long time last night wondering if I could be a man who could be there for her. A man capable of taking the leap.

She made me want to try. That meant being honest.

I dropped my voice. "I just want to do this right. No rushing, no feeling like I'm sneaking around in your parents' house."

"You *are* sneaking around in my parents' house." She looked at me over the coffee. "Thank you—for this."

I got tangled up in her eyes. And I swear, if we were anywhere else, I wouldn't have given her time to finish that coffee. I'd be hauling her upstairs to finish what we'd started last night. "I, um— I wondered if you'd take me to the Kris Kringle market today?"

Her eyes widened. "You want to go to the Kris Kringle market?"

I put an arm on the staircase woodwork behind her head and leaned in, hoping this would tell her how much I wanted her until I got the chance to tell her with words. "Yeah. With you." I paused. "After I finish helping your mom make cookies, that is."

She looked into my eyes and smiled, and I swear my heartbeat went from eighty to two fifty. "You are so elfed up," she said. But she was breathing a little fast. Her lips were a little open, and now she was staring at mine. She looked a little dazed. "But I like it."

"And you're beautiful." I leaned over, set her coffee cup on the edge of one of the stairs behind her, and kissed her, firmly and quickly. She sucked in a surprised breath, her eyes widening, then drew her hands up to my shoulders. One kiss just wasn't enough. So I took the time to taste her lips, placing a few soft kisses there before cupping her neck with my hand, pulling her in, and really kissing her.

I was surprised that she melted into me, kissing me back with the exact same enthusiasm. I curled my arms around her, placing my hands on her hips. She made a little sound, barely audible, the softest sigh, that made me feel like she probably wasn't holding a grudge about last night anymore.

The sound of Beth first opening the door and talking to the dog, then the soft clattering of baking sheets being set on the island brought us both back to reality. "Then it's settled?" I said as I pulled back, my voice a little raspy, my balance a little off.

I couldn't help thinking that I really *was* pretty elfed up. Because the longer I stayed, the more I fell in love with Mia—and her family.

~

Mia

I could hear my mom around the corner dragging out cookie cutters and flour and vanilla and baking sheets, but I was in a haze of weak-kneed, heart-pounding discombobulation from those kisses.

I admit, I slept really badly, wondering if Brax had changed his mind, if our conversation had really happened, if he'd really said he wanted me.

But when he greeted me with fresh coffee and told me he wanted to do things right—and told me I was beautiful and kissed me—okay, all was forgiven.

But the real stunner occurred when Emma came bursting into the kitchen in fuzzy-footed pj's and reindeer antlers with bells on them, and a big picture book in her hands, which she brought right over to Brax.

I caught my breath. It was a book I knew well, an old, worn copy of *The Night Before Christmas*, with gorgeous illustrations of a family in Victorian times, Mama in her kerchief and Papa in his cap, the children sleeping in their beds with visions of sugarplums over their heads.

You know how everyone has their own idea of what Santa looks like? Well, the jolly, red-cheeked, twinkling-eyed Santa in this book was it for me.

Gracie and I used to beg our dad to read it every night, and he used to, over and over again, narrating the poem with flourishes and even putting on a red-and-white striped stocking cap just like the one the dad wears to bed in the book as he throws open the sash to discover Santa's sleigh landing on the rooftop.

I placed a hand over my chest. *Be still my heart.*

Brax took a moment to examine the old book, to see exactly what he was dealing with. He glanced up briefly at me, but by then, I was pretty sure I'd managed to erase the flood of emotion from my eyes.

"This is my favorite Christmas story," he said.

"Me too," Emma said. "Read it, read it." She grabbed his hand and tugged him into the family room to a chair by the fireplace.

He didn't say *later*, or *I'm busy*, or *go read it yourself.* He let himself be led, sat down, and hoisted her onto his lap.

And then he read. Except it wasn't the monotone, rapid reading of a bored adult, but a dramatic enacting of the story. He read that poem with so much excitement and inflection, even my mom stopped what she was doing. My dad joined us as we stood near the doorway, listening. Caleb, who'd basically rolled out of bed and walked downstairs shirtless, was also caught in the magic. Even though Liam tossed him a shirt and said, "Cover the pecs, okay? This isn't a college dorm."

Just then, Dina walked in, wrapped in a thick, fuzzy robe. Liam gathered her in front of him, wrapping his arms around her.

We were all mesmerized until Brax used his best Santa voice to ho-ho-ho and say, "Happy Christmas to all and to all a good night!"

It was quite the performance. Over the top, wonderful. Even better, it showed me that Brax had so much to give, much more than he knew. I didn't have time to overthink it, because just then, my entire nerdy family clapped and whooped.

"I feel a little upstaged," my dad said quietly from where he stood next to me.

I rubbed his back and gave him a squeeze. "No one could ever upstage you, Daddy."

"Read it again!" Emma cried, glancing up at Brax with Cindy Lou Who eyes. "Can we read it again, Uncle Brax?"

My mom swooped in with a cinnamon roll and a glass of milk for Emma, effectively rescuing him.

"We'll read it again later," he said, his gaze straying my way. "After we make the cookies."

And that, Dear Reader, was the moment I lost my heart for good.

Chapter Fifteen

Brax

"So, this is the Kris Kringle market?" I looked around at the quaint row of Main Street buildings outlined with glowing lights, the shoppers buzzing with holiday cheer, the lampposts covered with garlands. It seemed as if the entire town was out doing their last-minute shopping. I felt a strange sense of anticipation watching the little kids tugging their parents toward Santa, who apparently was visiting with kids in the middle of the bookstore.

Mia wore a bright yellow knit cap. Her cheeks were flushed in the cold, her eyes bright. Before I could think too much about it, I reached over and took her hand. A person had to start somewhere, right?

She glanced over in surprise. "You're holding my hand," she said. "And my family's nowhere in sight."

"It feels good," I said.

She gave a lukewarm smile. Which made me worry a little, until I saw that she was focused on two women in the distance, walking down the street, their arms laden with shopping bags.

"Let's try here," she said quickly, pulling me into a Christmas store filled with decorated trees—as far as the eye could see—all different colors, shapes, and sizes, every bough laden with handmade ornaments. The tree nearest to us sat atop a table and was lit with white and blue lights and covered with sports-themed ornaments. More ornaments filled baskets underneath the trees.

"Who were those women you were looking at?" I asked.

"What women?" she said. Then she sighed. "Okay, fine. Old friends from high school."

Hmm, seemed like her brothers were right. "So you're avoiding people you know?" I asked. "Or are you worried that what's-his-name is going to show up?"

I could tell by her worried look that I'd hit a nerve. "No, I just —I don't want people asking me if I'm going tonight." She set down a soccer ball ornament and tugged off her cap, probably because it felt like a hundred degrees in the crowded store. "And please don't ask me either. Because I'm not."

She looked on edge, scanning the shop. "Okay," I said, "but you've got nothing to be ashamed of. The cheating wasn't your fault."

"Of course it wasn't!"

Put foot in mouth, stop talking. I guess I didn't listen to that wise inner voice, because I kept trying to help. "You're human like all of us, you know. Cheating aside, I mean, most everyone gets dumped."

"Even you, Mr. Eight Weeks?" She gave a weak half smile. But I could tell the issue was weighing on her mind.

"Yep. Sophomore year. Meribel Klinger."

She shot me an incredulous look as we moved on to a table full of beach-themed ornaments.

I was desperate to make her smile. "Is it so hard to imagine that I had my heart broken?"

"I was just thinking that she has a unique name." She examined a glittery orange starfish. "So, did she break the eight-week rule?"

I picked up a sparkling sand dollar. "She was an exception to it. She wouldn't go out with me, but I was hopelessly in love with her for an entire school year."

Mia looked up. "And then what happened?"

I shrugged. "I had to move on. Too many other girls were sad that I was unavailable." That got me an eye roll. "Okay, the truth is that I switched foster families and schools." I paused. I didn't want this to be about me. "Mia, no one else in the world is perfect—no breakups, no losses. You shouldn't hold yourself to that standard. I'm sure no one else does."

She clapped her chest, a gesture of indignation. "I do not hold myself to a standard of perfection."

"Says the daughter who brought home a fake boyfriend because she didn't want to disappoint her mom."

She gave me a good glare but couldn't tell me off because an elderly woman with white hair began waving furiously as she approached.

"Mia! How wonderful to see you," the woman said, giving Mia an exuberant hug.

"Mrs. Bradbury, how are you?" Mia hugged her back, clearly excited to see her too.

"Wonderful. Who's the hunk?" she asked in a lively tone, checking me out over the tops of her spectacles.

"Mrs. B, this is Brax." I noticed Mia avoided labeling our relationship. But maybe it was high time to.

"Nice to meet you," I said, shaking the woman's hand.

She didn't let go, rather added her other hand on top. "Nice to meet you, Brax. Mia," she said, glancing over at her, "I hope you've told this handsome young man that you won the state essay competition your senior year." She turned back to me. "I was hoping she might become a writer one day, but I understand that medicine claimed her."

I knew Mia sometimes brought books with her to read on call that barely got cracked open with how busy we were, but writing? Interesting.

Mia grinned. "I credit you for giving me the confidence to write, Mrs. B."

"Well, lots of doctors become writers, so you never know," the former teacher said in a singsong voice. "Actually, I suppose more lawyers do, but maybe someday, you will write a book." She finally dropped my hands. "Are you two going to the big party tonight?" Her eyes twinkling with mischief, she looked me up and down. "If I had this hottie on my arm, I'd walk in there in a red dress and heels and tell old Charlie to go stick it."

"Oh my goodness." Mia laughed and put a hand over her chest. "I don't have hard feelings but thank you for that."

"I'm so thrilled to see you successful and happy, dear," the older woman said.

Mia hugged her one last time. "Great to see you too."

Hmmm. As we walked out of the shop and back onto the street, I couldn't let that go. "She was nice. You want to write a book one day? I mean, you're multitalented, so it doesn't surprise me."

She smiled. "She was an amazing teacher. I double majored in English in college. Did you know that?"

"That's fascinating. But what kind of book would you write?"

"A romance. They're full of hope, and I love that." She gave me a tentative look. "Have you ever read one?"

"Does Sarah J. Maas's ACOTAR count?"

She stopped walking. "You've *read* Sarah J. Maas? I love her."

I gave a chuckle. "Would you be into me more if I said yes?"

She burst out in laughter, shaking her head. "I don't think it's possible for me to be any more into you than I already am."

Her answer made my heart slam into my chest. I took her hand. It was soft and small compared to my big paws and a little cool to the touch. I kissed it lightly and looked up at her. My throat felt tight, and I had to clear my throat to get my words out. "I'm really into you too." Her smile told me everything I needed to know. That I was in big trouble. The best kind. "Tell you what," I said as we moved on. "You write your book, and I'll read it."

She grinned. "Deal."

We came to a shop called Ye Olde Trading Post. In the window, I saw a mix of gifts of all kinds—candles, beautiful wooden cutting boards stained like checkerboards, small oil paintings by local artists. "Can we go in here? I'd like to get a gift for your parents." And for her, but I had no idea what.

She frowned. "You know that's not necessary. Just giving your time to come here with me—"

"Was something I really wanted to do." Then I opened the door, and we walked inside.

The shop smelled like wood and was filled with fun handmade item like serving spoons, wine racks, and nativity sets. I could've stayed and admired the artistry there all day. Out of the corner of my eye, I spotted a display of snow globes. Hmm. Duly noted.

Mia inhaled deeply. With a twinkle in her eye, she said, "I love this smell. What do you think?"

At that moment, her hair was lit up with golden highlights under the overhead bulbs, and her cheeks were flushed from the cold, and despite all the stress of the past weeks, she looked happy.

And that happiness just might've been infectious. So I inhaled deeply too. "Nice. Fresh wood. Lemon oil. Shavings."

"Exactly." She looked at me sideways. "Are you okay? You don't have to pretend to like shopping, you know."

I smiled, because while I didn't care much for shopping, I loved being here with her. "Just wondering if you would help me pick out some gifts for your family."

"You don't need to do that." She noticed a display of beautiful handmade cutting boards. "But now that I'm looking, I know my dad really, really wants one of these."

I looked where she was pointing. "A charcuterie board?"

Mia nodded. "My mom monitors the amount of cholesterol he consumes. But ever since he tasted prosciutto, she can't keep him away from it."

We started sorting through the various sizes. "Which size do you think we should get? Like, how much prosciutto does he eat?"

"More than he should, good point. How about a smaller one?" She chose one while I spotted a set of hand-carved wooden measuring spoons and snagged them.

"For my mom?"

I nodded. "For your mom."

For the boys—I meant the oak trees—Mia helped me choose hand-forged chef knives, since she said they enjoyed cooking, even though I had reservations about purchasing any sharp implements that could be used against me. For Dina, I bought a soft, hand-knitted wool scarf that Mia assured me was fashion-forward.

We moved on to a mug display. Mia picked up a cheesy one that said *Best Mom Ever* with reindeer antlers.

"Can I ask you something personal?" I asked.

She held up another one that had chickens standing together, all dressed in Christmas hats. "Sure."

"How was it with Charlie?"

She stopped browsing and frowned. "How was what?"

"Just—everything. The relationship, how you got along." I knew that the last thing she wanted to talk about was Charlie. But maybe she needed to, you know? Besides, she got me to open up. I figured some payback was in order.

She set down a mug she was holding. "None of your—no, wait." She closed her eyes. "I see what you're doing. I'm not going tonight. She paused. "But to answer your question, we grew up together. He was...familiar."

Whew. "I love that word."

She shot me a puzzled look. "Why?"

"Because it's not *hot*, *sexy*, or *fabulous in bed*."

"I'm not in love with him, if that's what you're asking."

Thank God. "It sounds like he wasn't The One."

"He wasn't The One," she quietly agreed.

She pressed her lips together as we assessed each other across all the red-ribboned, copper cookie-cutter gifts. She worried at her bottom lip. "So you think I should go?"

I narrowed my eyes. "That's for you to decide," I said carefully. "I mean, you're not really angry anymore, are you?"

She shrugged. "I'm more embarrassed." She fiddled with the red ribbons, smoothing them, straightening them out.

I could tell from her stoic expression that maybe it was time for some humor. I held out my arms. "If you decide to go, you'd have a hunk by your side. All you'd need is that red dress your teacher mentioned."

"I'm an accomplished woman who doesn't need anyone on my arm." She paused. "But maybe it can't hurt. The dress, I mean. Seriously, I'll think about it."

She was wavering, so I made my case. "If you go, I'd be happy to stay next to you the entire time and even flex my muscles if you want me to. I mean, might as well use a not-so-fake boyfriend when you've got one."

"Not so fake?" Her eyes told me everything. That she wanted the truth.

All right, then. Here I went. "Not fake," I said, meeting her gaze with what I hoped was a dead-serious one of my own. "Not fake at all."

"So, you're taking the leap?"

"Yeah." Once I'd finally said it out loud, I felt strangely okay. "Yeah, I am."

"Hmmm. Okay, then, not-fake boyfriend, if you can take the leap, maybe I can too." She paused. "But what would it take to have you do that muscle flexing in private? You know, as a reward. If I survive this."

I grinned. "Not much."

She burst out laughing, which was cute. I was glad I could

lighten up her decision. Then I let settle what I'd just said. *Boyfriend*. It was a big step for me, but it felt right.

She pointed to the cashier desk. "I'm going to see if they can embroider my mom's name on this apron." She held up a pretty Christmas-red one. "She really needs to get rid of that elfed-up one."

"I kind of liked it." I tipped my head toward the ornament section to throw her off. "I'm going to look around a little," I said as casually as possible.

As soon as she was out of sight, I bolted in the opposite direction to the snow globe display I'd seen on the way in. I quickly scanned all the shelves. And suddenly, I spotted one containing a tiny house, all lit up for Christmas. It looked similar to Mia's house, all charm, wreaths on every window, a turret. There was a dog, a retriever, not a wiener dog, and with the dog were two little girls, holding hands, playing in the snow. It was exactly like Beth's description. Except, standing behind the two girls was a third girl, her hands on each of their shoulders. It was hard to say if she was an older sister or a mother. But I knew exactly what she was. A guardian of those girls. The symbolism struck me as perfect.

An older woman wearing an elf hat and a green apron walked up to me. "My son hand-makes those," she said. "In case you're wondering if they're imported, they're not. All local. The wood base is cherry or oak. Each one takes him about a week to make."

"Cool." All right, then. "This is for my girlfriend, who's over there." I hiked a thumb toward the front of the store. Just then, Mia turned around in line and waved. I stepped away from the display and gave a quick wave back. "I don't want her to see it. Can you help?"

"Of course. Hand your gifts to me—plus your credit card. Would you like these wrapped?"

As I surrendered the globe, the spoons, and the wooden board, I happened to spot a pair of fleece reindeer slippers with red noses that lit up that I thought would be perfect for Mia. I eyeballed her size and impulsively added them to the pile as the woman whisked everything off.

That was kind of...fun, knowing I'd surprise Mia with these little, unexpected things.

Ten minutes later, she was waiting for me by the door, her bag in hand. "Next stop, the bookstore."

"For Emma?"

She nodded. As we made our way across the street, I asked, "What's the story behind the beat-up Christmas book that Emma wants to read fifty times a day?"

"Grace and I loved it," she said. "We used to beg our dad to read it over and over. Except I used to listen, while Grace pantomimed and performed it. She was such an actress."

I thought about the photo in Mia's room with the birthday cake. "Sounds like Grace was an extrovert?"

"Definitely." Mia talked animatedly, using her hands. "She was bold and funny and...and she lived in Technicolor. Nothing frightened her. I try to remember that. It helps me sometimes."

I loved hearing her talk about her sister. "I think you live in Technicolor too. I mean, you became a doctor because of her, right?"

She minimized that by shrugging. "I guess you feel helpless when something like that happens, so you want to do anything you can to make it have meaning. Like, if I help other kids, somehow that makes Grace's death easier to handle."

"I think you're amazing." It felt good to finally be able to tell her.

She shook her head. "I'm not a martyr. And you did the same thing—you saw how Dr. Pendergast helped people, and you wanted to do that too."

"He was a huge influence," I said. "If it weren't for him, I never would've gone to med school. He believed in me until I learned I could believe in myself."

"How did you meet him, anyway?" She linked her arm through my mine as we walked. It felt nice.

"He gave a lecture to the premed organization at UW, and I happened to ask him a question afterward—I don't even remember what I asked, but it turned out to be the best question of my life. He saw my curiosity, struck up a conversation, and we'd hit it off. He ended up taking me under his wing, helped me get into med school, and totally changed the course of my life."

She looked over at me and smiled. "That's very powerful."

I nodded. "And lucky. A kid like me could've ended up a whole lot worse."

"I'm not sure I buy that," she disagreed. "You got yourself a full scholarship to college. I think you would've been successful even without meeting him."

"Thanks for believing that," I said. "All I know is I hope to someday help kids like I was helped."

That was about enough about me. We were getting close to the bookstore, and I was running out of time to ask her something that had been on my mind for a while. "Can I ask something personal? Have you thought about applying for the heme-onc fellowship? I mean, you gravitate toward those heme-onc kids. I get how you feel about Rylee and Reagan now."

She shrugged. "I see a lot of me and my sister in them. But I couldn't handle all that emotion full-time. I know my limits."

I felt in my gut that she wasn't telling me the whole story. "There are a lot of success stories too."

"I can't relive my own tragedy whenever I lose a patient. I just can't."

She was adamant, more than adamant, and she was drawing a line in the sand. I had to respect it. "I didn't mean to upset you."

She touched my arm and met my gaze. "We promised not to talk about work, remember?"

"Yeah. Right. Here we are." I opened the door to a quaint but crowded bookstore, with a line snaking around full of parents and kiddos waiting to see Santa, who was on his throne in the back. "So what kind of book do you want for Emma?"

"One that's cool and fun and makes her discover wonderful things. And gives her a love of reading. And one that she remembers that I gave it to her and that I'm the best aunt ever."

I lifted a brow. "That's a tall order for one book."

She laughed. "I know. But I just want to find her the perfect one."

I shook my head as we headed to the children's section. The Santa line was noisy and a baby was crying loudly. On a more pleasant note, the store was filled with the scent of books, something that always made me happy. "You love giving gifts, don't you?"

"Yes," she said unabashedly.

"Like, how much?" I tried not to look mystified. I wondered, with a childhood where no one baked cookies or even expected presents, if I could pretend that all of this wasn't a mystery to me.

She checked out a Christmas display of kids' books. "Because it means you're thinking of someone. You understand what they like, and it's just a little thoughtful way of being nice to someone. And when you open a gift, it's just plain fun."

I must've gone quiet, because I found her looking at me in a peculiar way. "Brax, did your family ever celebrate Christmas?"

"I don't think I could answer that question and maintain our happy mood."

She grabbed my hand. "Tell me. I know you don't like to talk about your past, but I really want to hear about it. I mean, it's part of who you are."

She'd told me about Charlie and Grace, so I couldn't argue about that. "There were promises of gifts. Like a red bike I wanted badly. A pair of Rollerblades. A baseball bat. But nothing ever materialized. Eventually, I learned to scrape and make sure to get something for my sister every year. Of course, the foster parents were always nice, but by then, I guess I just cared about surviving Christmas."

Her expression nearly brought me to my knees. It was half sadness, half horror. I should have minimized it. Lied. Anything to avoid that look, which was slicing straight through my chest. "Don't be sad about it," I said quickly. "I'm not."

Before I could react, I suddenly found my arms full of Mia—the scent of her hair, the soft slide of her down jacket against mine. Right there in the crowded store, she'd somehow wrapped herself around me and was holding on tightly. Like, really tightly—as if she could squeeze all that pain right out of me. With all our shopping bags that ended up at our feet, we must've been quite a sight.

"Don't," I managed. "Don't feel sorry for me, okay?"

She kissed my cheek. Then my other cheek. Then my mouth. Of course, I gladly accepted her attempts to ease my suffering.

Finally, I had to chuckle. "What are you doing?"

"Trying to make you laugh." As she unwrapped herself, I saw a tear in her eye.

No one had ever done that for me—cried for what I'd gone through. I found myself getting choked up for the second time that day. Instinctively, I reached up and traced her tear with my finger. "At least when I wasn't honest and open, I didn't make you cry."

She reached up and took my hand, pressing her cheek against my palm. That slayed me even more.

"I hurt for that boy," she whispered, her eyes soft. "I want to do anything to help erase that pain." I didn't know what to say to that. Honesty came so easily to her, whereas I was always tongue-tied.

The crowds around us faded away, and I saw only her. "I'm fine," I whispered. "Don't waste your worry on me."

I kissed her again. I mean, I was desperate, so full of emotion that this woman wanted to...well, to heal me. The most shocking thing was that I dared to believe it, that she could somehow replace my wounds with her sunshine and light.

She pressed her lips, her whole body to mine, demanding that I forget everything but her.

And it worked. I lost track of everything except for her mind-blowing kisses, her caring heart, her...

I was afraid to say *love*. A fierce need rose up within me. I had to get a grip. There was too much feeling. It was like submerging, going under, drowning in emotions I had no control over. They were amazing and totally terrifying at the same time.

Mia was a bright light. She was Christmas lights. When you were surrounded by them, everything wintery, dingy, and barren became glorious and bright. Transformed.

Fortunately, some teenage boys were walking down the next aisle and yelled, "Hey, get a room!" and we broke apart, laughing.

We got back to work, Mia picking out Emma's present, and I doing a little more sneak shopping of my own before meeting up again in front of the store.

"You know what we need now?" Mia asked, mischief in her eyes.

I looked around at the crowds. Suddenly became aware of piped-in Christmas music playing over our heads. "I'm afraid to ask. How many more stores are there?"

She waved a hand dismissively. "I think we've earned a treat." As we picked up our bags, she hooked her arm in mine and led me...somewhere. It could've been straight off a cliff, and I would've followed.

"What kind of treat?" I waggled my eyebrows suggestively as she led me out of the store. "The treat I want isn't on Main Street."

She smiled and shook her head. "This one is definitely on Main Street. Do you smell it?"

She took a huge sniff, so I did too.

It was the smell of something savory cooking. Warm and delicious and fried. I really couldn't identify it any further than that, other than it made my stomach growl. "What is it?"

"Cheese curds. You like them?" she asked. I heard the hope in her voice.

Uh oh. "If I answer that, you have to promise not to shame me."

She eyed me suspiciously. "Wait a minute. I figured out you were a sledding virgin. But a cheese curd virgin too?"

I guess I turned red because she pounced on that. "You are! Oh my god, you've never had one. Tell me that isn't true!"

"I'm losing trust in you because I feel shamed," I said in a deadpan voice.

"Brax! Please tell me how you've avoided cheese curds for all these years? I mean, they're amazing!"

"The right opportunity to try one never came along, I guess," I mumbled. "Truth is, I was very frugal as an undergrad—I just didn't have money to go out much. And after a while, I just...never tried them." I gave an apologetic shrug. "The pizza always looked better."

She looked completely disbelieving. "Okay, well, there's only one way to fix this. But once you try one, you'll never go back to your pathetic cheese-curdless state."

Oh, the drama. "Okay, fine. I want one," I said without hesitation, mainly because she was never going to let this go until I caved.

"All right then, let's go," she said as she led us off.

Shopping, presents, and cheese curds, and Mia. The perfect day. And she was irresistible.

For the first time in my life, I was in way over my head. And I was loving every minute of it.

Chapter Sixteen

Mia

I couldn't believe Brax had been an undergrad *and* a med student in Wisconsin and had never brought a cheese curd to his lips. I made it my mission to change that immediately. While he waited on a bench inside the little indoor shopping area, I walked up to one of the food trucks parked in a nearby lot and got us some.

Waiting in line, and yes, there was a line, even at eleven in the morning, gave me a minute to calm down. I had stars in my eyes. I couldn't help myself.

Brax had bought my parents a charcuterie board, and I was pretty sure there was something else in that bag that he wasn't talking about.

Maybe for me. The thought that he might have bought me a surprise gift made me ridiculously giddy. Plus, he kept holding my hand.

Even more nerve-racking, it looked like I'd decided to go to Charlie and Erin's party tonight. But I didn't have an issue with people seeing me as anything other than perfect, did I? I mean, I'd spent most of my life minimizing my scrapes and failures to not worry my parents, but had that made me think I had to show a perfect face to the world as well?

As I thought about that, I realized that sooner or later, unless I never came home again, I'd have to face Charlie and everyone I knew. And maybe that was the best reason of all to go.

Despite Brax's uncanny ability call me out on my flaws, I had good reason to believe that if I survived this event, there was a great chance I might be doing more with Brax than just holding hands.

I felt this huge, warm wave of anticipation expanding in my chest that I was afraid to name. I forced myself to breathe and prayed that it wasn't all going to go away. This must be what really falling in love was like. Not like with Charlie, when I was just a kid and didn't understand what real love was.

I brought the goods back to the bench and sat down next to Brax. "Okay, now close your eyes. It's time for a taste test, okay?"

He shut his eyes, but quickly opened one and asked, "A cheese curd taste test?"

"Totally." I waited until he complied. "Open up."

He did, and I placed a cheese curd in his mouth. It was firm, whitish, and irregularly shaped, and he took it willingly. Could someone look sexy when they're chewing? Brax certainly could. "What do you think?"

"It's very...cheesy." He opened his eyes. "It's good."

"How squeaky was it?" I sounded like I was doing a survey. But I had to educate the man on Wisconsin lore, didn't I?

He looked incredulous. "Squeaky?"

"A good curd squeaks when the protein strands rub against tooth enamel."

"Cool. Give me another one, and I'll check."

I did and popped one in my own mouth too. "Yep. Definitely squeaky. Ready for Number Two?"

This time, I took a freshly fried curd with a garlicky bread-crumb coating—my personal, all-time favorite—and placed it carefully in his mouth. Then I kissed him, just because I couldn't help it.

"Mmm, now you're talking," he said. "More kisses, please."

"Focus on the curd," I said. "For now."

He chewed, his skeptical frown dissolving into a look of pure pleasure. "This is incredible. What is a cheese curd anyway?"

A magical thing. But I wanted him to discover that for himself, so I started from the beginning. "Did you ever learn the nursery rhyme, *Little Miss Muffet, sat on a tuffet...*"

"...eating her curds and whey?"

"Exactly," I confirmed. "The curds separate from the whey, which is the watery part."

His mouth curved upward. "Interesting, but can I have another one?"

I frowned. "A curd or a kiss?"

Before I could answer, he reached over and kissed me breathless, right there on the bench, in the middle of the Christmas shopping crowd. He even remembered to take the little cardboard carton of curds from my hand and set it down. When we finally came up for air, I had no idea how long we'd been kissing or what we'd been talking about beforehand. I did vaguely remember, in retrospect, a couple of whistles, claps, and cheers from passersby.

"Wisconsin has the only master cheesemaker program outside Switzerland," I said as I recovered.

He shot me a giant grin. "Good to remember if being a doctor doesn't work out." He popped another fried curd into his mouth. "These are almost as addictive as you."

We devoured the rest of the cheese and, energy restored, were window shopping our way back to Brax's car, when he suddenly halted in front of the most chichi shop on the street, a women's clothing boutique that I'd never even step foot in. La Petite Poussine, The Baby Chick, was like a James Beard-rated restaurant that made you salivate over its entrées even as your wallet forced you to head down the street to settle for a drive-through burger. But burgers were good too, right? And they didn't break the bank. Until recently, anyway.

Brax was staring at the mannequin in the window, who wore a red sequined dress with a plunging neckline that fit her unrealistic form like a second skin.

He turned to me, all earnestness. "You need this."

Was he joking? "I am not going to wear Revenge Red to my ex's party."

"But your English teacher said." He literally held up his face so close to the window that his nose touched the glass. "How about that one?" I did the same, to find him pointing to another dress that hung jauntily on a headless mannequin above a round dress rack. It was formfitting, made of a shimmery maroon material, with a scooped neckline and little straps. I gave a little gasp. It was love at first sight.

The dress was...stunning. Satiny, clingy, but classy. It was something you'd wear to a fancy office Christmas party or a wedding or a dinner and feel amazing in. Plus, it happened to be my favorite color, deep, intense, but not wildly bright.

I guess I hesitated, but Brax took that for a *yes,* and next thing I knew, he was towing me through the door, straight up to the dress. I dared to touch the butter-soft material. "Pretty." I immediately searched for the price tag, but this time, Brax steered me off to the side. Before he could make a case for the dress, I dropped my voice. "This place is out of my price range."

What he said next shocked me. With a look of total assurance, he said, "This is an out-of-your-comfort-zone event. You need a one-of-a-kind dress like this."

The man was not a spendthrift. I happened to know that he bought his dress shirts at TJ Maxx. He made his lunch at home every single day and brought it to work in a vintage Spiderman lunch box from the nineties. And of course, there was his eight-year-old CR-V. So, this was completely out of character.

"May I help you?" A woman who looked to be in her thirties

with jet-black hair, red lipstick, and a French accent walked over to us, smiling.

A woman in a bright orange jumpsuit waved to her and left out the door. Either she was an escaped con or at the height of fashion, I wasn't sure which.

I was wearing soft old jeans and a Fair Isle sweater. A fashionista I was not. What was I even doing here?

"No, thanks," I said, "we were just..."

I didn't even get out the "looking" before Brax asked, "Would you happen to have this dress in my girlfriend's size?"

"Ah, but this is the only one," she said, reaching up to touch the hem so that the silky material caught all the rays of light from a nearby Christmas tree. "A beauty, isn't it?"

I tugged on Brax's arm. I happened to get a feel of his biceps in the process, which was actually not unpleasant. "There, you see?" I said with an oh-well smile. "Wasn't meant to be. Time to go."

Claudia, our salesperson, according to her name tag, proceeded to take the dress off the headless mannequin and then hold it up next to me. "You have a coat on, of course, but I believe this might be your size. When do you need it for?"

"Tonight," Brax said.

"Would you like to try it on?" she asked pleasantly.

Absolutely not. "No, thank you," I managed. "I—"

"Give us just a minute." Brax steered me over to an aisle of faux-fur-lined evening jackets and crossed his arms.

I knew that stance. That was his *Bianca-you-need-to-take-this-pill-right-now* stance. His take-no-prisoners posture. "You're being stubborn."

"*You're* being stubborn," I replied. "I could easily find something in my closet."

He lifted a skeptical brow. "This is not the event to wear a *circa* 2007 prom dress to."

One for him. Unless I wanted to show up a bubble-gum-pink dress with sequins and red five-inch heels with bows that I had no idea why my practical mother ever let me buy, he was right.

"That dress costs as much as a paycheck," I said. "Plus, you need special undies to wear under it." Not to mention proper shoes. "And it's three o'clock." Meaning we had T minus four hours.

"It's not that much. And I'm sure Claudia could help with all that." I started to leave, but he held me back. "How about this? You try it on, and if it doesn't fit, we're done here."

"Okay, fine," I said. I thought I really did have that old prom dress in my closet. And maybe a few short, inappropriate-for-a-wedding-celebration black dresses from my sorority days. And not much else.

Claudia walked over to a fitting room door, the dress shimmering over her arm.

I went in and, despite my practical cotton bra and undies, tried it on.

Drat. It fit. To perfection. I pushed back the curtain.

Brax was sitting on a pink velvet settee, checking his phone. He looked up when I walked onto the trying-on dais in front of a three-way mirror.

And then he dropped his phone. He blinked a few times. Cleared his throat.

Oh wow. Maybe this dress was worth the credit card debt after all.

"Mia, I...it's..." I'd never seen him lose his words. "You're a fricking *knockout.*"

I probably turned the same color as the dress. I shook my head in denial at his words, but they ran over me as smoothly as hot fudge sauce. And from the look in his eyes, I could tell he meant them.

Claudia came rushing over. "C'est belle! Magnifique!"

"It's very beautiful," I said. "But I have to think about it."

"I recommend you think fast," she said. "That woman in the

orange jumpsuit who just left is thinking about it too." She dropped her voice. "But it looks better on you."

Okay, she was good. But still. I went back inside the fitting room and sent a quick selfie to Gabe, my fashion consultant.

He responded before I had my shoes back on. *"Damn, girl, buy that immediately!"*

Okay, so no help there either.

I liked the dress. I *really* liked Brax's win-the-lottery reaction. But it was only a silly party.

"I'll think about the dress, okay?" I said to Brax as we walked out a few minutes later. "Maybe I'll have time to run into Madison this afternoon."

"I thought we were helping Dina and Liam wrap Emma's gifts and watching you and your sibs put up your ornaments from when you were kids."

I groaned. "My mother makes everything a tradition." She was especially fond of those little crafty ornaments from grade school that she kept in special labeled boxes for each one of us.

"Ice cream," he said, pointing to our local creamery a few doors down. "That makes everyone think better."

I glanced up to the La Petite Poussine window, where Claudia was putting sparkly earrings into a display.

Ugh, I hadn't even brought jewelry. I guess I did a poor job stifling my groan, because Brax glanced over. "There's no way short of a fairy godmother I could put myself together before tonight." I counted off on my fingers: "Dress, underwear, shoes, jewelry." I thought of something else. "Plus, that dress is for something more important than an ex's wedding reception."

Brax waved his hands in the air. "You're overthinking," he said.

"You're a man," I retorted. "You have no idea."

"You can wear a dress like that anywhere."

He might've had a point. Still, it was a big splurge. We joined the ice cream line, which by now was twenty-five people long, and all my nerves had replaced my appetite.

Brax's phone went off. He pulled it out of his pocket and checked the number. "Hey, I've got to take this," he said. "I'll be right back."

As he answered it, I grabbed his elbow. "Don't you dare go back and buy that dress," I warned.

He pressed down on his lower lip, as if he was stifling a smile. "I respect your autonomy far too much to do that." After one step away, he turned. "Hey, get me a chocolate cone, okay?"

And that was how he left me. With a stomach too full of heartburn to even want ice cream.

He returned just in time to accept his cone.

"Where's yours?" he asked.

"Not hungry. I decided that I'm going back to get that dress."

"Great," he said, taking the cone.

"I mean, YOLO and everything," I said, rambling. "Plus, closure is important. Might as well feel good about myself when the eyes of the entire town are on me, right?"

In my confusion, I realized he was smiling. And he was standing kind of funny. Sort of like how you do when you're hiding something.

I peeked around him to see a shopping bag with strongly scented pink tissue paper sticking out of it. And it smelled just like La Petite Poussine.

"Ah-choo!" I sneezed into my arm.

"Gesundheit," he said. He grinned and stepped aside. "Good thing you want it, because it's unreturnable."

"Thanks, fairy godfather. I'll Venmo you."

"No, you won't. Merry Christmas."

I tugged him by the sleeve of his jacket over to the side of the wall. Three little kids were sitting at a table nearby. There was more ice cream on their faces and clothes than in their little bodies.

"Brax...Brax." I took a deep breath. "No. Just...no. I can't accept this as a gift. I just can't."

He set the bags down, and then he put his hands on my shoulders. "Mia," he said softly, and his quiet, calm tone made me get teary for some reason. I already sensed what he was about to say.

"Forget about the money for now. You can wear whatever you want to tonight. But I wanted you to have the choice of feeling like you could walk in there and do anything and feel confident and beautiful doing it. Even though you're beautiful with the dress or without it." He gave a lopsided grin that was absolutely charming. I knew that he truly wanted me to have that dress. Period. "Please don't be angry with me. The lady with the orange jumpsuit was circling like a piranha. I had to act fast."

Of course, I laughed. He did too. Then I clutched my stomach. I was now in full fight-or-flight mode.

"Have some ice cream. It always makes things better."

I was more worried about panty lines and my boobs showing. "Do you mind if I run into the lingerie store?"

"Who do you think I am?" He looked fake appalled. "I didn't get to be chief because I'm a slacker." He pointed to the bag. "Claudia worked her magic. It's all in there."

I shook my head, incredulous. "Thanks," I said, giving him a quick squeeze. "Not just for the dress, which I am totally paying you back for. For helping me think this through."

"Anything for you," he said, giving me a look that made me feel like melted chocolate inside.

This had been the most fun afternoon. It almost took away the pain of everything I had yet to face.

Chapter Seventeen

Mia

That night, Dina did my makeup and let me borrow her necklace with one hanging pearl in the shape of a teardrop that Liam got her for their fifth anniversary. But I had to swear on my unborn children that I'd keep it safe. And she did my makeup the way only she could—that made me look exactly like me, only better.

The only thing she couldn't do was find me shoes. She was a tiny size six, and my mom was a seven, and absolutely no one was a nine and a half. So out came the red five-inch platforms with straps that crisscrossed around and ended at my ankles in sparkly red bows. They were wild. But at least they matched the dress...in a prom '07 sort of way.

I walked downstairs expecting a wrist corsage and a photo with my boyfriend standing behind me with his arms at my waist, because my entire family was oddly present, all dressed up themselves and ready to go, yet all lined up in the foyer. Liam was taking photos. My dad was eating peanut butter crackers, no doubt wishing he was watching a game. My mom looked me up and down. It took her all of three seconds to spot my shoes.

I preempted her question. "It was these or ballet flats," I said dryly.

"Maybe you can bring flip-flops and pretend it's time to dance," Dina suggested.

"You all are draining my confidence," I shot back.

"Good thing I didn't throw those away," my mom said, which actually was a charitable thing to say.

"Why did you ever let me buy these?" I asked her. She literally never let me buy anything I wanted as a teenager.

She shrugged. "Sometimes, you've got to pick your battles." She kissed me. "You look beautiful."

At the end of the line was Brax, in Caleb's suit. It somehow fit decently enough. "You're stunning," he said.

"And you're the best boyfriend ever," I teased. But I meant it. Also, I loved saying that word.

My dad helped me on with my coat. "You look beautiful, sweetheart," he said, and kissed my cheek.

"We'll meet you there," said my mom.

Brax stood by the door, holding out his arm for me to grab onto as we traveled down the icy path. *Okay, five-inchers, don't fail me now.*

As I took his arm, he grinned widely and gave me a wink. "Okay, gorgeous. Time to go kick Charlie's ass."

My family literally cheered. It was weird, a strange pseudo-prom-date moment that my whole family was witnessing, and yet Brax took it all in stride.

He closed the door and stopped me on the stoop, which happened to be right under that mistletoe. In contrast to the dark night, the entire outside of the house was lit with strings of cheery glowing lights. He faced me and took both my hands in his. "If you asked me what I thought I'd be doing tonight a week ago, I wouldn't have said going to a party for your ex and his new wife.

But Mia," he looked me up and down, "You take my breath away. And even if you were wearing scrubs or sweats with your hair up in that bun thing you do"—he made a little curlicue in the air with his index finger—"I just want you to know I wouldn't want to be anywhere else but here tonight, with you."

My eyes misted over. "You had me at kicking Charlie's ass."

He looked up at the mistletoe, a twinkle in his eye. And then he kissed me.

And that sealed the deal. Suddenly, I didn't care about what I was going to say to Charlie—or to Erin. I didn't care who saw me tonight or what anyone would say. All I cared about was that I really did feel beautiful, in front of the only one who mattered.

And with that, I stepped straight into his arms.

"I give them three years," Dina whispered to me like the wonderful sister-in-law she was as we stood at my family's table near the back of the reception hall. We were surrounded by twinkle lights and pine boughs. There were candles everywhere, and red napkins complemented the gold chargers and the white-as-snow table-cloths. A local band played Christmas tunes while people danced. Everyone was dressed in their holiday best and having a fun time.

I had to smile, not so much at her comment, but at her fierce loyalty. "What are you talking about?"

Charlie and Erin were walking around the crowded hall, greeting people, shaking hands, and accepting congratulations. Charlie looked nice, dapper in a navy suit. He'd grown a hipster beard since we'd been together and lost about twenty pounds, so maybe his appearance was a reflection of being with the right person. Erin's blonde hair was worn up, with a jeweled crown over her veil. Yes, she was wearing a wedding dress, strapless, cut to show off her cleavage and a tattoo on her upper chest of an "E" and a "C" intertwined with a vine.

Brax was off getting me a drink, and he couldn't return soon enough.

Dina dropped her voice even further. "He hasn't even looked at her or touched her for the past five minutes," she said, "even though they're standing right next to each other."

"That's a risky tattoo," Caleb said, joining us, shaking his head in disbelief.

"Okay, everyone," I said, "thanks for being on my side, but you don't have to critique them on my behalf. Although I appreciate your having my back." The party was wedding-reception identical, with I'd guess around a hundred and fifty people. I'd caught up with some old high school friends that I hadn't seen for a while, and that had been fun. And just as Brax had predicted, no one judged me for being there or even seemed to give it a second thought. I did see a few acquaintances whispering among themselves and pointing to me. *Mia's here,* they were probably saying. *Would you take a look at that?*

Take a good look, people, I forced myself to think. *Because here I am.* Could that drink get here any quicker? Because I sure needed it.

While I waited, I said hi to—well, everyone I could. Old neighbors, teachers, our family doc who'd written me a recommendation letter for med school, my old dentist, and anyone else I could. Once I started, I just kept going. Finally, I ended up back at my family's table.

"Where are the bridesmaids?" Caleb asked, taking a sip of his drink.

I rolled my eyes. "It's not a wedding reception," I said.

"No bridesmaids?" he said, looking disappointed. But then he squeezed my shoulder, and it occurred to me that he wasn't a complete Neanderthal. He was only trying to make me laugh. Was Caleb actually...maturing?

"Hey," he said, smiling enough so that his dimple showed, also making me feel a strong sisterly fondness toward him. "If you need us, you've got Liam and me here."

I hugged him. "Thanks."

Just then, Brax returned. Caleb gave him a little nod, which was cordial but not much more. I wished he would let the big-brotherly thing go. I mean, come on already.

Brax handed me a drink. "I have a question for you."

"Okay." I took a sip and coughed. "I do too. What's in this?"

"A lot of vodka. Drink up."

"Do I look that nervous?"

He looked me up and down. "Yes." As I forced down another gulp, he lowered his voice and asked, "How was the um—*you know*—with him?"

I narrowed my eyes. "The um-you-know?" I thought about that. "Are you asking me about sex with Charlie?" I considered that. "If you're trying to take my mind off this, that may just have worked."

"Hear me out, okay? He doesn't strike me as the kind of guy who would make sure you were having a good time too." He pointed to Charlie and Erin, who were now greeting a long line of people. "Just look at him. He's talking to everyone, shaking everyone's hands. No arm around her, not taking up her hand, not introducing her to people. It's like it's The Charlie Show, and she's just along for the ride."

I took another sip of the drink, which now finally went down less like a fireball and more like a cozy, radiant campfire that you warm your hands near. Brax—and Dina—had made an oddly perceptive point. Charlie had always wanted what he wanted. He wasn't one to stop, slow down, and make sure his partner was on board. That fit perfectly with the way he'd ended things too.

A memory suddenly hit me, of the day I'd driven to Milwaukee and moved into my efficiency apartment, where I didn't know a soul. I was exhausted. Scared.

And absolutely exhilarated. Thrilled to be starting over. Thrilled to be on my own. Feeling like my life was about to begin.

I remembered that feeling so clearly now. I hadn't thought this at the time, but now I understood that it had been the feeling of freedom. A freedom that maybe I wouldn't have felt or maybe even needed if things had been right with Charlie.

"Are you okay?" Brax asked, touching my arm.

My throat felt too closed off to answer, but I managed a smile. Took a deep breath. Set down my drink, took up his hands, and looked into his warm brown eyes that somehow managed to calm me and unsettle me at the same time. "Thank you for being here. For getting me here. And for making me feel...not alone."

He leaned over and whispered in my ear, "If I were your partner, I'd make sure you never felt alone when you were with me." He looked concerned. And sincere. And steady. And...something more.

A feeling hit me hard in my gut. Brax, the guy who basically said he couldn't show up in a relationship, did—every single time. He'd come to a small town in the middle of the Wisconsin countryside to have my back. And he kept doing it, over and over.

Though my nerves, I smiled. "Somehow, I already knew that," I said. "But you can show me exactly what you mean by that later if you like."

A slow smile spread over his beautiful face. "Happily."

All right, then. I set down my drink and gave him a nod. It was time to do something I really needed to do.

"Go get 'em, tiger." How could I fail with all the belief I saw in his eyes?

I kissed him and headed over to the happy couple.

Charlie was standing near one of the front tables, talking to Henrietta and Jake, who happened to be the couple we used to hang with the most. Truthfully, after our breakup, I'd lost touch. It was just too hard.

I felt like I was starring in a weird dream, where I entered an alternate reality and did things I could never in a million years have pictured myself doing. This one went like "One day, you'll be at Charlie's wedding party and congratulate him on his marriage to someone else."

By the time I got to Charlie, he'd moved on to chatting with a couple I think I remembered as being his great-aunt and uncle. I lingered for a minute until they moved on, and then I tapped him on the shoulder. "Hey, Charlie," I said and braced myself.

You know what happened? His face lit up like at his eight-year-old birthday party when I'd bought him a Ken doll to play with my Barbie.

"Mia-ba-dia, you came." He smiled broadly, that same old Charlie smile, using that ridiculous nickname that I hadn't heard since—well, since he'd said it last, years ago.

A wave of nostalgia hit me. We'd crossed many milestones together. We just hadn't been meant to continue the journey together.

I swallowed. Took a breath. "I wanted to wish you the best."

There. I'd done it. I was shaky and nervous, but I'd done it.

He broke into another smile and squeezed me tight. For some dumb reason, my eyes grew watery, and I found myself hugging him right back.

He wasn't a bad person. He just wasn't *my* person. Maybe some things happened for a reason. Maybe his cheating would ironically turn out to be the best thing he'd ever done for me.

He drew back. "Mia, you look amazing. And happy."

He clearly hadn't seen my shoes. "Thank you. You do too." Erin was talking to an elderly guest, but she glanced over, and I knew she'd soon head over to us. I found myself wanting another minute with just Charlie.

I started to drop my hands, but Charlie squeezed them. "Listen," he said, "it means a lot that you're here."

I could see that he meant it. And that it also meant something to me. Maybe more than I could process right now. I managed a nod.

Then he bent close and said in a low voice, "I'm so sorry, Mia. For hurting you. Please forgive me."

For so long, I'd wanted to ask him why he did it. Why, after all those years together, he didn't have the decency to simply break up with me first. But suddenly, I realized that it no longer mattered. "Charlie, I'm sorry too. You found your person." I rubbed his shoulder. "It's all good."

"Great," he said. "Meet Erin."

Erin joined him. Up close, she had gorgeous hair and pretty blue eyes. She immediately tucked an arm through his. "Hey, babe," she said. "Hi, Mia. So nice to finally meet you."

"You too." I hugged her. She seemed nice, but what I'd really appreciated was my moment with Charlie. It had been surprisingly comforting, and we'd been able to say a lot in a brief minute or two.

And then I felt a touch on my arm.

Brax. Of course, there at just the right moment again. I hooked my arm through his. "This is Brax, my boyfriend." He shook hands with Charlie and hugged Erin. Then he wrapped his arm around me, ready to steady me if I needed it. I didn't. I was going to be just fine.

I hugged Charlie one last time. Gave him a good squeeze. It was a goodbye hug. It also was a goodbye-to-my-past hug. "Congratulations," I said to him and his bride.

When I turned away, Brax was waiting. Smiling. Looking so handsome, my heart dropped down to my feet. He took my hand.

Good thing. I felt a little shaky.

"I have a plan," he said. "Do you trust me?"

"Yes." I did trust him. With my whole heart.

He started to lead me out but halted. "You want to stay and visit with anybody else?"

"No," I said honestly. "I spoke with everyone who counts."

He led me through the crowd, past the bar, and through a side door, where one of the catering staff handed us our coats.

Wait. Brax had arranged to get our coats?

This didn't seem like just a quick exit. It seemed like the beginning of an adventure.

"Where are we going?" I asked.

"Outta here," he said as he opened the heavy metal door to the outside. It clanged shut behind us as we left.

Chapter Eighteen

Brax

My plan got us out of that reception hall and into my car. I started the car, turned on the wipers because it had begun to snow, and turned to Mia. "I want us to celebrate, but I need a little help from you."

"That sounds fun. Define 'celebrate.'"

"Food...and you."

"Nice." She grabbed my hand. "In that order?"

Turned out we were both starving, so she directed me a few blocks away to Outta This World Burger, which was apparently *the* place in town for the best burgers. It was a drive-up restaurant, the roof shaped like a flying saucer. Cute.

We took our food a little ways out of town to a lookout Mia knew of. Our view was stunning—an iced-over lake with a full moon, surrounded by a forest of pines. I cranked up the heat to make it toasty.

In between bites, I looked around. "Where are all the teenagers with steamed-up car windows?"

"Ha. Stick with me, kid," she said. "We locals know the private spots."

"Too private for bears?" I locked the doors as images of bears mauling our car figured prominently in my mind. Although it was snowing so fiercely by now that all the sensible ones would probably stay snug in their dens tonight.

She laughed. "Bears hibernate. You city boys are so suspicious. We're literally the only humans for miles."

I looked around at the rapidly accumulating snow. "That's what I'm afraid of."

"I thought you'd like it." She waved her hands around to demonstrate. "It's peaceful. No parents, no brothers, no dogs."

The windshield was already covered. "Wait a minute. Are you saying we're going to do more than eat our burgers and enjoy the view here?" I imagined us answering a few awkward questions as we talked to the snowplow driver who showed up to shovel us out.

She shrugged and flashed a knowing smile. "If you're lucky. Now eat your cosmic fries. And relax...enjoy the Christmasy view." She reached over and snagged a fry. "Once, I drove four of my college friends two hours just to get these burgers. I still dream about them sometimes. And the double-fudge shakes." After taking a long pull on her shake, she offered it to me. "You like it?"

I gave her an enthusiastic nod and a thumbs-up. The food was good, but the view was great. The view on the inside of the car, that is. Mia was eating with the abandon of someone who hadn't eaten in a few days, her relief was palpable. I was happy she'd gotten through the party. But now I wanted time for us, but how and where? I didn't know how to bring it up without sounding like a horny teenager.

Soon, we'd devoured everything and began balling up our papers and stuffing them into the white Cosmic Burger bag.

Mia sat back and patted her stomach in contentment. "I was starving. Nothing like stress relief to rev up the appetite."

I chuckled. "Was it that bad, talking to Charlie?"

"It was good. You were right to encourage me to do it. And I realized something."

I hope her answer involved telling me how much she wanted to kiss me. And other stuff. "What was that?"

"Do you really want to hear?" Her tone was cautious.

I crumpled up the bag and stuck it between my seat and the door. "Hit me."

She blew out a big breath. "I realized that I may have been the one to check out of our relationship first. Mentally, I mean. Like, Charlie made his choice to stay, and I made mine to go, but neither of us had the courage to break it off until he pretty much forced it to end."

I thought about that. "Cheating is not exactly the best way to end a six-year relationship."

"That was pretty devastating. Looking back now, I think part of me was relieved. What I mean is, when I got to Milwaukee, I was so excited to be starting fresh. I think honestly that I'd started to check out even before he found Erin, and he sensed it." She lifted her milkshake cup. "Anyway, to closure."

Lucky me that things didn't work out with good ol' Charlie. That made me smile. "To closure," I echoed, touching my cup to hers. "And new beginnings."

～

Mia

My heart skipped a beat at Brax's words. "To new beginnings," I said.

We finished our shakes with the toast, then he reached over and took my drink, stacked it with his empty cup, and placed both of them in his door cup holder. Then he took my hands in his. "We're a better match." He rubbed his thumb along my palm, smiling at me as his words sank in.

I felt his words deep down. "You're *totally* who I want," I said with a huge grin.

The heat flared in his eyes. My heart gave a steady thump as it accelerated, and then I felt a dizzying rush as he quickly closed the space between us. But then he paused. He tucked a curl carefully behind my ear and sat back a little, and I was afraid he was having second thoughts. But then he spoke. "I haven't slept with anyone since us. I just wanted you to know."

Inside my head, cheerleaders cheered. Fireworks exploded. But I tried to keep my voice level and unaffected. "Why not?"

"Because you're the only one *I* want."

I must have stared dumbly because of those incredible words I never thought I'd hear, so sincerely and deeply said. I could barely believe something so wondrous was happening to me.

Unbelievably, he kept going. "Didn't you ever wonder why we're on call so often together? I arrange that. I couldn't stay away from you."

Things like this didn't occur in my life. He'd wanted me all along? He'd arranged for us to work together? My head was spinning.

His eyes were soft with feeling as he said, "I'm sorry I wasted so much time thinking I couldn't—shouldn't—be with you. I'm sorry I hurt you."

"You're forgiven," I finally managed, unable to stop grinning. "I understand your story now." I knew how much it had taken him—and us—to get to this place of honesty. "What should we do now?" I flicked on the wipers so I could check out the pretty snow-covered pines, the iced-over lake. The night was silent and calm. The half of me that had closed a chapter in my life today felt calm and peaceful too. But the other half felt like a stadium full of crazed fans cheering on their favorite team. I felt that the next chapter of my life was just beginning, and I couldn't wait for it.

He smiled. "Hey, do you want to go somewhere?"

I lifted a brow. "Go somewhere?" The snow was falling in thick, fat flakes, covering the windshield, insulating us from the frozen world outside. I wanted to stay right here with him —forever.

He shrugged. "Like a hotel?"

My brows lifted in surprise. "You'd do that for just a couple of hours?"

"Why not? I feel a little funny doing it in your parents' house." He cleared his throat. "I don't mean *it*...I mean *making love*." He glanced up, his eyes showing me...well, everything I'd ever want to see there. Honesty, vulnerability, want—for me. Joy filled my heart, sloshing over the edges like a too-full bucket. And the fact that I had suave, cool Brax fumbling with words was even more incredible. It was like I'd landed in the universe of my dreams, but it was all suddenly real. A wild Christmas miracle, for sure.

He looked tentative as he added, "I mean, if that's what you want to do...Do you?"

"There's one hotel downtown," I said, "and guess who owns it? Charlie's grandparents. They're really good friends with my parents too. The whole town would know by morning."

"Oh."

"Also, I think that's sweet of you to want to find a place for us. And yes, I want to do it." I peered into the back. "I see a blanket back there. Looks pretty comfy, especially with those special seat liners."

He gave a hearty laugh. "You sure this is a good idea? I mean, the snow's really coming down and...I don't know, do the cops patrol here?"

I reached down to oh-so-carefully unbuckle one of my ridiculous shoes. It clunked to the floor. Relief. I felt ten pounds lighter. The other one joined it.

I did even better. I pulled my dress over my head and tossed it over the seat. As he pulled his seat back, I crawled over the middle console and straddled him. "I'm not worried about it." He just went with it, smiling as I undid his tie and tossed it behind me. And then I put my hands on his shoulders, feeling their smooth contours, their breadth, their strength.

He let out a sound—an *oomph*—maybe because we were a little squished. Or maybe it was from relief that we were finally, finally together.

He rubbed his hands up and down my back, over the silky material of the one-piece, no-panty-line underwear. His gaze was hot and searing and made me feel completely worshipped. *Thank you, Claudia.* "I want you so much," he murmured against my neck as he dropped featherlight kisses there. "I never stopped."

Words that had me thanking my lucky stars. "Thank you for coming home with me." I tipped back my head so he could kiss me more thoroughly. "For being so wonderful to my family. And for being so wonderful to me."

"Funny." He stopped kissing me and glanced up. "I think it's you who saved me."

At last, our lips met. The space was tight, but it suited us just fine. I got lost in the simple taste of him and the scent of his woodsy aftershave, in the way his hands roved over the pretty camisole. I pressed against the softness of his lean, muscular chest, hungry for him, barely able to focus on unbuttoning his shirt buttons.

Somehow, we climbed into the back, barely missing a beat. He took me down to the seat that was solid and roomy enough. Not that I was paying that much attention.

As he kissed my neck, he murmured, "Thank goodness for grandma's seat liners."

"I'd say they're *very* comfortable," I managed to add as I traced the smooth, muscular contours of his back.

"Mia." The way he said my name—low and gravelly and full of

desire—made me shiver. Brax looked at me, his beautiful brown eyes devouring me.

"What is it?" I said, breathless.

"Just—I've never felt like this before with anyone."

As the snow gently fell outside and melted on the windshield, his words melted my body and my heart.

And then, Dear Reader, we steamed up those windows.

Brax

Sometime later, I carried Mia into her house, the heavy, wildly spiky, netted high-heeled shoes dangling from her hands. I tried to be stealthy going up the stairs and managed to get us into her room, closing the door with my foot.

"I was going to pitch these," she remarked, tossing the shoes on the floor near her closet, where they hit with a giant thud, "but now I'm going to call them my get-lucky shoes. I may have to keep them forever."

"You don't need spiky shoes to get lucky with me." I deposited her on the bed and then joined her. We folded back the comforter and climbed into the too-cool sheets, shedding clothes along the way.

"I'm freezing," she said, curling against me. "Do you mind if I do this?"

"Do what?"

"Snuggle," she said innocently.

I felt her doing something under those covers that technically was a bit more than snuggling. Did I mind? "Honey, snuggle all you want. Just know you might just be lighting a match to tinder."

She turned her pretty face up to me. Her hair was wildly mussed, her eyes bright, her smile wide, her joy completely contagious. "Why, Dr. Hughes, do you mean you'd consider breaking your I-don't-do-it-at-your-parents'-house rule?"

I nodded solemnly. "For you, I'd make that sacrifice." And then I kissed her.

Best. Early. Christmas. Ever.

Chapter Nineteen

Brax

It was still dark on Christmas Eve morning when my phone went off. Mia lay next to me, her head on my chest, her hair wild and soft against me. When I reached to grab the phone, noticing that it was 5:00 a.m., I hated to leave the cocoon of warmth we'd created. I wished we could stay in bed all day today and tomorrow too.

I felt a weight on my feet, preventing me from moving. Suddenly, a lump moved up the bed between us, and the wiener dog popped out from the covers. "How do you get air down there?" I mumbled as I got out of bed and replaced the covers over Mia, the dog curling up beside her. I ran into the bathroom to take the call, closing the door so she wouldn't awaken. It was from Tim Green, April's husband.

"April's in labor," he said. A week early. I instantly knew that my holiday was over.

"I'll cover her patients," I said quickly. "No worries. Now go have that baby."

As I reentered the bedroom, Mia stirred and opened her eyes. "April's in labor?" she asked, groggy from sleep.

I sat down next to her. "I've got to go," I said. "Stay and have Christmas with your family. I'll come back for you after work tomorrow."

"No need." She rubbed her eyes. "I'll catch a ride with Caleb. He works on the twenty-sixth too."

Cooper sat at the top of the bed again, patiently waiting. As soon as Mia lifted the covers, he dove under them.

She smiled at what must've been my puzzled expression. "Doxies are burrowers," she said.

"And here I thought he had a foot fetish." I smoothed back her hair, gazing into her eyes. I wished I didn't have to go, but duty called. To cover April's ER shift, I'd have to leave as soon as possible, so I bent and kissed Mia's forehead, then headed for the shower.

❧

Mia

On the way out, Brax kissed me and reassured me that we'd see each other as soon as I got back. But a sudden chill cut through me, an irrational fear gripping me. Everything between us was too perfect. My life didn't support so much happiness. It never had.

I was wide awake, so I picked up my phone from the bedside table. There was a text from Sam. *Call me as soon as you get this,* it read.

Thinking that maybe she was about to tell me about April's exciting news, I called her right away. We'd talk about April, and I'd tell her how wonderful things were with Brax. How that had been the best Christmas present of all.

"Mia, I have to talk to you," was the first thing she said, her voice strained. My heart plummeted into my stomach. I thought the worst.

"What's wrong?" I asked as soon as I could force out the words.

"Everything's fine," Sam said, "but—I overheard something yesterday afternoon that I think you should know. It's about Brax."

"About Brax?" He'd just left me. I could hear his truck idling in the driveway and the sounds of him scraping last night's snow from his windshield.

"Have you heard anything about the BCP job?" she asked.

"Before I left, Robin told me the group would announce the new associate after the holidays. Why?" With everything else going on, I'd forgotten all about it. Frankly, it had been a relief to table thinking about it until after the holidays. That had given Brax and me a chance to take it out of our relationship and focus on what was really important—us. However it worked out, I was certain we could handle it. But I didn't say any of this out loud.

"Ted Brunner was chatting with Dr. Hebert after rounds yesterday, and I overheard them talking. You don't know anything about this?"

"No." I was still groggy, still processing that Brax and I wouldn't be together on Christmas. I'd wanted him to see how much fun our family holiday was.

Dr. Hebert was the chairman of the Department of Pediatrics, a bigwig. Brunner was probably boasting about something regarding the practice, as he often did. I was struggling to follow what this had to do with Brax or me.

Over the phone, Sam sighed heavily. "Brunner said he let Brax know last week that the job was essentially his if he wanted it."

"Wait a minute." It took a while for my brain to catch up. Did she just say Brax basically got offered the job? Last *week*? "That's impossible. Brax—" would have told me. Of course he would have.

I squeezed my eyes shut. Somehow, Cooper was on the bed, nudging his little nose in my palm, wanting me to pet him and wish him good morning. I did pet him, of course, and like clockwork, he rolled over, belly up. "Brax and I agreed not to talk about it this weekend," I said weakly. "He never mentioned anything."

Brax had been the one to suggest keeping business out of this weekend. Could that have been why? Because he'd known the outcome all along?

"Look," Sam went on, and I was so grateful she was talking, because it felt as if someone had shoved half a bag of cotton balls down my throat, "Brunner was talking in low tones, secretively. He said they hadn't made a formal announcement yet, but they were going to make an offer soon. I thought you should know."

I murmured something. Probably an expletive. My head was whirling. And my tongue was clinging to the roof of my mouth. I was beyond thirsty.

"I'm so sorry," Sam said. "Maybe I should've waited until you got back, but I thought you should know. Did I do the right thing?"

"Yes. Of course. You're being a good friend."

Good friends—and lovers—didn't keep secrets. Like cheating. And like hiding that they'd been offered the job you both wanted.

How could Brax sleep with me when he was keeping such a secret?

"If it helps, you should know people are starting to whisper about BCP. They're calling it short for Birth Control Pills to poke fun at how they treat women. They're losing respect, if that's any consolation."

I managed to thank Sam for letting me know. Then I sat in bed for a few seconds, trying to think this through. I realized one thing: I didn't want to wonder about what Brax had been thinking for the next few days until I saw him again. I wanted to know now.

I threw on my slippers and crept quickly down the stairs,

opened the door, and bolted out to the driveway, not even taking time to close the door. It felt like wind chill minus ten as the cold cut straight through my flannel nightgown, and the new snow—about four inches of it—instantly filled my slippers and froze my calves. Brax was still sitting in his snow-covered car, white exhaust pouring into the lightening day, the defrost and wipers at full blast.

Thank you, Wisconsin weather.

I could tell he'd been trying to cut out in a hurry, because he'd used his hands to knock the thick layer of snow off his car, and half of it was still there. For what seemed like my whole life, my dad had made sure to equip us with numerous snow brushes, scrapers, blankets, water and granola bars, flares, etc., to the extent that stocking the car for any weather emergency became a family joke.

I had no idea why I was thinking about that now. Only because it underscored that Brax had nobody to let him use a family car, let alone stock it with useful stuff—he'd had no help, no mentorship. He'd done everything on his own and so had learned how *not* to count on people.

I got that the job meant a lot to him because of Atticus Pendergast. But it meant a lot to me too. Not telling me about it was just plain wrong. A stunning betrayal.

I tried to hop through Brax's footprints in the driveway, but I quickly learned that not bothering to put on boots had been a big mistake. As he rolled down his window, his face appeared, drawn and dead serious. "Mia, what's wrong?" He looked surprised and worried.

"I need to ask you something." I winced at the tightness in my voice. Maybe he had a reason for not telling me. *Please, God, let there be a reason.*

"Brax, I—" A wave of emotion hit me. I didn't want this happiness to end. I didn't want to be betrayed again. That terror closed my throat.

"Mia, what is it?" He glanced from the windshield to me,

checking on the progress of the defrost, which was nearly far enough to see out. I knew he was anxious to go.

I spilled all my words. "Sam overheard Brunner say that he all but offered you the job last week. Is that true?"

To Brax's credit, he didn't hesitate, looking me directly in the eye. "He implied they were leaning into choosing a male associate —which obviously would be me."

My stomach dropped like a lead ball. "They never wanted a woman, did they?" Icy cold was seeping into my toes and my heart. I should have known. I should have listened to my gut.

"I don't know the exact politics." He sighed heavily. "But Brunner insinuated that might be the case."

"Why didn't you tell me?" Hot tears leaked out of my eyes. I swiped them away, ashamed that I was already so emotional about this.

"I wasn't thinking about the job these past few days. I was thinking about you."

I threw up my hands. "I don't know what that means. If you were thinking of me, you should have told me."

"We had an amazing weekend." His brows were knit down. "More than amazing. Please don't do this."

I couldn't let it go. "You knew, but you slept with me anyway. How could you keep this from me?" A huge secret. Just like how Charlie kept Erin from me.

"Honestly, Mia, I didn't know what to make of what he said. It was a little icky, actually. And then you needed someone to come home with you, and I guess I just didn't think about it." He sounded like he always did, calm and even. But I couldn't wrap my head around the fact that he was basically saying he'd forgotten to mention such a life-changing thing.

Fury bubbled all through me. I could barely contain my anger. "You're going to work for a group of pediatricians that overworks its employees, doesn't care about work-life balance, and preferentially hires men?" Suddenly, I saw something about myself. I'd wanted the prestige of this job so badly that I'd overlooked the glaring alarm bells. I was willing to trade the misery of being mistreated for the glory of being able to say I'd been chosen.

And so was Brax, apparently.

He averted his gaze. "Look, if I did take the job, I'd work hard to change the culture."

I shook my head in disbelief. "Apparently I'm not the only one willing to sell my soul for that job."

His eyes darkened with anger. "I wouldn't cast stones at my compromises." His voice rose a little. "What about yours?"

I jerked up my head. "What are you talking about?"

"If you'd get over what's holding you back, you'd apply for that heme-onc fellowship while it's still open." He looked so stern and unyielding. "It's an opportunity dropping right into your lap, and you don't even see it."

A terrible thought occurred that made me sick to my stomach. "Is that why you were trying to talk me into applying for the fellowship? So you'd feel better about taking the job?" I should've seen right through that. It was an easy, guilt-free solution that would knock me right out of the running. It meant something else too, something too terrible to think about. It meant he wanted that job more than he wanted me.

"I wasn't trying to manipulate you." He sounded outraged. "Only trying to get you to see that you're avoiding your true calling for all the wrong reasons."

He sounded like such a know-it-all. "What exactly are those reasons? Please tell me."

We were shouting in the driveway. My toes were ice cubes, numb and tingling from the cold. I prayed that my family wasn't awake and on the way to check out all the commotion.

Brax blew out a big breath. As he looked me in the eye, he seemed to be deciding if he should say what he was really thinking. "Grace," he finally blurted. "You're afraid of Grace."

I gasped. "Gracie is gone." My voice wobbled. How dare he bring my sister into this? "Please leave her out of this." I would never stop defending her, protecting her, even in death. Even if it was only against words.

"You don't want to talk about her. Or about the impact her death has had on you. Yet you became a doctor because of her, and it's clear she's always on your mind." He saw my distress, and I think that made him soften his voice. But that didn't soften the words. "What I mean is, you're letting your sad memories of her passing—all the fear and pain—impact what you do now. You went into pediatrics because of her. To save kids. Why not help the ones that you understand better than anyone else? It might be your true calling if you'd just allow yourself to consider it. If you make peace with the past."

His words stung like an arrow piercing its target. I blinked back tears. How had he somehow managed to put my greatest fear into words? I wished he would turn off that stupid car, open his door and rush to hold me. I wished he'd tell me that we'd had a wonderful weekend, and say that he loved me, and that whatever happened, we'd work through all this together.

But he didn't. Instead, he'd been willing to leave hiding something very important from me. And time was up. His windshield was now crystal clear.

"Look," he finally said, "I've got to get to the hospital in time for morning rounds. I'll see you back at work, okay?"

Back at work. Where we'd be colleagues.

The boyfriend was turning into a pumpkin, and he was taking the car.

Leaving me alone. Again. Betrayed, again. Not to mention carless.

My choices were to stay here with my family when I felt like a crashed train, or what? Hitch a ride with Brax for two hours? Absolutely not.

I refused to stand there while he pulled away, so I headed

straight back into the house. But I still heard the crunch of his tires on the snow, heard the car motor slowly fade away as he drove down the driveway. He left me wondering if everything he'd said and done was as fake as the fake boyfriend that he'd pretended so well to be.

Chapter Twenty

Brax

I had two miserable hours on the road to think about how much I sucked. At one point, I turned on the radio to the 24-7 Christmas carols, and "I'll Be Home for Christmas" was playing. I shut it off immediately. But it just underscored how I'd ruined Christmas Eve, the one time of the year when absolutely no one should fight. I thought about Mia standing there, looking so empty, her nose turning red, shivering in the cold.

I'd done that. I'd caused her pain. Again.

My excuse was that these past few days, I'd been processing what Brunner said. Thinking about it. Or really, *avoiding* thinking about it was more like it. And I'd gotten so wrapped up with Mia that I'd forgotten all about it.

The moral sketchiness of the job was pretty revolting, frankly. But I'd still wanted it, hadn't I?

That job was my connection with Atticus. It meant something to me down to my core.

I'd made sure to never fall in love or do relationships. That had made life so much simpler—it would have made this decision simpler. But I had been doing a relationship, hadn't I? And it had felt amazing.

I love you. We can work this out. Something I'd never said before. Something I hadn't said this morning.

Maybe Jenna was right. I believed in myself in other ways, but in relationships, I couldn't seem to do anything right.

I arrived at work to find that the pediatric emergency room was not enjoying a quiet Christmas Eve morning. Every room was full, and a team was admitting a child to the PICU for asthma management. I stopped to talk to the child's father, who looked exhausted and terrified, and took time to explain what was happening and to reassure him they were in good hands.

But inside, I felt off-balance. I saw the fright in that father's eyes. I was overly emotional, and I had to somehow tamp my emotions down in order to do my job.

The staff had draped the desk with red and green light strings. I knew there would be a plethora of candy and cookies in the break room. Plus, everyone had brought in covered dishes for a lunch spread to make the most of working on a holiday. Still, in this place, life and death converged, and festive could go only so far. And today, I definitely didn't feel festive.

I was feeling too much about everything. The eight-year-old boy who broke his ankle ice skating. The little six-month-old who cried all night with an earache. The twelve-year-old who ate shrimp and broke out in hives. The toddler who ate too many Christmas cookies and had a tummy ache. They'd all be fine, but I felt out-of-proportion worried about everyone.

It struck me that loving someone must feel a lot like that too. You couldn't help wanting that person to thrive and be happy and be their best selves, no matter what the price. All you wanted was to try and take away their pain and suffering and help them through hard times. And to just...be there.

Love was a gift that people gave each other unconditionally.

Not because they deserved or earned it, but because they wanted to give it.

Mia had done that for me. She'd opened me up in a way no one had been able to before. Now it seemed I felt everything at full volume, without being able to turn it down.

The thought of losing her broke me.

It was so much easier when I had held everyone at arm's length and not felt anything.

~

Mia

I decided from the moment I took my very first step back through the front door that I wasn't going to spoil the day. Tossing off my sopping wet slippers, I ran upstairs and pulled on a long, thick sweater, some sweats, and warm socks. I reminded myself that my goal was to give my mom the best Christmas ever, and I would do that, even if it killed me.

I took a deep breath against the pain in my chest. It hurt so much, I could barely breathe. I wanted to cry, but I had to be strong. I had to see this through.

Following the scent of fresh coffee into the kitchen, I found my dad setting out mugs and the electric griddle. Maybe my mom loved everything about Christmas, but my dad was king of family breakfasts. He was apparently planning today's with zeal, judging by all the ingredients he had spread out all over the island. I forced a smile and kissed him on the cheek. "Good morning, Dad."

There. I'd managed a full sentence without crying. One sentence at a time, right?

He poured me some coffee and set it down on the island near me, assessing me over his bifocals. "Good morning to you too, sweetheart. You're up early."

My first thought was wondering if he'd heard us arguing in the driveway. If he did, he wasn't letting on. "One of the residents in our program is having her baby a little early, so Brax had to go back to cover for her."

"That's exciting, but I'm sorry Brax had to leave." He poured blueberries into a bowl and pressed them down with a fork, then sprinkled sugar on them. "How are you getting back to Milwaukee?"

I bit the insides of my cheeks to stave off the urge to cry, because suddenly thinking about surviving this entire day with fake Christmas cheer seemed as impossible as scaling Annapurna. My dad began pouring chocolate chips into another bowl when I managed, "Maybe Caleb. I don't know."

He looked up, again with that puzzled look. "We can get you back. No worries."

"Thanks, Dad." I held my cup in two hands, trying to take in the warmth. I felt frozen, inside and out. Numb.

Next, he mixed up the batter. But to my surprise, he poured some on the griddle.

"You're making the pancakes this early?" I asked with surprise. "No one's awake yet."

He looked up and smiled at me over his glasses. "You are." He dropped a bunch of chocolate chips on them as they cooked, just the way I liked them.

I clutched my stomach. "I'm not really sure I can eat right now."

He watched the batter bubble up, and then pressed the pancakes down so they'd cook evenly. "So what's going on?"

My dad could always have the most serious of discussions while pretending to be very busy doing something else. I think it was his secret way of getting us to spill all our troubles.

"We fought," I blurted.

He shrugged and glanced up. "It happens."

I set my cup down and looked my father in the eye. Before I could get out any words, I burst out with a sob.

Nonplussed, he flipped the pancakes onto a plate and covered it with a big lid—he never could abide them getting cold—and walked around the island, sitting down and wrapping an arm around me. He even ripped off a couple of paper towels on the way and deposited them in front of me so I could blow my nose.

His comforting presence made me bawl even harder. This was the man who taught me how to change the tire on my bike, who sat right here with me at this very table and quizzed me on geography facts so that I won the school geography bee, who taught me how to play poker, who even learned how to tie shoes left-handed so he could teach me, a left-handed person, so I didn't have to learn the right-handed way. He passed the football to me right along with my brothers to show them and me that girls counted too. I wished my current problems were as simple as all those skinned knees that just needed a wash, a soak, and a Band-Aid.

"Out with it," he said in a voice that was commanding and calming at the same time.

I was literally out of lies. I was emotionally drained. And I desperately needed someone to listen.

"Brax wasn't my real boyfriend." I blew my nose in the paper towel. "Well, he was for a few weeks last summer, but then he dumped me. We just got back together, but I learned this morning he lied to me about that job we're both competing for."

He sat back and pondered my words. "I'm sort of having trouble following that, but why'd he dump you last summer?"

"He said it was because we worked together, but it really was that he didn't feel like he could be good in a relationship." How to explain this giant mess? "You know he aged out of the foster care system. He's accomplished so much on his own—he's amazing, really." I wondered, what if he'd been telling the truth? That he'd thought the offer was sketchy, had plenty to deal with helping me here, and had simply pushed thinking about it aside? I just didn't know what to believe.

"The boy certainly looked smitten."

I had to smile. "Who says *smitten*, Dad?" I blew my nose loudly again.

"Someone who does the NYT crossword every day," he said with the slightest smile.

I was too distraught to react. "We work together, so we became good friends."

"Good friends after you stopped dating?"

"Right. Sort of. Except he agreed to come home with me and pretend to be my boyfriend."

"A fake boyfriend? You've been watching too much Hallmark Channel like your mom."

This twisted roller coaster of a story would be too much for anyone to understand. But I tried to untwist it. "I told Mom about him last summer when I was crazy about him, but then she was going through all the cancer stuff, and I...well, I never stopped. I just kept spinning lies."

"So he was your boyfriend, then he wasn't, but then he was, but now he's not anymore." He whistled.

Yeah. Pretty messed up, wasn't it? "One of the men in the pediatric group in Milwaukee I applied to told Brax under the table that the job would likely be his. And Brax didn't tell me."

"That's how the best group in town behaves?" My dad took off his glasses and pinched the bridge of his nose. "Is Brax going to take the job?"

"Of course he is. His mentor was a founding member. He was the whole reason Brax became a doctor in the first place."

My dad had just implied something important and true. This truly wasn't wasn't how the best group in town should behave. Its actions were more akin to behavior for the *worst* group. Why had it even been in the running for me?

My dad let out a big sigh, like he was still trying to wrap his head around everything but not quite able. "With all this going on, why on earth did you bring him here?"

I swallowed hard. "Well, I..." I had to collect my thoughts. I wanted to say that I'd done it to keep my mom's spirit up at a tough time. That was true, but it was also flawed. At that moment, I realized I should have given my mom more credit.

My mom, who had been there for all my troubles my entire life. Who had withstood the death of a child. Who had survived cancer.

How could I possibly have thought that my silly breakup could devastate her?

And something else too. I hadn't been able to come clean and admit that things hadn't worked out.

So much of this was me doing what I always did—pretending that I didn't have troubles or problems. Hiding my struggles to not create waves, because I didn't want to disappoint. After what had happened in our family with Grace, I'd become really good at minimizing my own difficulties.

"I know why Mia did it," my mom said from the doorway. "I know you did it for me, sweetheart." As she came in, Liam, Dina, and Caleb followed, all in their robes and pj's.

My mom and dad eyed each other with the expressions of two people who'd been married a long time and had seen a lot. I didn't want to see their concerned faces.

"Braxton does not think of you as a friend," my mom said. I looked up in surprise. Because what she hadn't said was *I'm so disappointed in you.*

I looked at my mother, whom I loved so much. Whom I never wanted to hurt. Whom I'd concocted this whole scheme for, which had only really ended up hurting me.

I stood up. "Mom, I'm so sorry."

She got a little teary. "Oh, baby." She wrapped me up in a hug.

Which reassured me that the stupid thing I'd done was...okay. That I'd been forgiven, just like that.

"You know," she said, examining my face. And by this time, I was crying too. "You don't always have to shoulder all the burdens of our family by yourself."

"I wasn't doing that," I said. But I was, wasn't I?

"You felt responsible for my happiness," my mom said.

"She's right," Caleb said. "Ever since Grace died, I think we've all tried to tread a little lightly with all our problems for Mom and Dad's sake."

My mom threw up her hands. "You people! Do you not think we know stuff anyway? If you don't let us in on what's going on with you, we imagine the worst."

I looked around at my family, all sitting raggedly at the table having this brutal discussion without coffee, this early in the morning. "I should have told you the truth," I said to my mom. "Initially I used the stories to lift your spirits during chemo. But then I was afraid to confess because I didn't want you to be disappointed in me."

"I know you love me," she said. "But give me more credit."

"I'm really sorry," I said.

"We liked Brax," Liam said after a while.

Caleb made a deep frown. "But he hurt Mia." He flashed me an I-told-you-so look that I did my best to ignore.

My dad hugged me. "Honey, we're sorry about the misunderstanding, but we're always proud of you. No matter what."

My mom nodded. "So proud."

Had I actually forgotten they'd love me no matter how badly I messed up?

"Maybe Brax just needs time to think," Dina said. "He seems like a good guy."

Just then, Emma walked in, rubbing the sleep out of her eyes. "I think Santa came early." She brought a flat, brightly wrapped package to her mom. "This says my name. Can I open it?"

Dina read the tag and looked up. "It's from Brax."

My stomach plummeted. He'd bought Emma a gift?

I closed my eyes to keep from crying any more. It was clearly a book. He must've somehow bought it when we were shopping.

She tore it open and confirmed what I suspected. It was *The Night Before Christmas*. A brand-new copy of the same classic edition we'd grown up with.

He'd given her a thoughtful gift, one with meaning—not only because he'd read it with her, but also because it was a cherished book to my family.

And that wasn't all he'd done.

He'd encouraged me to tie up my loose ends with Charlie.

He'd run back and snagged that red dress because he suspected I'd never buy it myself.

He'd sacrificed spending the holiday with his sister to come home with me because I needed him.

I placed my hand over my chest because it physically ached. He'd done *a lot*. For me.

Emma held up the book like show-and-tell. "Aunt Mia, will Uncle Brax come back to read with me?"

"I hope so," my mom answered for me.

"He left a few gifts under the tree," Liam said, who'd walked into the family room and then back into the kitchen.

"Those are from our shopping trip yesterday," I said.

"I found this one on the coffee table." My dad walked over with a small square box and placed it on the island next to me. It was beautifully wrapped in sparkly green paper, with a bright green foil bow on top. "It's got your name on it."

That got me choked up again. Hadn't he done enough? I shook my head. And pushed it away. "I can't open it. I...I don't want to."

"You should open it," my mom said, pushing it back. "He bought it for you."

"I'll just put whatever it is in the donation pile," I said. "Along with those five-inchers." Which, as of now, I no longer considered to be my lucky shoes.

"You don't mean that—about the present, that is," Dina said. "Those shoes should have gone out with the trash a long time ago."

I gave a little snort.

"See?" my mom said. "At least you can laugh a little."

Right. Mainly so I didn't break down and bawl in front of my entire family. I ripped off the paper to find a plain cardboard box taped at the seams. Liam opened the junk drawer and slid a pair of scissors to me down the length of the island.

I cut the tape on the box and opened it. Something was packed in heaps of white packing peanuts, which spilled from the box like snow.

And then I pulled out a snow globe.

My eyes instantly blurred so that I couldn't even see it. I had to wipe my eyes on my sweater. While I was doing that, Caleb, of all people, spoke.

"It's the same one as when we were kids," he said, his tone incredulous.

"No way," Liam said, lifting himself halfway out of his chair to see.

"I showed him our photo album," my mom said. "I told him about it."

Everyone gathered around.

"Aunt Mia, let me see," Emma said. I lifted her onto my lap.

"It's two little girls holding hands," she said, pointing inside. "And there's a little dog. And a house." I heard a click. Leave it to the four-year-old to find the on switch. "Oooh, the house has Christmas lights," she exclaimed. "And there's an angel."

I looked around her shoulder. An angel?

Sure enough, there was a third figure, her hands on each child's shoulders like she was guarding them, keeping them safe. I examined the globe from different angles. The figure didn't have wings. But she definitely looked...protective.

I sensed exactly why Brax had given this to me. It was a bit bold. Maybe a bit brazen. But I got why he did it.

"I—I think it means how we watch over our kids in the hospital," I said.

"Like a doctor guarding the health of patients," Dina said, intuitively getting it. "It's beautiful."

"It's kind of like you watching over kids like you and Grace," my mom said. She didn't go so far as to say cancer patients. She knew my reaction too well to go there.

Maybe Brax chose it because it was so similar to that globe many years ago, a representation of me and Gracie together. Except I understood what Brax had intended for me to see. This time, I wasn't one of the kids. I was the guard. He was trying to tell me I could be a guardian for kids like Gracie. Like Rylee. Kids with cancer.

Tears were streaming now. I couldn't stop them.

Brax somehow knew what I couldn't face, and yet he'd made me face it. In a gentle way, if that made any sense. It was like he was trying to tell me not to be afraid. Maybe I should be angry, but I wasn't. When I looked at the three figures, I *wanted* to be the so-called angel. I'd always wanted to protect kids because I hadn't been able to protect Gracie. And maybe that meant taking one further leap than I'd been willing to take.

"That doesn't seem like the kind of gift someone gives you who's just trying to knock you out of the running for a job," Caleb said.

If Caleb could say something that charitable, it must mean something. Also, he was right.

Caleb collected the gift wrap to toss in the recycle container. "Hey, I'm thinking of heading back tomorrow after lunch." He used the ball of paper to shoot a basket. "Want a ride?"

"Yeah, sure. Thanks," I said.

Brax got me, more than anyone I'd met. He pushed me to examine myself, and sometimes understood me scarily more than I did myself.

I'd been quick to judge him. Quick to believe he'd betrayed me. And I hadn't given him the benefit of the doubt.

Chapter Twenty-One

Brax

"What are you doing back so soon?" Gabe narrowed his eyes and asked me between inhaling bites of "spaghetti" in the cafeteria that night. "Spaghetti" in quotes because it looked—well, pale and clumpy, with a sauce that was more orange than red. And it sucked, just like my life right now.

That was also how I would've defined my mood at the moment—pale and clumpy. I felt cold and clammy. I felt paralyzed with nerves. If I didn't get my attitude readjusted quickly, it was going to be a really long night.

"That looks...disgusting," I couldn't help saying.

I was downing my fourth cup of coffee since this morning. If I didn't cut myself off soon, my shakes would have shakes.

Gabe, however, was inhaling the pasta. "Don't judge me," he said between hurried bites. "I got in at midnight last night, I'm on call tonight, and I'm starving because I have no groceries in my apartment. Tomorrow, when I get off, it'll be Christmas Day, and all the grocery stores will be closed." He checked his watch. "Plus,

I've only got ten minutes before I have to be in the ER. And my holiday was great, thanks. How was yours?"

I didn't even ask about Jason. "Sorry." I ran a hand through my hair. "Did you say yes?"

He stopped eating long enough to grin widely. "I said yes."

"Oh wow. Gabe, that's—" I smiled back and clapped him on the back. "Wonderful. Congratulations, man."

I was genuinely happy for him. He deserved happiness.

Gabe wiped his mouth with his napkin. "The wedding's in July, as soon as this year of hell ends. In Charleston. Ever been?"

I gave a little smile. "Not yet, but I can't wait to go. I'm really happy for you two."

"And I want you to be my best man." He set down his fork. "But only if you tell me what's wrong."

I jerked my head up. "I'm honored." I got choked up. "You're like a brother to me. We can talk about me some other time."

He set down his fork. "That's why I asked you. You are my brother, in every way that matters. So, what's going on with Mia?"

"I had a great time. She's got an amazing family. She's amazing."

"But?"

"I screwed up."

He frowned. "Does that mean you slept together? Because you already did that before."

"I don't kiss and tell."

"You do if you want my advice." He went back to slurping down the spaghetti.

"Yes, okay, that was amazing too. But then…"

Gabe stopped eating again and checked his watch. "You're going to have to get this story out faster if you want my advice before I have to leave."

"Before I left, Brunner implied that the practice was going to offer me the job, and I didn't tell Mia. Honestly, I was trying to figure it all out. They don't seem to want women in the practice.

They overwork everyone. On the other hand, maybe if I join, I can be the one to set things right." I was getting it all out fast, so I had to take a breath. "Mia thinks I kept the secret on purpose. That I was even trying to sway her away from the job when I told her she'd be great at heme-onc." I looked up. "I hate what they're doing. But I've been dreaming of working in that practice for years. It's...it's kind of in my blood."

Gabe was shaking his head and looking at me like—well, like I sucked. I thought that he, of all people, would sympathize. "So you didn't tell her about the shady job offer, mistake number one. And you tried to talk her into applying for heme-onc, so now she thinks you were assuaging your guilt, number two."

I dropped my head into my hands. I sucked. "What's number three?"

"Number three is that you seem willing to take a job where they treat you and other people badly just for the sake of saying you have that job. What would Dr. Pendergast do?"

I jerked up my head. I stared across the table at my best friend, who'd just asked a ten-million-dollar question. Of course I knew. "He would've told them to take their job and stick it somewhere where the sun don't shine."

He never would have compromised his integrity for the prestige of having a job.

Suddenly, all that caffeine must've kicked in, because the clouds finally parted. Everything became crystal clear. Somehow, I'd forgotten who I was.

I'd complained about no one really loving me. But the truth was, I didn't understand what it was to love another person back. I'd let my desire for that job cloud my thinking. I'd put it before Mia.

Gabe sat back and crossed his arms. "Love or the job. Those are your choices."

∾

Mia

The day after Christmas, the same gold tinsel and colorful lights still looped around the nurses' station, except the holiday decorations had that tired, the-party-is-over, take-me-down look.

Everything seemed different. Every beep and buzz seemed jarring, yet the ward was oddly quiet. Muffled, as if I had earbuds in my ears that muted the rest of the world. Maybe it was because Bianca and Pedro had both been discharged home, and their fun teenage banter was gone.

Rylee and her family were also long gone, hopefully enjoying a fun and uneventful holiday. The hissing sound of an albuterol nebulizer machine, accompanied by crying, emanated from her old room. It was now occupied by a two-year-old with a viral respiratory infection who was crying in his mother's arms as she struggled to keep the mask that delivered the treatment on his face.

I went about my work, catching up on everyone. Hospital life went on as normal. Who was I kidding? Everything seemed sad and lifeless. *Brax-less.*

I didn't have time to think about my troubles. We had nine admissions that morning alone. The city seemed to be blowing up with post-holiday respiratory illnesses and gastroenteritis.

Right before lunchtime, I ran to the bathroom and bumped into Sam in the call room, sitting on a bottom bunk, pillaging a box of leftover Christmas chocolates. She'd been texting me literally every hour since Christmas Eve. "Hey," she said, holding up a box of candy wrapped in bright red foil under my nose. Ordinarily, the rich scent of good chocolate would have worked wonders, but today, it made my stomach churn, so I passed.

She stopped midchew. "Have you eaten breakfast? I'm going to run down and grab you an egg sandwich." She got up and hugged me. "I'd buy you a drink tonight, but I know you're on call. How about I take your call for you?"

"You're a good friend." As I hugged her back, I fought back a sudden swell of tears. This would not do. I had a long, harrowing day ahead of me, not to mention a busy night ahead. I rubbed my pounding temples. "Got any Advil?"

My pager went off. It was Val, the charge nurse, telling me that Dr. Brunner was waiting at the desk to talk with me. It was probably about an admission. They were coming left and right today. I somehow had to get my game on fast.

"I'm worried about you," Sam said.

"I'm okay." I *had* to be. Sam knew as well as I did everyone was stretched thin with the holiday schedule. If I took off, I'd be screwing my already-overworked colleagues. I would somehow have to get through this day.

Cracking a wry smile, I joked, "Being busy cures anything, right?" Although I doubted that was a smart strategy for a broken heart. All I could hope for was to continue getting pounded, so I didn't have a second to think about Brax.

Sam gave me another concerned look and a squeeze as I wrapped my stethoscope around my neck and headed out of the call room.

"There you are," Dr. Brunner said as he met me at the nurses' station.

I immediately grabbed my laptop and tried not to think about the dreaded job that had torn Brax and me apart. "Okay, who have we got?" I hovered my hand over the keyboard, waiting for the details of the incoming admission.

"Actually," he said, looking over his silver-rimmed bifocals, "I'm here with a little holiday gift."

That made me look up. He looked calm and confident, as if he was about to bestow a great honor upon me. I can read people pretty well, and somehow, whatever he was about to say made my gut clench. "I'm speaking on behalf of all of us physicians in the group," he said as if he were making a speech. "We're all highly impressed with you, young lady. We feel that your work ethic, your relatability to our patients and our families, and your competence all add up to a physician with exceptional character. Bottom line is, we'd like to offer you a spot in our practice."

I stared down at the compact computer in my hands, but I couldn't bring anything into focus. That seemed to be the mantra of my life lately—nothing was clear.

Brax had said no to the job of his dreams? And now they were offering the job to me? Or did they end up not offering it to Brax in the first place?

I couldn't think. I couldn't understand.

All I seemed to hear was the fact that Brunner had called me *young lady*.

Did anyone ever call him *old man*? What would happen if someone did? And why was I thinking of this when he'd just presented me my heart's desire?

My heart started pounding and sweat was accumulating along the back of my neck. *Say thank you and accept the offer*, I told myself.

"Thank you for the offer," I began. But no other words came. I set down the computer on the counter. I knew the smart thing would be to walk away. But instead, I looked at him, at this respected, experienced pediatrician, and said, "May I ask you a question, Dr. Brunner?"

"It's okay to be a little stunned, Mia," he said, chuckling. "Ask away."

It was better to be quiet. To be grateful. But I had to know. I had to hear the answer and see him say it. "Why me?"

I saw Dr. Brunner's eyes shift. He hesitated slightly. Cleared his throat.

"First of all, we at BCP believe in diversity and inclusion."

"Is being a woman diverse?" A white woman at that?

The lines between his eyes creased into a frown. "Part of our plan has always been to expand the number of female physicians in our practice. But as you know, our top priority is to provide our patients with twenty-four-seven access to the best health care in the city. We dislike our employees dropping to part time, so we're committed to finding the hardest-working residents we can. Those whose work ethic resembles yours."

I thought of Robin, who always seemed overworked and exhausted. Who had tiptoed around the truth to keep her job.

"As you must know," Dr. Brunner continued, "Dr. Hughes turned us down because of his plans to search for a job in Philadelphia, so we are absolutely thrilled to offer you the spot. Both of you were excellent candidates. It really was a neck-and-neck choice."

Brax wasn't taking the job, and he was leaving? To go to Philadelphia? Where Jenna lived?

Leaving me? Leaving *us*?

"Mia," Val called from across the desk. "Morgan's mom is asking if it's okay for her to have something to drink."

"Just ice chips until I get the X-ray results," I answered over my shoulder.

"Okay," she said on her way down the hall. "But just FYI, she's starving."

"I'll get on it," I said. I turned to Dr. Brunner. "Thanks for being honest." I blew out a big breath. The kind of breath you let out when you're about to do the thing you should have done a long time ago.

"I'm truly honored to be one of your top picks. Your group sets the standard for what good pediatricians are."

I paused. *Stop right there,* my safe side warned me.

Sorry, I said right back. *This time, I'm pulling a Gracie.*

"But there's a dark side to your practice that the residents are talking about. Some of us feel that you prefer white male doctors, or that you choose people willing to put up with long hours and unspoken expectations."

His demeanor changed before my eyes, and he spoke in a cool, level tone. "Clearly, you and Braxton have been in collusion. You know, young lady, being disgruntled that you weren't our top pick and spreading rumors can harm your career."

In collusion? Had Brax told them the same thing? Also, was Dr. Brunner subtly threatening me to get me to keep quiet? "The other thing, Dr. Brunner, is that I don't believe you'd ever refer to a male resident as a young man. You'd call him *Doctor*. I'd appreciate the same consideration."

He narrowed his eyes in a way that should have worried me. I'd never uttered a word out of the respect zone ever to any of my superiors. "I should write you up for being disrespectful."

I didn't back down. "I've only said what a lot of us are thinking."

As I turned away, I discovered that two of my interns and four of our nursing staff were hovering nearby, listening intently. Soon, the entire hospital would know what I'd done.

Well, good. I'd finally stood up and said what I felt needed to be said.

I loved kids, and I loved my job. But Brax had called it right. I truly wasn't upset about letting that job go. My heart wasn't into doing well-child checks, charting growth and development, and educating moms on the many nuances of raising a healthy child. Not that that wasn't wonderful stuff—it just wasn't wonderful to me.

Also, I was done with trying to achieve *perfect*. I wasn't coming close in any aspect of my life anyway. And I didn't need the prestige of belonging to that practice.

Or the misogyny.

I was glad—even proud—that I hadn't stayed silent. But I wasn't sure quite what to do now that I'd just shot my promising future right in the foot. Or about the fact that Brax was leaving for good.

Chapter Twenty-Two

Mia

I was scheduled to see patients in the heme-onc clinic with Dr. March that afternoon. I skipped lunch to seek out Gabe because I knew he was nearby, getting ready to supervise interns in the primary care sick clinic today. I was trying desperately to compartmentalize, but I was a mess.

The first thing he did was sit me down and hand me half of his turkey sandwich—and refuse to talk to me until I ate it.

"Congrats on getting engaged," I managed after the first bite.

"Thanks, but don't even bother saying anything else. Sam told me everything, including what you said to Brunner. You're my hero."

I knew word traveled fast in the hospital, but that fast? I forced myself to swallow another bite of sandwich, but it was no use. "I made a mess out of everything."

He smiled. "Yes, you did. Welcome to the world of human beings, Superwoman." He hugged me hard. "The only thing I can say is that I saw Brax the last night, and he looks as bad as you do."

I sat back and looked at him. "How bad?"

"Pretty darn bad."

A flicker of hope kicked deep inside of me. "Have you talked to him?"

Unaffected by my grilling, he looked me calmly in the eye. "I think the real question is, have you?"

"He was on call last night, and I'm on call tonight." I could tell by Gabe's eye roll that he saw right through that. "Okay, fine. He hasn't called. And I haven't contacted him either. He kept a huge secret from me, Gabe. And I just found out he gave up the BCP job and he's leaving."

"Leaving?" Gabe frowned. "That doesn't sound like Brax."

He was calling us quits. Blowing out of town. Running away. "I guess he was right all along. He couldn't do a relationship after all."

Gabe hugged me hard again. "I don't have any idea what he's thinking. But you know what you need to do." He mimed talking motions with both his hands.

"No matter what happens, I'll be okay." I tried to honestly believe it, not ask it like a question. And yes, I'd be courageous. I'd pick up the pieces of my career, my family, my life, one at a time, starting right now. I pushed the sandwich away. "Thanks for sharing—and for being my friend."

"You're welcome." He smiled a giant smile. "And yes, you will."

Rylee's chart said that she was tolerating her induction phase chemo very well. She'd continue to be hit hard with the chemo agents for another few weeks. Today in clinic, we'd done another lumbar puncture and given her an infusion of intrathecal chemo into her spinal canal. She was on medication to protect her stomach, for nausea, prophylaxis for pneumonia, and for mouth sores.

But despite all this rather dry information, I walked in to see two little girls, heads together, giggling and clearly conspiring over something. Rylee wore a multicolored crocheted cap with a big yarn flower over her ear. I suspected that her hair was well on its way to falling out. She was pale, with dark circles under her eyes, but her eyes were bright. And she was smiling.

Reagan wore the same kind of hat, but in different colors.

Becca and Ryan were sitting together, watching their girls. I noticed they were tightly holding hands, a sign that they were figuratively holding their breath, waiting to hear about Rylee's progress.

"I'm trying new hairstyles for when Rylee's grows back," Reagan said, taking off her hat and showing me that she was now sporting a short pixie haircut.

I touched a curl. "Cute. What do you think, Rylee?"

"It's nice," she said, surveying her sister, "but when my hair grows back, I'm never cutting it again."

"Like Rapunzel?" I asked, and the girls giggled.

"We made you something," Rylee said, nodding to her mom, who reached beside her and pulled out a poster.

A sign that said, *Thank you, Dr. Mia*, all in glitter. They'd clearly made good use of the glitter pens I'd given them. I was truly touched. This was a bright spot in my otherwise gray day.

"We know you're moving on to another rotation, and we wanted to say thank you," Becca explained.

"It's so awesome," I said, looking over the sign that was embellished with literally every color of glitter imaginable. "But girls, do you think you used enough glitter?"

That got more giggles from both of them. I couldn't tell you how good a sound that was.

A short, staccato knock sounded on the door, and a second later, Dr. March joined us, greeting the Hunters. I gave a little summary of how Rylee was doing and what her labs showed.

"Fantastic," Dr. March said. She outlined the plan for finishing the induction phase and the tests and chemo that would follow. Everything was looking positive as they left to enjoy the rest of the holidays as best as they could.

It was late in the afternoon and the clinic staff had left, anxious to begin their holiday. I decided on impulse to go back into the exam room to chart my note. And, to be honest, to simply take a minute. Fresh paper covering had been rolled down to cover the exam table, the stool had been tucked underneath the desk, and all was quiet except for the soft buzz of traffic outside on the street.

The glitter sign was still on the desk. Maybe it was all the emotional stress I was under, but I couldn't help remembering two very different little girls from a long time ago, my sister and me.

"*I love you so much.*" I looked up suddenly from my charting. I'd heard Grace's voice for the first time in many years, clear as a crisp winter breeze. The room was still silent—and empty. No one was there but me, but I could feel her. I could literally sense my sister's presence.

She wasn't saying that she was proud of me or beseeching me to help sick children or even telling me what path to take. She was just...smiling at me. Not that I saw her; I *felt* her smiling.

Okay, I've read accounts of weird things happening. And let's face it, I was desperate—the heartbreak, the job thing, the stress of the fake-boyfriend weekend. Compared to the heartache I'd suffered when Charlie cheated on me, this felt a thousand times worse. Holding myself together at work today had taken every ounce of strength I possessed. But I could tell you beyond a doubt that I *sensed* something, in the way that people claim to feel a strong, intense presence long after their loved ones have passed. It's like the sensation you experience when you wake up from a vivid dream and feel certain that it was real.

Countless times, I'd wished that Grace was with me, sharing something that I knew she'd think was hilarious or something that had special meaning between us. But I'd never sensed this—well, I can only describe it as a *presence*.

I somehow knew she was okay. More than okay. Like, maybe she didn't get to fulfill her potential on earth. But maybe she was doing it...somewhere else. At least, that was what I believed.

My heart beat wildly in my chest. I had so much I wanted to say. Years' worth of things.

Like *Stay, please stay*. Or, *When will I see you again*? There was so much more I wanted to know. And I needed to tell her how much I missed her.

"*They remind me of us*," Grace said.

"Exactly," I said, tearing up. "Just like us."

"Mia, can I talk to you about something?"

I jumped at Dr. March's voice behind me. I'd thought she'd gone home for the day. How long had she been standing in the doorway?

A strange void filled me. That waking-up-from-a-dream sensation of being so close to something, and then suddenly, it was gone.

All day long, I'd been trying so hard not to crack. I'd been functioning on the maniacal side of cheerful, overdoing it to disguise all my pain. The last thing I wanted to do was to suddenly break down under anyone's concern. Also, what did she think I was doing, sitting in an empty exam room talking to myself? "Look, Dr. March I'm a little emotional today, but I swear it's not impacting my—"

She smiled as she leaned against the doorjamb. "You love those little girls."

Uh oh. The last thing I wanted was to be unprofessional. Especially since I'd just crossed a huge line with Dr. Brunner.

Plus, professional detachment was necessary for survival in this job. You couldn't allow yourself to cross a line with patients. You'd never survive the tragedies.

Maybe I'd never have what it took.

"I do," I told Dr. March.

"It's a great relief that Rylee is doing okay," she said.

Tears burned behind my lids. I blinked them back. "I worried about her over my break."

"Me too."

That startled me. "You did too?"

She walked in and leaned against the exam table, seeming to have all the time in the world to chat. I had no idea if she sensed how on the edge I was. "I worry all the time about my patients. You know, Rylee has an excellent chance of doing very, very well."

I nodded. I somehow felt my sister's presence fading. *Please, please don't leave,* I wanted to shout.

I fisted and unfisted my hands from the tension of wanting Dr. March to leave, hoping that I could hear Grace just one last time. Or tell her one last *I love you* before she was gone for good.

"My sister—" I said, hoping somehow to signal to Grace to stay.

Dr. March stood there, listening.

I took a deep breath. "My twin sister died when we were nine."

Her brow arched. "Of leukemia?"

I nodded. And let out a sob I didn't know I was keeping in.

She walked over and placed her hand on my shoulder. "That explains why you're so invested in Rylee's whole family. And little Reagan too."

"I've been there," I said simply. That let the floodgates loose—tear-wise and talking-wise. "I just said no to the primary care job with BCP. And...I was wondering..." I had to take a big breath to get it out. "Is it too late to apply for the heme-onc fellowship? If you've found someone, maybe I could staff the residents' clinic for a year. I know sometimes I'm too emotional, and maybe I need more detachment, but I know I can—"

"Caring is a good asset," she said firmly, interrupting me. "Never for a moment do I doubt that you have what it takes to be great at this job." She seemed to thoughtfully gather her words. "Mia, being a cancer doctor for kids a scary job, but it's also wonderful and rewarding. To know that you've helped these families through the most terrifying time of their lives is a great thing."

And then she stepped forward and hugged me.

Of course, I burst into tears anew. It was relief, it was affirmation, it was someone telling you that it was okay to be afraid of something. But maybe you should go ahead and do it anyway.

How lucky I was to have someone like that. A mentor.

"Are you okay?" she asked, assessing me carefully.

"I've got some things going on," I said, swiping at my eyes. "I'm sorry."

"Never be sorry for being human," she said, handing me the box of tissues from the desk.

"I'll fill out the application as soon as possible."

"Of course. And I'll write you a recommendation letter too." She paused. "I can do better than that. I'll also tell all my colleagues that I believe you're the best candidate."

Oh, joy! What I meant was, I wasn't exactly in a happy state, but I felt something squeeze inside my chest, a feeling that this was, well, right. As far as any big, scary, major decision can. "Thank you, Dr. March," I managed. "I really appreciate it."

Once she left, I was alone for real this time. I finished my charting and looked up.

"Grace?" I said very quietly.

The late afternoon sun was shining in, a pale winter ray. It drew me over to the window, where I saw all the impressive hospital buildings lining the street. Small, bare trees far below were outlined in Christmas lights already turned on, anticipating the darkness that would soon arrive.

I turned back to the room. The beam of sunlight hit the nondescript vinyl floor and sparkled.

I walked over to examine the strange sight. Sure enough, tiny sparkly specks shone brightly in the light.

Glitter.

I smiled. And then I laughed out loud. Good thing I was the only one around.

Or maybe I wasn't. My sister's love wrapped around me like a warm blanket, swirling about me as if she were in this sterile exam room right beside me.

Or maybe she had been, and she'd left behind some magic.

Yes, I knew that the glitter had spilled from the poster. But still, I clutched my laptop to my chest. "I hope heaven has a ton of art supplies," I whispered.

The door creaked a little behind me.

"Grace?" I called as I spun around.

"Not Grace," Brax said softly. He was standing there, looking tired and a little disheveled, his eyes full of feeling, making my heart thump hard from an absurd amount of hope. "Just me."

Chapter Twenty-Three

Brax

"Mia," I said on an exhale that was half tension, half relief that I'd finally found her. She was standing by the window, looking stoic. I wasn't sure why she was in this exam room alone, or why I'd heard her call out Grace's name. But I had so much to say—how to begin?

"How did you find me?" she asked.

"I ran into Dr. March." I'd thought clinic was empty on my first pass, so I'd searched the ward and then the ER, before finally heading back here. I didn't tell her any of that as I walked over to her. I could see that just seeing me was making her a little teary. Honestly, I was getting choked up too.

I stopped a few feet in front of her. "I'm sorry," I blurted. "I was wrong to not tell you about the job. Forgive me."

She started to cry. I took her hands in mine and was relieved she didn't push me away. "I let my desire to walk in Atticus's shoes cloud my thinking."

"I'm sorry too," she said, her voice cracking. "I jumped to

conclusions. I accused you of lying. I know that job meant a lot to you."

"You mean more." I squeezed her hands and looked into her green eyes that were bright with feeling. "The best way I can honor Atticus is to be a good man. I don't want the job. Take it. Take it and give them hell."

She smiled through her tears. "Too late. Long story, but I spoke my mind to Brunner. But more importantly, I just hit Send on the fellowship application a second before you showed up. You were right about me—I'm terrified. I don't like to fail. And I'm afraid of the times when things won't go well, and how that might remind me of my sister. But I'm going to do it anyway. I love the kids. I love the families. I love heme-onc. And I think Grace would want me to do it too."

"You'll be an amazing oncologist." I knew it down to my bones. I didn't know exactly what had happened between her and Brunner, but I knew she was okay with not getting the job. And so was I.

Mia smiled, but not a giant, happy smile. More of a sad one. "Brax, are you leaving? Dr. Brunner told me you're going back to Philly?"

There was a sudden racket in the hall, accompanied by voices and laughter, but I ignored it. I shrugged and said, "That's what I told Brunner. Honestly, at that time, I didn't know what I was doing."

"So you're not? Going?"

I was relieved that she sounded like my answer mattered. I had to let her know how much she mattered to me. "I want to be with you. If you'll have me."

She walked straight into my arms. "I love you," she said simply.

"I love you too." Those words had never been so easy to say. Or so wonderful to hear as I wrapped my arms around her. Holding her close, feeling her softness, and taking in the familiar scent of her hair made my heart swell with joy. This was where we belonged. *Together*, wherever that might lead us.

I had one more piece of news. "You know that job in the residents' clinic that they hired me for last year? Well, they want me to take it in July, when my chief year ends. I like teaching. What do you think?"

She looked up at me, her smile wide and bright. "I think Atticus would be proud. I know I am."

A clatter in the hall had both of us glancing toward the door again. But I needed Mia to stay with me just another minute. So I held her hands tight and said, "So I thought we might start from the point where things went wrong."

She gave a snorty laugh. "When you said, 'Take me home for Christmas'?"

I gave a little chuckle. "I was thinking about when we started talking about the job thing." The chatter of voices in the now-deserted clinic got louder, and footsteps were coming closer by the second. I was going to have to step this up.

"What's going on out there?" She tried to look past me, but I blocked her view with my body.

"Mia Maria D'Angelo, I, Braxton Michael Hughes, love you, with all my heart and soul. And I feel bad that your visit home got sort of messed up at the end."

She frowned, like she was a little worried about my mental health. "I'm over it."

"Just go with this, okay?"

As soon as she said "Okay," back, I kissed her quickly and gripped her shoulders. "You took me home for Christmas, so now I thought I'd bring Christmas to you." And then I turned around and said in a loud voice, "Everybody can come in now."

Her family—and friends, who were really family too—all piled in. Her mom and her dad, carrying Emma. Liam and Dina. Sam and Gabe. And Caleb, carrying pizza. Lots of pizza. And salad. And jojos, which, if you don't know, are homemade fried potato wedges some pizza parlors around here make from scratch. And Diet Coke, which we all needed after these long few days. But mostly, they brought their love.

Caleb set down a six-pack.

Sam rushed up to him, no holds barred. "What are you doing, you big ortho lug? You can't bring beer in here."

"I wasn't sure. I mean, it's after hours," Caleb said, sounding a little startled and looking at Sam like he'd just gotten attacked by a pit bull. A cute one, but still.

Sam rolled her eyes. "Maybe this is how you ortho guys roll, but this is a clinic. In a *children's hospital*."

"Sorry," he said apologetically.

"Okay, fine," she said, relenting a little. "I guess you meant well."

He grinned at her concession, and then turned to Mia, "We're going to your place for dessert."

"Oh no," Mia said, clasping a hand to her forehead. "I can't go. I'm on call tonight."

"No, you're not," Sam said. "I'm taking your call. You can do mine tomorrow."

"Are you sure?" Mia hugged her. "You're the best friend ever."

"No problem." Sam said. "Just save me some dessert."

"Uh-oh, family," Mia said. "My place isn't looking too great after these past few days."

"We don't care," Beth said. "We've been so worried about you." She gave me a squeeze. "Thanks for asking us to come, Brax."

"Hey, buddy," I said to Caleb, pounding him on the back. "Thanks for helping me set this up."

"Wait—you *helped* him?" Mia said to Caleb.

"Yeah," Caleb said, hugging. "We're square now." Turned out that because of the snow globe, I'd managed to score a few bro points with him.

Beth picked up a child's drawing on the desk. "Looks like

you've got a couple of fans," she said to Mia. She dusted off her hand after getting glitter on it.

Mia walked over to her mom and put her arm around her. "Mom, I met the cutest little girls," she said. "I can't wait to tell you all about them."

"Thanks for bringing the pizza, Mom and Dad D'Angelo," I said. Maybe I should have stuck to Mr. and Mrs. but...why not?

"Mom and Dad D'Angelo?" Mia asked me with a laugh.

Steve put an arm around me. "No problem, son." *Son.* I must've looked as affected as I really was from hearing that, because he shook my shoulder affectionately and beamed. "Looks like you two worked it out."

I met Mia's eyes. They were twinkling. "We worked it out."

"I guess we're going to my place," Mia said to me with a shrug.

"With your family," I said.

"With *our* family. My dad called you *son*. It's official."

Then I laughed out loud. "Yeah, I guess it is." Happiness was bubbling all through me. I hadn't planned on gaining an entire family, but somehow, I had. I gathered Mia into my arms. "I love you."

She smiled up at me. "I love you too."

$\sim$

Mia

Later that night, when everybody left, we got ready for bed ridiculously early, laying blankets and pillows down in front of the tiny little fake tree my mom had set up for me. Only she would bring me a tree to basically light up after Christmas. *Thanks, Mom.*

Brax called Jenna, and I got to talk to her for the first time. "Jenna," he said, "I want you to meet my girlfriend, Mia." He looked up from the phone, and with pride in his voice, said, "Mia,

Jenna's my younger sister, but she's a lot wiser than me. And she's awesome."

"Mia, oh my gosh," Jenna exclaimed. "I'm thrilled."

"Hi Jenna!" I responded. "Great to meet you."

What I learned was that Brax was loving and affectionate with his sister, and she was the same right back. To me as well.

Before he hung up, Brax took the phone off speaker mode and spoke quietly to his sister. "Hey," he said. "I just wanted to tell you thanks. For everything. And I love you." Afterward, he poured us some wine as we both sat on my couch.

"I'm sorry you missed spending Christmas with her," I said.

"That's okay." He was still smiling proudly. "I'll see her soon. You know, I owe her. She told me to give myself a chance with you."

I grinned widely. "Then I owe her too."

We settled into relaxing. "You hungry?" he asked.

"Not a chance." I patted my stomach and laughed.

"What is it?" he asked.

"Pizza tastes so good when you're not heartbroken," I said.

He chuckled in agreement and handed me a glass. We clinked a cheers.

"It's so pretty," I said as I took a sip and admired the tree.

"Yes, you are," Brax said. He started to nuzzle my neck, which I loved.

"Oh, wait," I said. "I have to tell you something."

"What is it?" He kept dropping kisses near my collarbone. I let out a little shiver.

"Guess who came into clinic with Bianca today?" I asked.

"Who?"

"Pedro," I confirmed. "They're officially dating."

"Guess Pedro listened to my dating advice," Brax said between kisses.

My mouth dropped open. "You gave him dating advice?"

I could feel him smile against my neck. "When you find someone special, you lock it down."

I rolled my eyes. "You're ridiculous. Want your present now?"

He frowned. "I've already had the best Christmas I could ever have. A real Christmas, a family, and most of all...you."

"That's sweet, babe," I said with a laugh, "but I've got something else for you. I mean, after that dress and the snow globe, you were a hard act to follow."

I got up and crossed the room to an envelope I'd hidden under my sadly neglected mail pile. I walked back and held it out to him.

He ripped it open. Then he tossed his head back with laughter. "Packers tickets? Ha, against the Eagles?"

I nodded. "I figured it's time you start switching your loyalties."

He looked puzzled. "I didn't know you liked football."

"Actually, Caleb's dying to go. Now that you're his new favorite person, I thought you might want to ask him."

"Thanks for the great gift." He laughed again. "Caleb's okay, you know? I'd love to go to the game with him." Then he reached around behind his back and pulled out a wrapped gift. "One last one," he said.

I pulled out fuzzy, warm reindeer slippers, which I promptly put on and made sure to light up the noses. Thrilled, I flashed him a smile. "They're almost as awesome as you."

He took me in his arms. "Happy New Year, honey," he whispered in my ear. "Happy new beginning." And then he kissed me until the Christmas lights blurred, and all that remained was him, his lips, his big arms, and his love wrapped around me tight.

Epilogue

Six years later, December 23rd

Mia

"Dr. D'Angelo?"

I looked up from my final chart of the day to see a bright-eyed teenage girl leaning into my doorway, peeking into my office. She casually flipped her long dark hair over her shoulder as she waved a piece of paper excitedly in the air.

"Rylee!" I exclaimed from my desk chair. Clearly, she had news. And I could tell that it must be really, really good. I squeezed the underside of my center desk drawer, trying to act cool.

"I'm so glad you're still here!" she said, a little breathless. "My mom said you'd probably be gone already for the holiday, but I had to take the chance."

"Is your mom here too?" I didn't see anyone standing behind her in the hall.

"I drove here myself." She was grinning from ear to ear. "Mom said I could. And Reagan's at art class. But I kind of wanted to come on my own."

My heart sped up a little as I stood, turned the corner of my desk, and met her in the middle of my office.

I knew why she was here. Part of me still couldn't believe she was nearly eighteen, bright, beautiful, and most of all, healthy. Life was so...wild.

And at the moment, she was also very, very happy. "I got in!" she said, shoving the paper in front of me.

Congratulations, I read. *It is with great pleasure that the faculty, staff, students, and alumni of the University of Wisconsin-Madison welcome you!*

Oh, my heart. I jumped and squealed and hugged Rylee, both of us making quite a commotion. Good thing I was the last one in the office, or someone just might've called a code.

"You did it," I said, wiping my eyes. "I'm so proud of you!" And so, so grateful she was here to experience this moment, this life, and the sparkling future ahead of her.

I calmed down enough to keep reading. "Admitted into the College of Letters and Science, Department of Biology." I looked up to see her beaming. "You always loved science." She'd even placed second in the state science fair last year.

She shrugged. "Yeah, well, Reagan's the artist." Actually, Reagan learned last month that she'd be studying at the Art Institute of Chicago. "I do better with cold, hard facts." She gazed up at me, suddenly quiet. "Dr. D'Angelo, I want to be a doctor."

And I thought I'd lost it before. That was nothing compared to this. I felt so proud, so overwhelmed, so...so damn lucky I was here, experiencing this moment that at times I'd feared might never come. After my torrent of tears subsided, I placed my hand on her slight, young shoulder. "You're going to make a terrific physician, Rylee. I-I'm just...speechless. In the best way."

"I want to do what you do," she continued, far more calmly than I. "I want to help kids like you do. I want to work with families and make them feel better, because I understand what it's like, you know?"

I was so choked up, I could barely speak. "I'm so honored to have a part in your decision. Everything you've been through will be a blessing, because you can use your experiences to help others."

And all those years ago, I thought, hadn't that been what Brax had known all along about me?

"That's the plan." She glanced at her phone. "I gotta go. Mom said I could pick Reagan up after class. We're going Christmas shopping."

"Merry Christmas, honey." I gave her a final squeeze. "You made my day—actually, you made my whole holiday. Give my love to your family."

"I sure will. Merry Christmas, Dr. D!"

It was nearly five o'clock when I walked onto the adolescent ward, rushing a little because I was late. But the sight in the middle of the hall made me slow my pace.

My handsome husband was standing in the middle of a group of ward-weary residents, some in scrubs, all with stethoscopes around their neck, all paying rapt attention as he talked animatedly, using his hands. Then they all laughed.

It was evident from the way the residents reacted that they liked and respected Brax. Just as he'd been one of our chief residents six years ago, he continued to love teaching and had gotten the Golden Apple Award the past three years in a row, the award that goes to the best teacher for residents.

Also, he was now the head of BCP. Except now it was called Pediatrics of Milwaukee. Even before Dr. Brunner retired, all of us residents made quite a commotion about the practice, and they'd changed their ways. Brax had become an agent for that change, and the group now consisted of three female and three male partners, one of whom was Brax.

As so often happened, he glanced up without warning and saw me. His face broke into a giant smile just as mine did every time I saw him. He shrugged, as if to say *Oops, sorry, I got caught up in this*. I shrugged back. Except I was wondering, what on earth had he done with our three-year-old?

"She's got her daddy's eyes, but who'd she get the curly brown hair from? And the desire to draw all the time?"

I spun about to see Val, holding our fast-asleep three-year-old, head resting on her shoulder and still clutching a red marker in her hand. A faint marker trail cut across her cheek. Those traits she mentioned seemed very much to me to come from my sister, but I just smiled as I shifted my book bag and purse so I could take my child.

"Sorry about that," Val said, swiping at the marker line while handing her over. "You can blame Bianca. She supplied the markers."

"Hey, don't blame the child life specialist," Bianca said as she walked up, healthy and strong. "Hi, Dr. D."

I smiled at our incredible child life specialist, who knew how to entertain this ward better than anyone, as I settled my completely passed-out daughter into my arms. "Thanks for exhausting—I mean entertaining her," I said with a grin. "How long have you two been watching her?"

"Dr. Brax was waiting for you," Val said, "but then Dr. March wanted him to consult on a patient."

"We were happy to play with her," Bianca said. "She's adorable."

Yes, she was. "Thanks, you two."

"No problem." Bianca handed me a pack of markers. "For your trip."

"You're the best," I said. "These are like, her favorite things in the world."

Bianca laughed. "We noticed."

"Hey, Dr. D," a male voice said. Pedro, wearing scrubs, walked up and snuck a peek at my sleeping toddler. As a physical therapy student, he'd finally found a way to put all that energy to good use. "She looks like Dr. Hughes," he said. But the one he really had eyes for was Bianca. "You ready, B?"

"I'm done," she said, pretend-dusting off her hands. "Time for Christmas break."

Pedro kissed Bianca on the cheek. "Bianca's coming home with me for Christmas."

Awww. The would-be physical therapist and the child life specialist were still an item. Too cute.

Then my honey walked over, said hi to everyone, and kissed me hello. Just a simple, straightforward kiss, but it still made my heart race. As he pulled back and smiled, I caught the twinkle in his eye. "Sorry I'm late," he said.

"You're forgiven," I said, still feeling a little weak in the knees.

"I'll make it up to you later," he whispered in my ear as he kissed our daughter on the head and took her from me.

Val shook her head. "You two lovebirds," she said.

Pedro laughed. "I don't know, but maybe there's something in the water on this floor."

We all laughed and wished each other happy holidays.

Romance on the adolescent unit. Guess a bunch of us fell for that.

Gracie slept the whole way to Oak Bluff.

"Still fast asleep," I said as I turned back around from checking on her. "She's going to be up all night."

"That's okay," Brax said as we held hands on the seat between us. "I have a feeling your mom will steal her from us the moment we walk in."

"And keep her most of the time we're there."

We were both tired but happy to have an entire week off. We'd spend half of it at my parents' house and half with Jenna and Aiden and their three kids. An entire week to spend with family was a treat.

In Oak Bluff, my parents met us at the door with hugs and kisses all around.

My mom looked happy and healthy, her hair now longer, but still its natural gray color. I'd never stopped being grateful for having her. After she greeted me and fussed over Grace, she pulled me aside and handed me a little bag, which I quickly tucked into Grace's travel bag.

"You got it," I exclaimed. "Thank you."

She nodded. "He did a beautiful job. Brax is going to love it."

"Thanks, Mom. I'm so excited to be home."

"Hi, sweetheart," my dad said, greeting me quickly, then racing to beat my mom by stealing Gracie away first to see the big Christmas tree. Of course, my mom followed right behind.

That left Brax and me to haul our suitcases up to our room and get settled.

As soon as we got into my old room, Brax grabbed my hand, sat down on the bed, and pulled me into his lap. I noticed that the familiar tree was lit with glowing red and pink lights. Nick Jonas had left the room a while ago. After all, he was married and a parent too, so it just didn't seem fitting anymore for me to keep hanging onto that old dream. Haha.

I caught sight of the old photo of me and Grace at our five-year-old birthday party. In my mind, I gave her a quick mental update. *Your namesake is just like you. I'm living my life the way you'd want me to, trying to be bold and unafraid. Trying to be my best self. You helped me get here.*

"Hi," Brax said to me, smiling. Being the object of his smile still felt like being in the light of the sun. Warm and wonderful.

"Why are you smiling?" I asked.

He kissed me. "Because we're off, it's almost Christmas, and for at least a few minutes, our daughter is in the loving care of her doting grandparents."

"Hi to you too," I said, going in for another kiss.

He blew out a big breath, as if with that, he left all the work stress behind for the holiday. "I'm looking forward to having some time off with you."

"Me too." I smiled and got up, walking over to my bag and pulling out the little package my mom had handed to me. "I have an early Christmas present for you."

He looked puzzled. And like all he really wanted were more kisses. "Now?"

I nodded. "Right now. It's—important. While we're alone. And it's quiet."

He gave me a shouldn't-we-be-responsible-parents-and-seek-out-our-child look.

"My mom's been waiting for a month to have Grace all to herself." I pushed the box into his hands.

He tore open the package to reveal of all things, a small cube-shaped box. "This isn't a snow globe, is it?"

I shook my head. "Of course not." When he sent me a questioning look, I shrugged. "Just open it."

He tore it open to reveal...a snow globe, similar to the one Brax had given me six years ago that sat on my desk at work and that I fondly looked at a hundred times a day. It inspired me and reminded me of who I aspired to be. The inside of this one, however, was a completely different scene. It held a family. A man and a woman, and two little children, all bundled in winter coats, building a snowman. And a golden retriever frolicking in the snow.

"We don't have a dog," he said slowly.

"Not yet," I said with a smile. "Keep going." I made a rolling motion with my hands.

Frowning, he looked from me to the globe, studying it carefully. He lifted his head and met my eyes. "...or a second child."

"That's correct." I nodded sagely. "But in about eight months, we will."

It was one of the big thrills of my life to watch his eyes grew wide and the truth dawn. "No way."

"Yes, way."

He moved fast, so fast, I'm not sure how he carefully set down the globe and tackled me on the bed. "Dr. D'Angelo-Hughes, congratulations." He gave me a loving gaze, his eyes full of happiness. The exact same happiness that was overflowing in my heart.

"It's going to get a little busier around here," I said. "You okay with that?"

"I love being insanely busy and having no sleep and working twenty-four seven. It reminds me of our residency days."

He shook his head incredulously, and then he kissed me tenderly. I wrapped my arms around his neck, felt the familiar silkiness of his thick hair, and pulled him in closer. His lips were soft and so familiar, moving over mine in a way that sent warmth flooding through me, making me breathless and dizzy. Still.

"Thank you for giving me your love. Every day is like Christmas with you," he said.

"You make me my best self," I said. "You helped me find my true destiny."

"I'm glad mine's with you." He kissed me. "Love you."

"Love you too. Merry Christmas."

Then we headed out to tell the fam our news.

Acknowledgments

I hope you enjoyed this holiday story as much as I did writing it. I got the idea over four years ago when I imagined a character who was greatly influenced by something tragic in her own life and whose journey was finding the courage to step into her true destiny.

And I thought of a man who had no family and what it would be like if he were suddenly dropped right into the middle of a big, loving, crazy one.

I believe in my heart that the people we love who are no longer in our lives still continually inspire us to be our best selves.

I want to thank my husband, Ed, who always treats my characters as if they are real people. One of the many reasons I love you.

I'd like to thank my wonderful writer friends who encourage me every day, keep me centered, and remind me what I love about writing. Sandra, Amy J, and Amy D, thank you for being my friends, for reading my stuff, and always encouraging me to keep going. Many thanks to Mary Ann E for your careful final read. Love you!

Thanks to my editor, Linda Ingmanson, to cover artist, Elizabeth Turner Stokes, and to proofreaders, Toni Lee and Kim Cannon.

Finally, thank you, dear readers, for reading my books, sharing your own stories, and writing me to let me know that you've enjoyed the stories. Making you laugh or smile means the world to me.

I firmly believe stories that make us feel good can't help but cause us to reexamine our own lives. Life is hard, but I hope we are inspired to see the positive, to make lemonade out of lemons when we can, and to reach out to others with hope and kindness.

Life is precious. Live every minute with love.

xo Miranda

Full Trigger Warning

Trigger warning: This book is a heartwarming and humorous romance. However, the heroine had a twin sister who died as a child. Her mother is recovering from cancer. And the main characters work in a pediatric hospital with sick children.

About the Author

Miranda Liasson is a best-selling author who writes about the important relationships in women's lives. Her heartwarming and humorous romances have won numerous accolades and have been praised by *Entertainment Weekly* for the way she "deals with so much of what makes life hard...without ever losing the warmth and heart that characterize her writing." She believes that we can handle whatever life throws at us just a little bit better with a laugh.

A proud native of Northeast Ohio, she and her husband live in a neighborhood of old homes that serves as inspiration for her books. She is very proud of her three young adult children. When she's not writing or enjoying books herself, she can be found biking along the old Ohio and Erie Canal Towpath trails in the beautiful Ohio Metro Parks.

Miranda loves to hear from readers!

Learn more at:
MirandaLiasson.com
Twitter @MirandaLiasson
Facebook.com/MirandaLiassonAuthor
Instagram @mirandaliasson
For information about new releases and sales, please sign up for her newsletter at https://mirandaliasson.com/#mailing-list

Find all Miranda's books at https://www.mirandaliasson.com/bookshelf

Coming soon: *Take Me to the Wedding*

Printed in the USA
CPSIA information can be obtained
at www.ICGtesting.com
JSHW020305110824
67841JS00005B/171